WARTIME
for the
SHOP GIRLS

Joanna read English at Cambridge University and worked on the production team of *The Archers* for ten years before serving as a scriptwriter for twenty. She has written several spin-off books about the long-running radio drama and on TV wrote for *Crossroads*, *Family Affairs*, *Doctors* and *EastEnders*. *Wartime for the Shop Girls* is the follow-up to her first novel *A Store at War*.

Find out more about Jo and the next book in the series on Facebook.com/joannatoyewriter and on Twitter @JoannaToye.

Also by Joanna Toye

A Store at War

WARTIME
for the
SHOP GIRLS

JOANNA TOYE

HarperCollins*Publishers*

HarperCollins*Publishers* Ltd
1 London Bridge Street,
London SE1 9GF

www.harpercollins.co.uk

First published by HarperCollins*Publishers* 2019
This paperback edition published 2020
2

A catalogue record for this book is available from the British Library

ISBN: 978-0-00-829869-2

This novel is entirely a work of fiction.
The names, characters and incidents portrayed in it are
the work of the author's imagination. Any resemblance to
actual persons, living or dead, events or localities is
entirely coincidental.

Typeset in Sabon Lt Std by Palimpsest Book Production Ltd, Falkirk, Stirlingshire

Printed and bound in the UK by CPI Group (UK) Ltd, Croydon CR0 4YY

MIX
Paper from
responsible sources
FSC™ C007454

This book is produced from independently certified FSC™ paper
to ensure responsible forest management.

For more information visit: www.harpercollins.co.uk/green

For my parents, John and Mary –
this was their war

Chapter 1

January 1942

'Reg! It's Reg! He's here!'

Lily couldn't help herself. She'd been stationed at the window for the past two hours, as tense as a look-out in a south coast pillbox. Now she tore to the back door the second she saw the latch on the back gate start to quiver. The hinge didn't even have time to squeak.

'Mum! Jim!' she hollered excitedly over her shoulder. 'He's home!'

Then she was flying out over the yard bricks, her feet skidding on the frosty surface. A few days ago, the whole country had been blanketed in snow, nearly five inches in their Midland town of Hinton, which had cast feverish doubt on Reg being able to get home at all. The snow had shrunk back now, leaving a scummy tidemark on the fringes of the yard, though it was still cold enough to make her eyes sting.

But Reg was here, finally, and guaranteed a warm welcome. His forty-eight-hour leave was in place of the family celebration they'd hoped to have at Christmas – insofar as anyone was celebrating Christmas in this third (the third, already!) winter of the war. If anyone had thought in 1939 that they'd still be fighting . . . Still, at least up till now it hadn't been as cold as that dreadful first winter, or as nail-shredding as the second, at the height of the Blitz.

'Lil! For goodness' sake, get back inside! You've only got your slippers on!'

The first words from her brother, and he was telling her off! No change there, and Lily had to smile. But she wasn't surprised: Reg, bless him, was the oldest in the family, and had always been the sensible one, the responsible one – he'd had to be, after their father had died.

Her other brother, Sid, would just have clocked the slippers' red pompoms, called her Frou-Frou or Fifi – he was always messing about with names – and made some crack about her pinching them off a French sailor. The fact that the British Navy, in which Sid was serving, issued its men with a plain flat-topped cap was a matter of some grievance with him, even though Lily was sure he'd have felt a right cissy in a hat with a pompom on it.

But Sid was away down south at HMS *Northney* on Hayling Island, and much as they'd tried, he and Reg hadn't been able to co-ordinate their leave to get home together. When she gave in to despair, which wasn't often, Dora, their mum, sometimes wondered out loud when or if she'd ever have her three children under the same roof again. But it was no more than everyone else had to put up with, and as Dora was more likely to be heard to say in one of the many maxims she could produce to suit any occasion – 'What can't be cured must be endured.'

'Come on inside, then!' Lily hung on Reg's arm. 'We'll get the kettle on.'

'I wouldn't say no.' Poor Reg looked chilled through. His train must have been delayed – they mostly were, these days, if not actually cancelled – and he'd probably had to hang about on a freezing platform. 'Where's Mum?'

'She's upstairs, trying to keep herself busy and not watch the clock—'

'No, I'm not. I'm here.'

And there was Dora Collins, expectant in the scullery doorway. She was in her best dress in honour of the homecoming, with a Jacqmar scarf at the neck, no less, her Christmas present from Lily. Ever since she'd started at Marlow's, the town's smartest department store, or so it liked to claim, Lily had promised

3

herself that as soon as she could afford it, she'd buy her mum something nice. And when Marlow's had given every junior a small bonus 'in gratitude for your hard work throughout the year in these difficult times', it had been earmarked straight away.

Lily had only joined the store the previous June. She hadn't been expecting anything extra in her pay packet, so the few extra shillings had been a very welcome surprise. But Marlow's was like that. It prided itself on looking after its employees, even though profits must be well down – for the simple reason that as the war ground on there was less and less to sell. Still, the buyers, like Miss Frobisher, Lily's boss on Childrenswear, did the best they could, and the shop's reputation meant that if anything did become available, from tea trays to tobacco, children's coats to combinations, Marlow's was one of the first places a supplier would contact.

Reg crossed the yard. Sid, again, would have bounded over and wrapped his mum in a hug, regardless of the rough, chilly wool of his tunic, but Reg, like Dora herself, was more reserved. He looked like her too, with soft brown hair, though his was now cropped short. Sid and Lily, on the other hand, had inherited their father's mop of fair curls.

Reg kissed his mum on the cheek before she stood back to let him in.

'Come in, love, out of the cold,' she urged. 'And let's have a good look at you.'

Only that telltale 'love' told Lily, and Reg himself, how much their mum had missed him and how very pleased she really was that he was home.

In the scullery, Jim was lifting the kettle from the gas and wetting the tea: he was going to make someone a wonderful wife someday, Sid always joked. Jim wasn't a member of the family, but as their lodger, he was starting to feel like one. He was another employee at Marlow's, seventeen and already Second Sales on Furniture.

The arrangement suited them all. Widowed when Lily was still a baby, Dora had learnt to be tough and independent. But with both her sons away, she felt happier and safer with a man about the house – and Jim wasn't only useful for the odd pot of tea. There was no doubt that the two raised beds in the yard were going to be a lot more productive this year under his watchful eye. Not only that, he'd even built them a henhouse. They now had fresh eggs – gold dust, nectar and ambrosia all at once – and useful as currency for bartering as more and more things went on the ration or disappeared altogether.

Jim held out his hand to Reg. They'd met once before, in the autumn, when Reg had been passing through on his way to yet another training camp.

'How's things?' Jim asked. 'Fair journey?'

'Oh, you know.'

It was yet another way in which Reg and Sid were

5

polar opposites. Where Reg was circumspect, Sid would have treated them to a minute breakdown, complete with music hall impressions of grumpy guards and a star rating for the station tea bar.

'Well, the tea won't be long.'

Reg slung his haversack down on a chair.

'I've been saving some of my rations, Mum. And there's a bit of stuff from the NAAFI.'

He unbuckled the straps and took out a couple of lumpy parcels.

'Jam . . . chocolate . . . a bit of ham.'

Lily's mouth watered, but Dora wasn't letting Reg get away with that.

'Reg! You shouldn't have! No wonder you've lost weight!'

Weight loss was a crime on a par with sedition in Dora's eyes. Though the Army got first dibs when it came to rations, which was partly why ordinary households were having to cut back, she was naturally convinced that her boy wasn't being fed as well as she could have fed him if he'd been at home.

Reg gave one of his rare smiles.

'I haven't lost weight, Mum, far from it. I've toned up, put on muscle, that's all.'

Dora sniffed disbelievingly.

'Irish stew for dinner,' was all she said. 'I'd better have a look at it.'

She opened the door of the Belling and concentrated

on extracting the promising-smelling pot of stew while Lily and Jim discreetly stowed Reg's offerings in the pantry.

'Thank you,' Lily mouthed.

Reg grinned and gave her a thumbs-up.

Lily might not be as close to Reg as she was to Sid, but jam, ham, chocolate or not, she realised just how pleased she was to see him too.

'All right, Mum, you win, hands down,' Reg conceded as he laid down his knife and fork. 'There might be plenty of it, Army food, but it's not a patch on your cooking.'

'Oh, get away with you! You'd eat horse manure if it was wrapped up in pretty paper!'

Lily bit back a smile. Their mum was no more capable of accepting a compliment than Lily had been of not shrieking her head off when she'd sensed Reg was at the gate.

'There's no more where that came from, you know!' Dora added, in case she hadn't dismissed the praise quite emphatically enough.

'I couldn't eat it anyway!' Reg protested. 'I'm stuffed!'

Dora's eyebrows shot up.

'That's all they've taught you in the Army, is it, that sort of talk?'

Lily saw Jim and Reg exchange knowing, 'man of the world' looks.

7

'I should think that's the least of it, Mrs Collins.' Jim gave one of his wry, twisty smiles. 'Right, Reg?'

'You don't know the half of it! But don't worry, Mum, I won't be using any language while I'm home. Especially not now Lily's gone all posh on us, working at Marlow's. I didn't see you crook your little finger drinking your tea, though, Lil. Tut, tut!'

Lily flapped her hand at him and Reg ducked out of the way, laughing. He was relaxing now; they all were, with the warmth of some food inside them and the fire nicely banked up.

'So tell me, what's new at the swankiest store in town? What's the best-dressed baby wearing this winter, Lil? Had a run on cut-glass decanters for the folk with cut-glass accents, have you, Jim?'

This time Lily and Jim were the ones to exchange looks. So much had happened in Lily's first few months at Marlow's that the last few, apart from the flurry before Christmas and the January sales, had seemed quite tame in comparison.

She opened her mouth to reply, but before she could begin, they heard the latch on the back gate click, followed by footsteps across the yard and then by someone opening the back door itself.

Lily's heart leapt. Surely not! It couldn't be, could it? Not Sid? Though it would be just like him to take them all by surprise. And who else could it be, turning up right in the middle of Sunday dinner?

'Only me!' trilled a voice approaching though the scullery.

Of course! Beryl! That's who.

Shy, tactful, reserved – not words you could ever use to describe Beryl. But what could she possibly want this time?

Chapter 2

As it turned out, on this occasion simply a free meal – or at least a pudding.

'How does she do it?' Lily demanded as she and Jim washed up. 'She must be able to smell Mum's cooking from right the other side of town!'

'I know. The War Office should use her as a sniffer dog. Perhaps she could do the same with explosives.'

'I always think that's so hard on the poor things,' fretted Lily. 'Imagine being a little puppy, thinking life was all chasing your tail and gambolling about with your brothers and sisters, then going to some nice family as a pet – instead you're crawling about on a battlefield or a bombsite.'

'On the other hand you might grow up to be a

rescue dog,' offered Jim. 'That'd give you a nice warm glow, finding people alive in the rubble.'

'True,' Lily conceded. 'They ought to give them medals . . . but we're getting away from Beryl! Inviting herself in like that and taking the bread out of our mouths!'

'The rice pudding, you mean,' lamented Jim. He'd been looking forward to seconds. 'Not to mention the—'

'Exactly! Mum even gave her the skin. The best bit!'

Lily finished his sentence for him: she often found they were thinking the same thing at the same time. It was one of the things which made Jim so easy to get along with, and they did get on, most of the time – except when he was teasing her about her attempts at knitting, or her deficiencies with the weeding, or when he used a long word she didn't understand – he'd been able to stay on at school to take his School Certificate, lucky thing. Lily usually gave as good as she got, though – she'd had enough practice with her brothers. But this time she knew she and Jim were in total agreement.

'Not a scrap left for you or me – or the hens!' she grumbled.

'Oh well. To be fair, she is eating for two.'

Jim shook the washing-up water from his hands and wiped them on his trousers: woe betide anyone who needlessly 'wore out' Dora's towels. She'd sworn by that thrifty dictum for years, and tea towels too, and since the latest Government advice had instructed people to leave crockery to drain to avoid that very thing, she could congratulate herself on having been right all along. When the handy tip had been broadcast on the wireless, she'd permitted herself a smile that could almost have been described as smug. Lily had only dried off the cutlery and the saucepans – being in the kitchen was more about letting off steam over Beryl than being much practical use.

'We'd better go back through,' she said reluctantly. 'It's not fair to inflict Beryl on poor Reg.'

When they did, though, Beryl seemed well ensconced. Dora was knitting yet another balaclava – her hands were never idle – and Beryl, whose were, and were folded over her pregnant stomach, was holding forth to a glazed-looking Reg.

'I wonder if you and my Les'll ever meet up?' she mused, raising a hand to twirl a strand of her shoulder-length blonde hair with a painted fingernail. Beryl might have been getting on for the size of a tank, but she was a glamorous tank, camouflaged with powder and peroxide.

It was a pretty dim question, given that there were two million men in the Army now, and it wasn't as if recruitment was organised in the same way as in the First War, with towns raising Pals' Battalions.

Reg, who'd been a mechanic before the war, had been quickly snapped up by the Royal Electrical and

Mechanical Engineers, while Les, he'd already learnt, had joined the local regiment. Reg tried gently to point this out, but Beryl seemed convinced his path and her husband's would cross, because Les, she informed them, had been transferred to the Royal Army Service Corps and was now officially an Army driver.

'How did he manage to swing that?' quipped Jim, hauling over a couple of dining chairs for himself and Lily. 'If they'd seen the way he used to take corners in our delivery vans . . .'

Till he'd been called up, Les Bulpitt had been a driver at Marlow's. Beryl had worked there too – it was how they'd all met.

Beryl pregnant . . . that had been just one of the many things that had happened since Lily had started at Marlow's. Lily thought back to that terrifying first day, standing frozen with fear outside the Staff Entrance, and Beryl sweeping by, all scent and smart remarks, even though she was only a junior herself, (a more senior junior maybe, but still a junior). But when Beryl had found herself in trouble, she'd had to throw herself on Lily and Dora's mercy, the start of the most unlikely friendship since Fay Wray and King Kong.

If Les and Beryl's wedding had had the whiff of the shotgun about it, everyone had rallied round to disperse the cordite and make the day the best they could. They'd been a merry party – Les and Beryl,

Lily as bridesmaid, Jim as best man and official photographer. Dora had made the dress, Sid had made it home to walk Beryl down the aisle – well, into the Register Office – and Les's mum, Ivy, had tapped up no one liked to think what black-market contacts to help lay on a magnificent spread.

Now, with Les's dad in the Merchant Navy, and Les away at training camp, Beryl was left living with Ivy and Les's younger sister, Susan. Susan, bless her, was a bit backward – quite a lot backward in fact – more like age two than twelve. From the time she'd spent over at Ivy's since the wedding, Lily had to admit that watching Susan laboriously try to do a simple jigsaw could make a Sunday afternoon pass very slowly indeed. No wonder Beryl needed to escape.

'Gor blimey!' said Reg when she'd gone, complete with the matinee jacket Dora had knitted for the baby, and which had been Beryl's transparent excuse for 'just dropping by' at dinnertime. Dora pursed her lips and unwound some more navy wool. It was an expletive too far for her, but that was war for you. 'She can't half talk, that one!'

It was true. Beryl had always had plenty to say for herself.

'You'd told me a bit about her,' Reg went on, 'but in the flesh . . . I should think "my Les" is glad to get away! I daresay you will be too, Jim, surrounded by all these women. You're next for call-up, aren't you?'

Lily swatted at her brother again, and caught him this time, on the arm.

'Cheek! You tell him, Jim! You like it here!'

Jim gave a half-smile and shrugged.

Lily thought nothing of it at the time. But afterwards, she'd remember that.

It might have been cold and dank and generally horrible outside, but the hens still had to be seen to and locked up before dark.

Reg declared he was 'gasping for a fag' so the three of them wrapped up and went out into the yard in the last of the feeble daylight. Jim didn't think Reg's cigarette and the henhouse straw would be a terrifically good mix, so he volunteered for the hens' bedtime lock-up, leaving Lily stamping her feet and swinging her arms as Reg lit up. He still couldn't get over the fact that Beryl was convinced he and Les were bound to meet.

He drew on his cigarette and chucked his spent match over the fence.

'Anyway, if he's just been called up, he'll get a home posting for the first few months, if not years – how old is he?'

'That's the thing,' Lily said. 'Les is twenty, the same as you.'

'What? How come he hasn't been called up till now?' Reg sounded outraged. 'Or volunteered? You mean he's sat on his backside when he could have been—'

Reg had volunteered the minute he was eligible, at eighteen – and Sid the same.

'Before you get on your high horse, Reg, Les *was* called up before.'

Lily had only learnt this herself when Les's call-up papers had come just before Christmas.

'Don't tell me,' exclaimed Reg. 'Tried to pass himself off as a conchie! Or unfit!'

'He *was* unfit the first time. Susan, his sister, because she's like she is, she's not strong. She gets all sorts of infections and things,' Lily explained. 'Les had tonsillitis that he'd caught off her, so he failed the medical.'

Reg snorted and took another disdainful draw on his cigarette. Lily could see she wasn't convincing him.

'Les isn't a shirker, Reg, honestly,' she insisted. 'I mean, he'd hardly have planned it this way. It's not the best timing, is it, for him to be called up now, when Beryl's due in a couple of months?'

'It's how it is, Lil,' said Reg plainly. 'There's plenty of blokes fighting this war that have never seen their kids.'

'I know, I know.'

The tip of Reg's cigarette glowed in the dusk. Lily wondered if he was going to tell her, or if she'd have to ask. That was the trouble with Reg. He was such an oyster. You had to prise things out of him.

'Reg . . .'

But for once, Reg saved her the trouble.

'I know what you're going to say, Sis. And yes, it's why I'm home. This leave isn't just in place of Christmas.'

'Oh, Reg! You've got your posting! Where? Tell me! Where are they sending you?'

Jim had finished his henhouse duties now, and he joined them, cradling two brown eggs in his hand. He could tell from Lily's face that something was up.

'Sorry,' he said. 'Am I interrupting?'

Though they'd been putting him up for six months now – or putting up with him, as he joked – Jim was always sensitive about not intruding into family matters.

'He's got his posting,' Lily said. 'That's it, isn't it, Reg?'

Red took a final long drag on his cigarette and pinched it out between his thumb and first finger. His hands were so worn and calloused after years of grappling with the insides of engines he could crush a wasp the same way and not feel the pain, he'd told them.

'Where are you going?' asked Jim.

The Army didn't send you abroad till you were twenty – or tried not to; Reg's last birthday had been a turning point, they all knew.

'I'll tell you two,' said Reg slowly. 'And I've told Sid. But not a word to Mum, not yet. I'll tell her tomorrow – and in good time, not just before I leave, so she's got the chance to take it in. But I don't want her brooding on it longer than she has to.'

'For goodness' sake Reg, tell us!' Lily had trouble keeping her voice down. 'Where?'

'They haven't told us officially,' said Reg. 'We're not allowed to know – and nor are you. But we all do know.'

Jim and Lily looked at him, waiting.

'Africa,' said Reg quietly. Walls, even those between their house and their next-door neighbours, were reputed to have ears, after all. 'North Africa. This bit of leave's my pre-embarkation. We sail next week.'

Chapter 3

Africa! In the wintry dusk of a Midlands' backyard,
Lily closed her eyes and she was there.

Africa! Heat, dust, the spice smell of the bazaars;
snowy-robed Arabs haggling over brass coffee pots;
captive cobras swaying to snake charmers' fluting;
tall, half-naked Nubians in marble halls, waving
ostrich-feather fans over doe-eyed women reclining
on cushions . . .

But before her fantasy could get any more, well,
fantastic, Lily pulled herself up. Stupid! Africa, North
Africa at least, was nothing like that. Her dimly-
remembered geography lessons had taught her that.
Most of it was desert, unpopulated because it was
uninhabitable, and the vast sand dunes and midnight

19

oases she might have gone on to imagine were only a tiny part of that. The rest was stony desert scrub, more like the surface of the moon than the setting for a romantic encounter with a real-life Rudolph Valentino. And now, the desert meant other things too. It was The Western Desert – those capital letters said it all – it was—

'The Desert War, then?'

Thank goodness Jim was there. The words had formed in her mind, but she hadn't seemed able to organise her lips, tongue and teeth to get them out. Maybe it was the cold. Or maybe it was because she couldn't bear to hear herself say them out loud.

Reg pulled a face.

'Sounds romantic put like that, doesn't it? Well, I'm about to find out.'

Lily swallowed hard.

'But Reg, you're a mechanic, you're not a . . . a sapper or a gunner or anything. You said yourself the drivers can do most of their own maintenance. You're going to be well back behind the lines. Aren't you?'

She saw Reg and Jim exchange another of those looks. But it wasn't the same man-of-the-world look they'd exchanged before, a look that Lily had felt was to shut her out. This was a look of recognition, and of resignation. She needed to know.

'What do you want me to say, Lil?' said Reg. 'Tell you we should all believe in the Tooth Fairy, and Father Christmas is real?'

'You mean he isn't?'

She was trying to make light of things, but she knew in her heart of hearts it was hopeless.

'I'm not going to lie to you,' said Reg. 'You're a bright girl, so think about it. If a jeep or a truck breaks down on ops, or takes a proper pounding, it's stuck where it is, isn't it? If you leave it there, the Jerries or the Eyeties'll have it, you're better off torching it.' He gave her a kind smile. 'But we can't afford to waste kit like that, can we? So they need blokes like me out with the fighting units, of course they do.'

'Yes, they do. But equally,' said Jim quickly, seeing the dismay in Lily's face, 'it's all the luck of the draw. You might be in the thick of things. Or . . .'

He looked at Reg again, a look that this time said, 'Help! You're the mechanic!'

Reg got the message.

'Or . . . I might be in a cosy billet in Alexandria, changing the spark plugs on the brigadier's car and come night-time quaffing beer in a nice little bar while a belly dancer whirls her tassels at me. OK?'

They were doing their best, Lily knew. Jim was kindly trying to reassure her in the same way he had before, over the puppy being a rescue dog and not a bomb-detector. Lily knew the chance of Reg being assigned to such light duties was probably about as likely as Hitler shaving off his moustache and joining the Mothers' Union. But they were doing their best.

She'd better do hers and make it as easy for Reg as she could. She took a deep breath.

'Well, make sure you are,' she said firmly. 'Make sure when you put your hand in that bran tub, you pull out a lucky ticket.'

Reg put his arm round her shoulder and gave her a hug.

'I'll make sure it's got my name on it.'

Lily leant her head against his. She hadn't taken that much interest in The Desert War till now – what had been happening in Europe, in Norway, even in Russia, seemed that much closer and more real, somehow. Africa was – well, stupid to say it, but it was a foreign country – a foreign continent. She could see the shape of it . . . almost a heart-shape, ironically – with Egypt, held by the British, in the top right-hand corner, and next to it Libya, which had become the rope in a tug-of-war first between the British and the Italians, and now between the British and the Italians and Germans together. She wasn't entirely sure how or why it had all started in that part of the world, or why getting hold of Libya and holding on to it was quite so vital. All that mattered now was that Reg was going out there, and soon.

'What are you three up to?' It was Dora, calling from the doorway. A thin beam of light lay like a bright bar on the blue bricks of the yard. 'Come inside. I'm letting the cold in and the light out! I don't know how you can see your hands in front of your faces! And you must be frozen!'

Lily suddenly realised that she was. Her teeth would have been chattering if her jaw hadn't been clamped tightly shut for fear of saying – no, shouting – what she really felt. 'Don't, Reg! Don't go – please, don't go!'

But for goodness' sake! If she felt like this about Reg, who was so self-contained, somehow, who she didn't feel she knew as well or was as close to as Sid, her lovely Sid – what was she going to be like when he was posted? She dreaded to think how her mum would take it when Reg told her. And how on earth could Beryl be so calm when Les was likely to be posted abroad so soon?

'Maybe she doesn't realise he could be off straight away,' reasoned Reg later, when she asked him the same question.

Tea was over and their mum had gone out to a Red Cross meeting – she'd upped her voluntary work now that even more younger women were being called up. Jim was out too. He was attached to a local ARP unit, and even though, thankfully, with Hitler occupied on other fronts, the threat of constant night-time bombing over England seemed to have gone away for now, he still had to patrol to give anyone not observing the blackout a good ticking-off.

The beastly blackout! At Marlow's, they'd had to install double doors to stop any chink of light escaping as customers left in the dark winter afternoons. And at home, every night, every single night, the scratchy, stiff material had to be put up – and every single morning, taken down. Lily hated the way it made the house so stuffy and tomb-like, but most of all she hated herself for hating it. She'd have liked to be more noble, somehow, to rise above it. It was a small thing, after all, when you thought of what other people in other countries were suffering. Terrible things, persecution, starvation . . . but even so . . . it was the small things that so often got you down. The chilblains because coal was rationed; the bra strap that broke or sagged, and no chance of any elastic to replace it.

Reg was looking at her, waiting for a response.

'Oh, I don't know what Beryl thinks any more,' she said. 'When they announced they were getting married she went all soppy, and I remember thinking then that her brain had turned to mush. I thought it was just about the wedding, but maybe it's being pregnant that does that to you.'

'I wouldn't know about any of that,' shrugged Reg. 'You're asking the wrong bloke.'

Lily felt suddenly awkward. Reg had been courting before he joined the Army: he and his girl had been going steady for over a year. But when Reg had signed up, distance hadn't made the heart grow fonder, it had just made things very difficult, and she was engaged now to someone else, who worked at the Town Hall and was in a reserved occupation.

'Things are pretty sticky out there beyond Hinton, you know, Lil,' said Reg gently. 'They need blokes desperately. They can't make any exemptions now, compassionate or otherwise. Or everybody'd be trying it on.'

'No, I suppose they can't,' said Lily reluctantly. 'But I don't like to think of Beryl having the baby on her own.'

'She won't be on her own, will she?' reasoned Reg. 'There's you and Mum and her mum-in-law . . . like I said, Lil, she's not the only one, not by a long way.'

'No, I know. But when it's someone you really know, it's different.' Lily sighed. 'There's so many people I know around here or at the shop – their husbands and sons and brothers are away fighting. I thought I understood how awful it must be. But now, with you going – well, I don't know how they stand it.'

'Blimey, I haven't even gone yet! Wait till Sid gets posted! Then what'll you be like!'

'Don't!' the word was out before she could stop herself, and Lily was embarrassed that for all her dismay on hearing Reg's news, it was obvious that Sid's eventual posting would affect her far more. She quickly backtracked. 'Anyway, that's not for ages. He's not even nineteen yet.'

'Listen,' said Reg even more gently. 'When I said

things were a bit sticky, I wasn't just saying it for effect. We're in a mess, frankly. They can't keep fit blokes in England square bashing and saluting all day. They're sure to lower the age for sending blokes overseas.'

Lily gaped.

'But – I don't understand!' she cried. 'America's in the war now! What about all their thousands of troops?'

'Lily,' said Reg patiently. 'They're still collecting their dead from Pearl Harbor. Well, not literally,' he reassured her when she looked horrified. 'But the Japs knocked out eighteen of their ships, for heaven's sake. They've got to regroup, get organised. The Yanks aren't going to come riding to our rescue tomorrow.'

That was that, then.

'The Japs are ripping through the Far East like a dose of salts,' Reg went on. 'They've got their eye on India, you know. The Americans and the Aussies can't do it all. So if we've got the blokes already trained up . . . I'm sorry, Lil, but there it is. It's going to be every man jack of us soon.'

Lily got up – and wished she hadn't. Her legs were shaking.

'I'm going to make some cocoa,' she said. Her voice was thin and weedy, even thinner than it had sounded in the cold air of the yard. 'Do you want some?'

'You bet! And let's cheer ourselves up. See what's on the wireless, eh?' Reg leant forward to switch it on.

Their old set exploded into voice: it did that sometimes, catching you off guard. It was the evening service – the middle of a hymn.

'*Through many a day of darkness,*' sang the congregation,

'*Through many a scene of strife,*
The faithful few fought bravely
To guard the nation's life—'

'Blimey,' said Reg. 'That's all we need. Let's find something brighter . . . Oi! Careful!'

Blundering out, Lily had knocked against the standard lamp. It wobbled crazily.

'Sorry.'

She made her escape. In the scullery, she sat down on the hard wooden chair and pressed her knees together.

She was already losing Reg. In the next year she could lose, then, not just Sid, but Jim as well. He'd be turning eighteen, and would have to join up, and he wouldn't be sorry about it, she knew. More and more these days he kept saying that selling recondi-tioned sideboards to the good ladies of Hinton wasn't exactly a reserved occupation, and he felt increasingly guilty about it. She'd had time to get used to the idea that Jim would be called up, but she'd thought at least that he'd be in the country. There'd be letters, and he'd get regular leave, and for the first few months, maybe years, he'd be doing something menial, and relatively safe. But the thought that he might be sent overseas almost straight away, into the thick of the fighting . . . Jim? Really?

It would be the Army, for sure: he'd said that much. Jim, who she was used to seeing either in his work suit or in old flannels and a tatty shirt digging the veg bed, in a stiff khaki uniform. Jim, pushing his glasses up his nose as he wrote out price tickets at the shop, or did the crossword at home, instead shouldering a rifle, or on the march, or charging at someone with a bayonet. Jim, over six-foot tall, bent double inside a tank, loading shells. Jim under fire, or laying explosives to blow up a bridge, or defusing bombs. Jim broiling in the desert, sweating in the jungle, freezing somewhere in Eastern Europe . . . Jim, hungry, thirsty, exhausted; captured, injured, dead . . .

Lily found she was shuddering all over. And five minutes ago, all she'd had to worry about had been the blackout.

Chapter 4

When Jim came home, Lily was still up, and being soundly beaten by Reg at dominoes. She didn't say anything to him about what Reg had told her, and next morning, after a restless night, what with her and Jim rushing to get to work, and Reg getting in the way of them having their breakfast, she didn't say anything either, or any more to Reg.

But Reg caught her in the hall as she was putting on the ankle boots she couldn't believe someone had actually been mad enough to give to the WVS jumble. All right, so the suede uppers were worn shiny, but they had a neat little cuff, a smart toggle fastening and a decent sole with only a couple of splits. But with a layer of cardboard inside, which mostly kept the wet out, they were at least warm.

'Sorry if I worried you last night, Sis.' The pleading look in his eyes intensified the apology. 'But it's no good being an ostrich, now, is it?'

'No, you were quite right, Reg,' Lily said firmly. 'I need to face facts. It's no good pretending.'

'That's what I think.' Reg seemed relieved. 'Just got to get on with it, haven't we?'

Lily nodded. 'I don't envy you telling Mum about your posting, all the same.'

'Oh, I expect she knows the score,' said Reg. 'You know what our mum's like. She's read your mind before you've even had the thought.'

Lily smiled. It was true that you couldn't get much, if anything, past Dora.

'At least it's different for you – you're years off call-up,' Reg added consolingly. 'Anyway, you're far too valuable for Marlow's to let you go!'

'Definitely! Every time I put a boy's sailor suit on the rail I feel I'm doing my bit!'

Laugh it off, that was the only way. 'Keep smiling through', as Vera Lynn had been singing last night, when Reg had finally found something cheerier to listen to.

'Essential war work! Vital for morale!' he assured her. 'Now give us a kiss, 'cos I'll be gone by the time you and Jim get back tonight.'

'Bye, Reg,' said Lily. She gave him not just a kiss, but a big tight hug as well. 'Look after yourself.'

It was completely inadequate, of course, but it was what everyone said.

'Will do. And make sure you write, once I've got an address.'

'Of course I will. And you must tell us if you need anything.'

'Well, it won't be balaclavas,' grinned Reg. 'Though they say it gets cold at night, out under the stars and that big desert moon.'

'Steady on,' said Lily, 'you'll be writing poetry next!'

She was getting quite good at this 'making light of it' approach.

'What, smoking a pipe and wearing a cravat? I don't think so!' countered Reg. He wasn't so bad at it himself. 'But it's an adventure, eh – join the Army and see the world?'

Neither of them was really convinced, she could tell, and it rang even more hollow now she'd realised how soon 'seeing the world' might happen for Sid and Les – and for Jim too. Maybe 'making light of it' wasn't the way forward after all.

Reg gave her another quick hug, then added, 'Say hello to Gladys for me, won't you?'

'Yes, yes, of course.'

Gladys was her very best friend at Marlow's. She was the other junior on Childrenswear and had generously shown Lily the ropes from her very first day. Reg had met her on the short leave he'd had in the autumn when Gladys had come to tea.

It was nice of Reg to remember Gladys, and she'd be touched, Lily knew. Shy, and to be honest rather plain, Gladys wasn't someone who usually made much of an impression.

'Are we going? Or is there an all-out strike I don't know about?'

It was Jim: they needed to get moving, or they'd be in the late book!

They'd only reached the corner when Jim dropped his bombshell.

'I'm leaving you here. I'm going in the other direction.'

'What . . . why?' queried Lily. 'Is there an all-out strike that *I* don't know about?'

'I'm not going to work,' he replied. 'I'm going for a medical. An Army medical.'

Lily stared at him. After the realisation she'd had last night, this was too much.

'But . . . already? Why? You're not eighteen yet. Not for weeks.'

'Doesn't matter. I decided last week. Get the medical out of the way, then as soon as it's my birthday, I'll be ready to go.'

Lily swallowed hard, as best she could around the lump in her throat.

'Hang on. You've done all this . . . without telling us?'

What she really meant was 'without telling me', but she could hardly say that.

'Come off it, Lily. You've known it was coming. Anyway, I'm telling you now.'

'I *hate* it when people say that! That's no answer!' Lily burst out. 'And never mind me, what about Mum? Don't you owe it to her to have said something? And why – why on earth didn't you say anything last night? Reg gave you the chance – he fed you the line when he was talking about your call-up!'

Now she remembered the half-smile, the shrug, and the lack of a straight answer to Reg's question. Now they spoke volumes.

'Lily,' said Jim evenly, 'be fair. It was Reg's first leave for ages, and his last for a good long while, from what he told us. Yesterday was about him being home with his family. I didn't want to shove myself into that. And for goodness' sake, it's only a medical, there's nothing to say till I pass!'

Lily looked at him, disbelieving. If he really thought that . . . and she'd thought they were friends! Didn't friends share things? Jim looked straight back at her. Fine, thought Lily, if he wants a challenge . . . she certainly wasn't going to be the first to look away – and she wasn't.

'I have to go,' he said finally, unpeeling his eyes from hers. She'd won – but if there was ever a case of winning the battle but not the war, this was it. 'You should too. Or you'll be late.'

'Thanks for your concern.'

Jim obviously noted the sarcasm but said nothing and took a step away. One step, but the first of many, perhaps.

'I've cleared it with the staff office,' he said calmly. 'I've booked the whole day off. I don't know how long it'll take.'

'No, well, you'll want to be measured for your kit straight away, I expect, and put your name down for the most dangerous mission they've got,' said Lily, seething at his forethought, furious that the typist in the staff office had known what she hadn't. 'Might as well get on with it, eh? The sooner you get issued with your bayonet and battledress the better.'

'Don't be like that.'

'That's another pointless and annoying thing people say!'

Because 'like what' exactly? How dare he presume to know what she was feeling? If he'd had any thought for her feelings at all, they wouldn't be having this scene in the first place.

'Lily,' he spoke to her as if she were a child, 'I'm going. There's no talking to you in this mood.'

'Well, what do you want me to say?' Lily retorted childishly, then added, 'Oh, I know. Of course. Good luck.'

'Thank you,' said Jim levelly. 'See you tonight.'

And he was gone, straightening his glasses, pulling down his cuffs, tall and lanky in his threadbare overcoat. Oh, why had it come out like that? Angry and bitter and sullen, when what she really felt was . . . what was it? She felt betrayed – he'd betrayed their friendship, the closeness she'd thought they had. But more than that, she felt . . . bereft. And in a flash, she knew she felt for him far more than she'd properly feel for a friend.

Lily blinked – hard – and looked down at her feet. She could still see Jim walking away, but this time he was wearing an Army greatcoat and he was walking away down a crowded station platform to the troop train. She blinked again. Can't cry, won't cry, she thought, looking even more determinedly down. But the pavement was slimed with dirt from the melted snow, and her boots, which just a short while ago she'd been so proud of, looked shabby and pathetic, and she hated, hated this war.

Lily made it to work in time – just. She'd been there for six months now, but having a job, and a job at Marlow's at that, was still enough of a novelty for her to feel a secret thrill every morning when she walked through the door, even at the staff entrance around the back, and even on a cold, dark Monday. Every morning – until this one.

It had never before seemed like dull routine, but it did today; clocking in with the timekeeper, taking off her outdoor things and stowing them in her locker in the clatter and din of the women's cloakroom, always especially loud at the start of the week as everyone swapped stories of their precious Sunday off. Waiting her turn for the speckled mirror to check her appearance, brushing stray hairs and lint from her skirt, and hurrying along the long corridor past the goods lift and up the back stairs with the rest of the staff . . .

Even stepping through the double doors on to the sales floor didn't give her heart its usual joyful lift. The store always looked so beautiful first thing, so pristine and tidy, with the faint strafe marks on the carpet from the cleaners' vacuums, the counters gleaming and the goods deftly displayed. Though the heating was turned to its lowest setting, some of the overhead lights had had their bulbs removed – another Government order – and the stock on the rails was thin, the first floor at Marlow's, in comparison with the increasing drabness of everything else in life, still looked impressive, glamorous, even.

She glanced automatically across to Furniture, as she usually did. Though they walked to work together and clocked in at the same time, Jim always beat her to the sales floor, because men never had to spend so long over their appearance, did they? Lily had seen it done enough times at home – a quick duck in the front of the mirror, smooth their hair, and that was it. It was a source of much envy to Lily. Even though she'd got much better at managing them for work, her strong-minded blonde curls still required a lot of handling and were the subject of many silent prayers – and curses.

She wouldn't be the only one who'd miss Jim when he left, Lily thought. With his absence today, it had fallen to the new junior on Furniture to try to anchor a stand-up price card on the bilious green satin waves of an eiderdown. He was not making a very good job of it. He eventually gave up and propped it drunkenly against the headboard.

That was always one of the first jobs of the day, making the stock look its best. On Childrenswear, that meant taking the dust sheets and tissue-paper covers off the more delicate baby clothes, lifting every hanger and polishing the rails beneath. She'd better get to work.

Gladys was already there, brushing the velvet-collared coats – a mere seven (seven!) coupons, plus the marked price, a pretty steep one in this case. But at least when you shopped at Marlow's you knew you were getting quality – or the best quality that was available these days. 'Nothing but the best' was the store's motto – so if you bought a big enough size for your child, a Marlow's garment would last and last. Anything else was a 'false economy'. That, at least, was the sales pitch Lily had heard many a time from Miss Thomas and Miss Temple. They were the department's two salesladies – or salesgirls, as they were called – absurd when they'd both been summoned out of retirement to replace younger staff who'd volunteered or been called up.

Lily mouthed a 'hello' to Gladys, found a duster, and started working her way around the rails. If she concentrated really hard, perhaps she could stop thinking about Jim and how he was getting on. She knew what he'd be going through from what Sid and Reg had told her about their medicals: breathing in and out under the cold disc of the stethoscope, sticking out your tongue and saying 'Ahhh', being quizzed about your bowels. She wondered if Jim knew what Reg had also told her last night, that once Jim had been trained, he might be sent abroad sooner than young men had been until now. But she knew he would. Jim wasn't daft. No wonder he'd kept his decision to himself.

As she polished, Lily could see Miss Frobisher in conversation with the new floor supervisor, Mr Simmonds. Well, he wasn't that new – he'd been in place since the autumn. He'd been the buyer on Sportswear before. It wasn't the biggest of depart-ments, so he'd been something of a surprise appointment, but announcing it to her staff, Miss Frobisher had been diplomatic.

'Mr Marlow obviously thinks he has what it takes,' she said, but Lily had noticed that she'd raised an eyebrow – she had very expressive eyebrows – when she'd first opened the staff office memo.

Mr Simmonds hadn't even been at Marlow's that long. He'd been a PT instructor in the Army, which was a qualification of sorts for selling sportswear, Jim had said, and he was certainly 'on the ball'. Apparently, he'd risen to Warrant Officer Class II but had been invalided out with a niggling shoulder injury. Tall and lean, he strode about the first floor with an athlete's vigour and a springy step which made you think he was going to vault the counter, not point out a smear. With his quick eye and brush-cut hair, he radiated energy and vitality, and Lily and Jim had concluded that he'd been given the job to shake things up.

As Lily watched, Mr Simmonds placed one hand under Miss Frobisher's elbow and with the other indicated the door to the stairs. That meant they were going up to the management floor – quite possibly to an audience with Mr Marlow himself.

Miss Frobisher shot a quick look at the hand beneath her elbow, then a longer one into Mr Simmonds's face. It was not a happy look, and it didn't make Lily any happier either. On top of the worry about Jim, did it mean Childrenswear was in for a jolly good shaking?

Chapter 5

The surface of Cedric Marlow's mahogany desk was usually empty apart from a calendar, blotter, pen tray and telephone. The accounts and paperwork that he took daily from his 'In' tray were efficiently placed, annotated, directly into his 'Out' tray. Anything that reposed for more than half an hour in the tray marked 'Pending' he regarded as a grave dereliction of duty.

Today, however, something had gone very wrong. For a start, he barely bothered with the usual pleasantries – and he was normally the most courteous of men. Secondly, the desk's surface was barely visible for paper.

'Have you seen this?' he demanded of Miss Frobisher.

She was barely halfway across the Turkey carpet, and Mr Simmonds was still closing the door behind them.

Mystified, she came closer as Mr Marlow pushed Saturday's copy of the local paper, the *Hinton Chronicle,* across the desk. Eileen Frobisher hadn't seen it at the weekend; she'd had better things to do, but now, as he jabbed an impatient finger, she saw what Cedric Marlow was getting at.

She sat down on the chair that Mr Simmonds had thoughtfully placed at her side and drew the newspaper towards her.

'WOMEN WANTED!' ran the headline – pithy and to the point for the usually long-winded *Chronicle*.

She read on.

An appeal has gone out for women, especially young women aged between 18 and 25, to 'do their bit' and join the war effort in a new munitions factory in North Staffordshire. The Ministry of Labour and National Service is seeking no less than ten thousand workers in total and it is hoped to recruit ten per cent of them from our area.

Girls and women of Hinton, what are you waiting for? The factory's machine shop could be turning out tens of thousands of shells a day for our brave fighting men. Instead it is standing shamefully idle. Answer this call and you could be actively helping our troops and our Allies in their valiant fight for justice and freedom! Not only that but you could be enjoying excellent working and living conditions.

The factory is situated in rolling countryside, but within easy reach of major towns. The workers will be housed on-site in a veritable home from home, not in dormitories but in their own separate bedrooms, equipped with a bed with sprung mattress, wardrobe and cupboard. There is an airy dining room serving three hot meals a day. There will be recreation rooms and hairdressing and laundry facilities. In addition, boyfriends will not be discouraged . . .

She understood at once why Mr Marlow was so agitated, and Peter Simmonds confirmed it. He plucked some papers from the 'Pending' tray.

'The *Chronicle*'s fevered prose has already had some success. Mr Marlow has had six letters of resignation.'

Six! Now Miss Frobisher was worried. Surely not . . . well, not Gladys, a home bird if ever there was one. But had Lily Collins been tempted? She'd seemed unnaturally quiet that morning . . . but surely Lily would have had the decency to mention it to her first – and anyway, neither Lily nor Gladys was old enough, thank goodness!

'Two girls from Haberdashery, one from China

and Glass, and three – three! – from Perfume and Cosmetics!' Cedric Marlow expostulated.

Miss Frobisher let out a breath.

'I see. Well, I'm sorry, Mr Marlow. That's a blow, obviously.'

'It is, it is,' fretted Cedric. 'We've invested time and money in training those young women. I hoped they'd be with us for the duration – or until they reached the age for conscription anyway.'

'Of course it's a shock, sir,' said Peter Simmonds smoothly. 'But let's try to look at it another way. With stocks ever lower, profits aren't what they were – and in the present climate, they're not going to recover. A little – shall we call it natural wastage? – may be a good thing.'

'But six at once! If this goes on—'

'There may be no more to come,' soothed Miss Frobisher. 'I'm sure most of the girls know they're very well off where they are.'

Cedric Marlow turned his ire on Simmonds.

'There's enough natural wastage, as you put it, as it is. Whatshername – Beryl Bulpitt – Miss Salter as was – she'll be leaving soon, won't she, to have her baby? That's another vacancy. There'll be more customers than staff at this rate!'

'I'm glad you said that, sir.' Peter Simmonds extracted a sheet from the clipboard he always carried. 'I've been taking a look at staffing levels. And without going so far as to outnumber staff with customers, I think there are several departments where a little rationalisation could be called for.'

Eileen Frobisher stiffened. Now she knew why Mr Simmonds had brought her up here. He had her department in his sights.

'Rationalisation, that's the word that was used,' said Miss Frobisher. She wasn't going to say who'd used it, though anyone would know that it wasn't a word that would fall easily from Cedric Marlow's lips.

It was ten thirty, and, having gathered her thoughts, she'd collected her staff together to explain 'how things stood'. Everyone looked blank.

'I'm sorry, Miss Frobisher,' began Miss Temple, 'you'll have to explain. Something to do with rationing?'

'Not quite. Though it seems I do have to give something up – a member of staff.'

Lily's heart gave a pancake-like flip. Oh, no – no, no, no! Hadn't she had enough bad news that morning? Yes, profits were down, yes, times were hard, but – no, please no! She'd be the one to go; last in, first out, wasn't that the rule?

Miss Frobisher saw the panic in her eyes and quickly spoke.

'I'm sorry, I put that badly,' she said. 'To be honest, I'm still taking it in myself. The good news is that no one will be losing their job. But there will be some shifting around.'

Bit by bit, Lily's heart slowed its insane thudding and she took a deep breath. So did Miss Frobisher, who resumed.

'Beryl – Miss Salter – Mrs Bulpitt as she is now – will be leaving in a couple of months to have her baby and the store will not be recruiting a replacement. Instead, it's been decided that you, Gladys, will move to Toys to fill her position. In fact, it's a promotion, because Mr Marlow's agreed to create a junior-cum-Third Sales role, and that will be yours.'

Thrilled, Lily reached out to squeeze her friend's arm. Gladys's mouth had fallen open before breaking into a delighted smile and Lily couldn't help feeling a swell of satisfaction.

Just a few months ago, Gladys would have been terrified at the thought of anything that might jolt her out of her safe little rut.

But friendship with Lily, bolder and more outspoken, and, when he was home, being on the receiving end of Sid's easy banter, had gradually brought Gladys out of herself. Sid had even engineered her a pen pal, Bill, from among his naval mates, who at Christmas had given her a bracelet and asked if she'd officially be his girl. With that inner glow lighting her face, and a little advice on make-up from Beryl, Gladys didn't even look quite so plain any more.

Lily would be sorry to lose her friend from the department, of course, but she'd only be across the sales floor, and Gladys deserved the promotion – she was already sixteen and had been at Marlow's for over a year.

'So that leaves Childrenswear.' Miss Frobisher smoothed the jacket of her black barathea suit, the one with the buttons like liquorice cartwheels. She was always beautifully turned out. 'I've been lobbying for another salesgirl for some time.'

Miss Temple and Miss Thomas, obviously privy to this, looked expectant.

'Well, I was told today that there's no hope of that in the current climate.'

The shoulders of Miss Thomas and Miss Temple sagged again.

'But I wasn't going to let that go. In the spirit of striking a hot iron, I suggested that this department should have a junior-cum-Third Sales too. And I'm pleased to say that Mr Marlow has agreed.'

She looked at Lily encouragingly. Lily was bemused. Did she mean her?

'Well, Lily?' said Miss Frobisher coolly, when Lily said nothing. 'I take it you'd do me the honour of accepting the position? Or would you like some time to consider?'

Oh Lord, Miss Frobisher must think she was a right dope! It was only because ninety-nine per cent of her brain was still thinking about Jim . . .

'Of course, Miss Frobisher! I'd be thrilled – I was just so surprised!' she stuttered.

Miss Frobisher inclined her head. Gladys hugged Lily, and Miss Temple and Miss Thomas looked pleased for her too, and for themselves: it would take some of the pressure off them.

Customers at Marlow's were dealt with in strict order of staff seniority. Lily wouldn't be serving any of the most prestigious ones – they were Miss Frobisher's preserve – or the ones who spent less, but regularly, or were new, but who had the look of becoming regulars. To start with, she knew, Lily only would be sent forward to serve the less promising-looking new ones, or the tiresome occasionals who spent ages agonising over a single pair of socks and went away without buying anything – the dreaded Mrs Pope sprang to mind. The theory was that Lily could practise on them. But if her manner was good, she might convert them, and they'd become her regulars. Equally, if the other salesladies were busy, or at lunch, she'd be allowed to serve one of their customers, who might look to her again in future, and so gradually, bit by bit, she'd build up her own clientele. She'd even have her own sales book!

'Thank you, Miss Frobisher.' Lily was pink with embarrassment, pleasure – and disbelief. 'That's – I'm sorry, I was stunned! Thank you!'

'Good,' said Miss Frobisher. 'I did wonder! Now back to work, everyone, please.'

In so many ways, Miss Frobisher could not have been more different from Lily's mum, but in one very important way they were the same. Neither ever showed much emotion, but it didn't mean they weren't feeling it.

From the start, Eileen Frobisher had had Lily marked out as promising, and she was secretly triumphant at having secured her this small victory. She also felt some pride in the fact that she'd put down a marker with Peter Simmonds. He might have been used to people jumping to attention and saluting when he was in the Army, but she had no intention of being a pushover. Warrant Officer Class II indeed!

'What was the matter with you?' asked Gladys later. They'd been sent to the stockroom to stow away the last of the unsold January sale items. 'I thought for a minute you were going to turn Miss Frobisher down!'

'I was miles away. Silly of me,' said Lily. 'Anyway, I'm really chuffed. And for you, Gladys.' She pushed a couple of dusty cartons to the back of a shelf to make room for a box of socks.

At least, thought Lily, her new role would give her something to concentrate on once Jim was away. Learning a new skill would keep her occupied, and if she threw herself into work then the days would surely pass, which would only leave the evenings to fill . . . and her Wednesday half-day . . . and Sundays . . .

What would she do without Jim to joke about with, to play cards with, to watch as he dug the veg plot? Well, she could do something a bit more useful, like go along to her mum's WVS and Red Cross meetings and address envelopes and sew gloves. She'd have to listen to the other women droning on about how they missed face powder and Lister's Lavenda 3-ply, of course – not the most appealing prospect, but it wouldn't kill her, and if Jim was doing his bit, she should jolly well do hers. Lily sighed inwardly. No Jim to go to the pictures with, to walk to work with, to fight for the last spoonful of stew. Oh, pull yourself together, she thought. She could always rely on Gladys for company, and in due course there'd be Beryl's baby for everyone to coo over . . . She might even try knitting it a little something herself.

Gladys, of course, was focussed on the excitement of telling Bill about her promotion. Lily couldn't help thinking that it would certainly be a change for Gladys to have something to report. She found it hard enough to find something to write to Sid and Reg every week apart from Marlow's gossip about people they'd never meet, or tiny tragedies like the hens going off lay or the scarcity of soap. She couldn't imagine what on earth Gladys found to put in her thrice-weekly letters to her sweetheart.

The relationship had only come about because Gladys had had a huge crush on Sid, which was pretty embarrassing for them all. Sid had realised, though, and had cleverly set her up with Bill to extricate himself. Gladys always maintained that Bill was the spitting image of the blond, athletic Sid, though in truth Bill was nothing like him – shorter and more solid, with the almost invisible eyelashes that went with hair more ginger than fair, and, though admittedly he shared Sid's wide grin, rather snaggly teeth.

But the important thing was that Bill was gentle, sincere, and well-meaning, all the more to his credit since he hadn't had the most promising start in life – no father that he knew of, given away by his mother and brought up in a children's home in London. Gladys had lost her parents in the Coventry Blitz and now lived with her grandmother, so they were both, in a sense, all alone in the world – until they'd found each other. They were a perfect match.

Bill and Sid were on different naval bases now. Bill was learning all about wireless and telegraphy – or something of that sort. He'd been vague in his letters – he had to be – and Gladys, relaying it to Lily, had been even vaguer. Sid's letters were vague too on his training, but at least they were full of the japes he and his new mates had got up to – dances and pub visits, which Sid claimed were the only things to look forward to in between cleaning your kit and endless drills. That was the trouble, thought Lily. All these young men signed up raring to go, but then they found life in the services dreary. Most of them would leap at the chance to go abroad as soon as they could and get stuck into some real fighting.

Which of course, brought her back to Jim.

'Lily! You do know those are girls' socks you're putting on the boys' shelf?'

Gladys's question jolted her back to the stockroom.

'You're not yourself today, are you?' pursued her friend. 'Come on, what is it?'

'Nothing,' lied Lily. 'Everything's fine.'

Chapter 6

Her mum was at the sink when Lily got in, scrubbing potatoes. A leek, a carrot, and half a swede meant it was Woolton pie for tea – again – though Dora usually managed some stroke of genius to make it moderately tasty. A tin of Colman's mustard on the side gave a clue towards today's inspiration.

'Jim not with you?' she asked, tutting at the scabs on the potatoes that were revealed when the mud washed off.

'No, we didn't leave together,' said Lily truthfully. 'I'll go and change, then I'll set the table, Mum.'

Upstairs she got out of her Marlow's uniform of dark skirt and white blouse and hung them up carefully. The bedroom was cold and she shivered in her slip as she got into her home jumper and skirt. Her mum had put the blackout up, so she couldn't see the backyard, but she heard the latch on the back gate click – Jim had oiled the hinge – and hurried her feet into her slippers. When Jim came up the stairs, she was waiting on the landing.

'The mood you were in this morning, I take it this isn't a welcome committee,' he said coldly. He looked tired. What had they made him do? Run around the parade ground?

'Well?' It was all Lily could do not to fold her arms. Then she'd look like a real nagging wife.

Jim glanced up at the bulb above them in its cracked parchment shade. Buying time, thought Lily unkindly. Then he looked at her, straight.

'No, not well, actually.'

'Jim . . .'

Lily's heart catapulted in her chest. For all the terror she'd felt at the prospect of losing him to the Army, she'd never considered this. Had the medical uncovered some awful illness? A heart murmur? TB?

'What is it? What did they find?'

'You know that song, "The Quartermaster's Stores"? You know how it goes, the chorus?'

Before she could answer, he began to sing:

> 'My eyes are dim, I cannot see
> I have not got my specs with me . . .'

Lily shook her head. She didn't see, either. Then Jim spoke, flatly.

'That's me, Lily. Eyesight not up to it. Rejected.'

'No!'

'Yes.'

'Oh, Jim, I'm so . . .'

What could she say? Her feelings trumped each other in a game of emotional whist.

First of all, and mostly, she was sorry for Jim, desperately so. She could see how bitterly disappointed he was, ashamed even, though it was hardly his fault. How could anyone have known? Yes, he wore glasses, but Lily certainly hadn't guessed how bad his eyes were – and presumably Jim didn't think they were either, or he'd never have seemed so casual about the medical in the first place. Now she wondered how much he compensated for his eyesight and remembered how often he rubbed his eyes when he'd been reading, how it always took him a while to adjust when he came into the house out of the sun, and how he squinted at small print.

On top of that came guilt at how beastly she'd been that morning, how hard she'd made it for him, and how hard it must have been for him to tell her now. Then came dread for him at having to tell other people – her mum and her brothers, Gladys, Beryl, neighbours, colleagues at work, strangers, even. Oh yes, because some people weren't above accosting any young men of serving age who were still at home, calling them conchies and cowards without even asking if they'd tried joining up. But then – and here was the ace on top of all the others – she had to admit it. On top of all of that, she was relieved – so relieved. She was so relieved that she pulsed with it.

'Jim—'

She held out her hand.

'Don't. Please.'

'I'm—'

'Don't say it. Don't say anything. Just leave it.'

He went into his bedroom and quietly closed the door.

Lily bit at a shred of loose skin near her thumbnail – a habit she'd been trying hard to break. She'd got what she wanted – Jim wouldn't be going anywhere after all. She should have been happy. But she wasn't, because he wasn't. Why were feelings so complicated?

Over the next few days, the full story slowly emerged. Jim's short sight needn't in itself have been a problem, but the eye test had revealed that he was as good as blind in one eye.

'Such a shame, he should have been patched as a child,' Dora told Ivy Bulpitt. The two had become fast friends since Les and Beryl's wedding, and Ivy 'popped in' almost as much as Beryl did, usually with Susan in tow.

Ivy tutted and graciously allowed Dora's hovering knife to cut her another piece of Swiss roll. Thanks to the hens, there was usually something in the cake tin in the Collinses' household, even with sugar on ration.

'Just a small one. Got to watch my figure!' Since Ivy was the size and shape of a barrage balloon, the damage had been done, but Dora cut her the generous slice she knew would be expected. 'Still, I daresay his mum'll be relieved. He's her only one, isn't he?'

'Yes.' Dora passed Ivy's plate back. 'They say you worry about a single one more, but I find you just worry about them all equally, in different ways.'

'You're not wrong there,' mused Ivy, contemplating her plate with satisfaction. 'Still, Jim having to stick around is good news for you, Dora. He'll still be here to dig your veg bed and do the hens.'

'That's true. And bless him, now he's had the chance to take it in, he's trying to turn it into a funny story. He said he wasn't doing too badly in the tests with his right eye, but with his left – never mind the chart, they could have held up a couple of dustbin lids and he couldn't have seen them!'

'Bless him, he's a good lad.' Ivy plucked a crumb off her sizeable bosom and popped it in her mouth. 'And it won't affect his job at Marlow's?'

'I shouldn't think so. He's been managing on his good eye all these years, school, work and everything. You can, can't you? If you close one eye and look around.'

Ivy tried it, screwing up her puddingy face in the process.

'I see what you mean. Doesn't make a blind bit of difference.'

She burst out laughing at her unintentional joke, and Susan, poring over a picture book, looked up and smiled her innocent smile. Ivy got up to wipe a skein of dribble spooling from her daughter's mouth.

'A bit more cake, Susan, love?' asked Dora kindly. 'Then you can help me wind some wool, can't you?'

Jim might have tried to turn his disappointment into a joke against himself in front of most people, but ten days on from his medical, deep down he seemed depressed. He'd been delighted to hear about Lily's promotion, and Gladys's, of course, genuinely delighted, but in private, with Lily, he was still so low in himself that he'd managed to convince himself that his job at Marlow's was under threat.

Lily had never seen him like this before, and it unsettled her. But then she'd never suffered a setback like his. Perhaps Jim was entitled to be fed up.

'I've seen more meat on a butcher's pencil than on this plate,' he observed glumly, prodding at his food in the staff canteen. 'And you need a pneumatic drill for these potatoes.'

'Oh come on,' Lily tried to rally him. 'Just because you were looking forward to getting fat on Army rations!'

It was as if he hadn't heard her.

'Still, I might not be eating here much longer.'

Lily laid down her knife and fork.

'Not that again! For the last time, Mr Marlow is not, not now, not ever, going to get rid of you – you of all people!'

What Lily knew, and no one else did, was that Jim was related through marriage to the Marlows: his mother's sister had been married to Cedric Marlow. She'd died young giving birth to their son Robert, and the two sides of the family hadn't been in contact till Jim had come to work at the store. But having Cedric as his uncle surely meant his position had to be secure?

Jim knew what she was driving at, but he didn't agree.

'Lily, you've got eyes in your head – better eyes than mine. There are six girls leaving – seven if you count Beryl. They've managed a neat trick shuffling you and Gladys about, but are any of the others being replaced? No.'

'That doesn't mean they're going to give anyone else the chop – far from it!'

Jim shook his head.

'Marlow's can't afford to carry extra members of staff, whoever they are. Margins are tight, profits are down. And why's Simmonds been appointed? To be a new broom, right? Well, they sweep in corners. And there's no dustier corners than in Furniture and

Household. You know we've got hardly anything to sell!'

'Who has? That applies to every department. And every shop in Hinton!'

'Maybe,' said Jim, 'but I've seen the way Simmonds has been looking at me lately. He's watching me all the time.'

'Don't be ridiculous! He looks at everyone, it's his job!'

'Hm. With that same shark-eyed stare?'

'Shark? You've seen too many newsreels about the Nazis, you really have!'

But Jim wouldn't be told.

'He's got to get rid of someone from our department,' he reasoned. 'There's a limit to how long Marlow's can still employ all five of us. I had a woman in this morning asking when we'd have lead crystal dressing table sets again. I felt like telling her a crystal ball would be more use.'

'Fine. Get one. And what future do you see for yourself if not here? Another job? Where? And doing what exactly?'

'Well, good question.' Jim pushed his plate away, unfinished – unheard of. 'I'm considering lots of options, actually.'

'Are you?' There was something in his tone, and Lily pushed her plate away too. It was one thing to dismiss his suspicions about Mr Simmonds, but this sounded serious.

Jim looked at his watch.

'I should go. I'm due back soon.'

'Jim!' protested Lily. 'You can't leave it like that! Aren't you going to tell me what these options are?'

'Not till I've narrowed them down a bit.'

Lily made a conscious effort to stay calm. 'Let me narrow them down for you. You stay here and get promotion after promotion till you take over from Mr Marlow.'

'Hang on!' Jim looked into the distance and pretended to shade his eyes against an imaginary sun. 'What's that I see? Oh yes. A flying pig.'

'Well, why not?' protested Lily. 'His son's not interested, and he's got to hand it on to someone.'

'Well, that's a nice little fantasy.' Jim tipped back on his chair. 'You carry on with it. Maybe in your world, Lily, we're not even at war – men, women, children dying every day while I'm telling our customers why we haven't got any tray cloths.'

Like a round of mortar fire his words hit home. Suddenly, with horrible clarity, she knew. Idiot that she was! Why hadn't she realised Jim wasn't the sort to take 'no' for an answer?

'You're going to re-apply, aren't you, to the Army? Tell them you want a desk job.'

'Well, there's enough of them,' Jim said reasonably. 'Someone's got to keep things going behind the scenes.'

'Pen-pushing?'

'It's still a lot more useful than what I'm doing here. And they can't say I'm not suitable for that!'

Lily swallowed hard.

'But Jim . . . it could be . . . you could be sent anywhere!'

'That's rather the point with work of national importance,' said Jim, stressing the 'national'. 'Or there's plenty of other kinds of war work. Factories, shipyards, the mines—'

This was getting worse.

'The mines?'

'They've lost a lot of men to the Forces. They're going to have to replace them somehow, and it's one job women can't do.'

The vision of a blackened Jim humping coal was even worse than one of him jabbing someone with a bayonet.

'You, a miner? You can't be serious.'

Jim looked at her straight, sincere.

'Lily, please. Put yourself in my shoes. In all conscience, how can I stay here selling tray cloths, day in day out – if we had any to sell? How do you think that makes me feel?'

'Well, all right . . .' It made him deeply unhappy, she could see. 'But—'

'If you don't see me as a miner or a steelworker – and I'll give you that, you could be right, then at the very least I could jack this in and go home. There's plenty of work on the land.'

Of course! Jim had grown up in the country – his mother had moved away from Hinton and met his father there. She would be over the moon if he made that choice. And farming was a reserved occupation.

Jim suddenly tutted and looked at his watch again.

'All this talking – you've made me late!'

He stood up and pushed his bowl of plums and custard towards her.

'You can have this. I'm not hungry anyway.'

Lily looked up at him, speechless.

'See you,' he said casually.

He smiled briefly and walked away.

Lily looked down at the bowl in front of her. She found she wasn't hungry either. In fact, she felt rather sick.

Surely he – she – hadn't had a reprieve from the Army just for him to go off somewhere else?

Chapter 7

Dinner break over, plums untasted, Lily went back to her department with a heart that felt as if it was strapped into the Big Dipper at Blackpool Pleasure Beach – as if it hadn't had enough ups and downs lately.

Instinctively she glanced across to Furniture. Jim was nowhere to be seen, but Gladys, busy straightening the rails, mouthed 'Delivery', which gave Lily some relief. At least that explained his absence. He wasn't up on the management floor handing in his notice. Yet. Even so, Lily found it difficult – impossible, actually – to share Miss Temple's outrage over the fact that Gentlemen's Outfitting had received a quantity of caps when Miss Frobisher had had children's pixie hoods on order since before Christmas.

'It's getting ridiculous!' Miss Temple complained, but her indignation only emphasised Jim's point. If they couldn't get the goods to sell anyway, Marlow's would be happy to let staff go. Why shouldn't Jim take the decision for them?

The afternoon dragged. It more than dragged, it positively limped towards five thirty and going-home time.

At last the final customer had left, the department was tidy, and Lily could make her escape. Jim had returned to his department mid-afternoon, and her plan was to intercept him before he got to the back stairs and gave her the slip. She'd spent the hours since dinner, when she was pretending to listen to Miss Temple, formulating her plan. She might not have any hope of persuading Jim out of this notion of leaving, but she could at least urge him not to do anything hasty. It was her only hope.

But it was not her day. Before she was halfway across the sales floor, she saw Mr Simmonds approaching. Like an avenging angel he bore down on Jim, his famous clipboard turned, in Lily's mind, into a flaming sword. She couldn't tell from that distance whether he had a particularly shark-like look in his eye – which would have sat rather oddly on an avenging angel, she realised.

But whether he had or not, could Lily trust Jim not to take the chance to blurt out that he was thinking of resigning? Surely Mr Simmonds, ex-Army as he was, would heartily endorse it. The mood Jim was in, he'd probably convinced himself that Simmonds thought he was ducking his duty anyway.

Whatever, it was too late. Mr Simmonds steered Jim through the double doors to the stairs – and Lily's chance was gone.

Miserably she trudged home. Even the first catkins on the alder trees in the park couldn't cheer her, nor the blackbird chirping from a chimney pot as she turned into their street.

Inside the house, she found her mother pinning on her hat in readiness for another evening of rolling bandages. Wordlessly, but smiling, Dora nodded towards a postcard on the mantelpiece.

Standard Forces' issue – and Sid's writing!

Lily snatched it up.

Greetings, all! it began – a typically cheery Sid opener.

Sorry I couldn't make it back when my darling brother was home, but I've finally managed to get some leave! It'll be midweek, unfortunately, only 24 hours, and not quite sure when (here something was crossed out in blue pencil – more likely an expletive than a revelation about his travel plans) *but before the end of the month for sure. Will write again as soon as I know. Toodle-pip! Sid.*

Lily turned her eyes to the heavens and gave a sigh. Thank goodness! Maybe it was a sign. Maybe all Mr Simmonds had wanted to talk to Jim about had been that afternoon's delivery. Maybe there was still time for her to urge Jim to take his time, and not to rush into anything. Then when Sid came back on leave she could get him on side. And if anyone could talk some sense into Jim, or at the very least jolly him out of the state he was in, it was Sid – lovely, funny, but still sensible Sid.

'There's only pilchards for tea,' Dora said, hat now firmly anchored. 'But there's plums and custard for afters. I hope you didn't have them for your dinner.'

Lily turned and gave her mum the first genuine smile of the afternoon.

'No,' she replied. 'I didn't.'

Dora had hardly been gone five minutes – Lily hadn't even changed out of her work clothes – when she heard what were unmistakeably Jim's footsteps coming down the entry. She certainly hadn't expected him back this soon – his conflab with Mr Simmonds hadn't taken long. Was that a good thing or a bad? Breath bated, she waited for the gate, the latch, the back door, bracing herself for what she might be about to hear.

She thought afterwards that she should have braced herself a bit more firmly, because the door was flung back on its hinges, and suddenly Jim was there, shouting 'Lily!' and almost cannoning into her.

Lily leapt back.

'What is it?'

Jim was grinning from ear to ear.

'Those shark eyes of Mr Simmonds? Turns out

they see more than you or I could ever suspect! But I think you'll like it!'

Pilchards had never been an especial favourite of Lily's, but that night they could have been – what was it that posh people ate? – oysters? lobster? – well, whatever it was, they didn't taste like pilchards usually did. Though that might have been thanks to the bottle of ginger beer that Jim had nipped to the outdoor to get.

'Something to celebrate, eh?' he said as they chinked glasses.

'Definitely,' Lily replied.

The crisis was over. Jim wouldn't be leaving after all.

'I hate to say "I told you so", Jim,' chortled Lily.

'But you're going to anyway. As if you haven't already, about a million times.'

'Well, it's true—'

Jim sat back and folded his arms.

'D'you know something? Next time I see a pub called "The Nag's Head", I'm going to pinch the sign and hang it outside your bedroom door!'

'Now, now, children!' Sid reprimanded them. 'Behave, or you won't get any pudding!'

It was the following week and Sid was back on his promised twenty-four-hour pass. As it was Wednesday and half-day closing, he'd arranged to meet Lily and Jim straight from work and treat them to lunch.

The reunion had been as ecstatic as Lily could have wished for. Jim had hung back, smiling, as Sid, grinning from ear to ear, had whirled her in the air so fast she'd almost lost a shoe, and the other Marlow's staff setting off for their half-days had shaken their heads and smiled too.

On the way to the British Restaurant in the Mission Hall, Lily had rattled away non-stop.

'No pudding' was an empty threat, though, because they already had their puddings on their trays, all-in for a very reasonable 9d, so Lily graciously, with a mock bow, conceded. To be fair, it was Jim's story.

'So,' Sid went on over the clatter at the trestle tables around them, 'this Simmonds character, Jim, that you thought was going to give you the boot, practically begged you to stay?'

'I wouldn't put it quite like that—'

'Of course he did!' Jim's story or not, Lily jumped in. 'Never mind shark-eyes, Jim's Mr Simmonds's blue-eyed boy!'

(Funny, Lily thought, that after being turned down by the Army on account of his eyesight, eyes were featuring so much in Jim's future career.)

Sid silenced her with a look.

'And he and Mr Marlow just wanted some new ideas? What are you thinking of, then, Jimbo?' Sid was off again, messing with people's names. 'Live mannequins in the windows? Roof garden with a Palm Court orchestra? How about slashing prices – I'd go for that!'

Lily was dying to supply the details – she was that proud of Jim – but managed with great restraint to contain herself. In preparation for her promotion, Miss Frobisher had given her the sales staff manual. It was very explicit on politeness, tact, and quiet dignity, none of which came naturally to Lily. Here was a chance to practise, and to let Jim have the limelight.

'Honestly, Sid,' Jim said now, 'they're nothing very special.'

Typical, thought Lily, annoyingly modest! He had tact and quiet dignity off to a 'T' . . .

'Jim, that's not true! Tell him!'

'Oh come on, the first thing is just obvious.'

'So obvious that no one else had thought of it!'

'Lily, who's telling this tale?' asked Sid patiently.

Lily sat back. Keeping to the sales staff dictums was going to be a serious challenge, she could see.

Jim resumed. 'Cedric Marlow's done some amazing things. From one tiny draper's shop, he's made Marlow's what it is today. When the war started, and the bombings, he was right on the button – air-raid shelter in the basement, fire-watching and plane spotters on the roof, bells and whistles – literally – to warn staff and customers about air raids almost before the sirens had started.'

'He made space for a Red Cross stall,' put in Lily. She just couldn't help herself. 'An interpreter's desk, too, when the refugees started arriving from France and Belgium.'

'That's right,' said Jim. 'But he's not daft. He's nearer seventy than sixty now and he must realise he's not quite up to the mark. So he's asked me and Peter Simmonds to—'

'Get that, Sid! Peter, if you please! And after all Jim said about him!'

Jim ignored her and carried on. '—to come up with suggestions. On three fronts. First, how can the store do more for the war effort, and keep the staff happy at the same time. And then he wants some ideas to bring in more custom.'

'So this "obvious" thing is what? Don't tell me – you're going to suggest a Suggestions Box!'

They'd finished their main courses now and Sid reached for a cigarette: he'd swapped to Player's Navy Cut from his pre-war brand the minute he'd joined up. He was very proud of being in the Senior Service – and never let Reg, still on Woodbines, forget it.

'No. A Fowl Club,' said Jim.

Sid paused with his cigarette halfway to his lips.

'Hang on. Pig Clubs, yes, I've heard of them—'

'Not very practical,' said Jim, 'on the roof of the store.'

'You're going to keep chickens on the roof of Marlow's?'

'It's wasted space apart from the fire-watchers' hut. And it's only what we're doing already at Lily's but on a bigger scale,' reasoned Jim. 'Any of the staff that are interested will give up their egg coupons and get coupons for grain instead.'

70

'Which will feed the hens, with some of the canteen waste from the store, instead of it all going in the pig bin,' added Lily.

'The store carpenters can knock us up some housing. And I'll get the chickens a few at a time.'

'Jim knows all the farmers in his village,' supplied Lily helpfully. 'He's got all the contacts, and club members will get far more eggs this way than on ration.'

'Incredible!'

Lily beamed so proudly on Jim he might have been her first-born who'd won a Bonny Baby Contest.

'And? Tell him the rest, Jim!'

'All right, I'm getting there.' Jim had been hoping to get stuck into his jam sponge, but he could see Lily wasn't going to let up. 'Simmonds wasn't convinced the staff were doing enough for Civil Defence. So he's got the ARP in, and the Voluntary Fire Service and the Home Guard. To give talks and drum up some recruits. In fact, he wants to make it compulsory for anyone who's not medically unfit.'

'Huh, you can take the bloke out of the Army . . .' mused Sid.

'And for the girls—'

'Women,' corrected Lily.

'Sorry. For women, we're going to start sewing and knitting classes in the Haberdashery department. For staff and customers. Beginner, intermediate and advanced.'

'And let me guess! They can buy everything they need at Marlow's!'

'Never entered our heads,' said Jim innocently.

'Well, well. I can't wait to see you join those, Lil!'

Lily rolled her eyes. She'd told Sid in letters about her cack-handed attempts to knit something for Beryl's baby, and how the wool had got so grubby and stringy with having to unravel it where she'd gone wrong that she'd had to give it up as a bad job.

'I might try the sewing,' she said. 'But that's just the "doing more for the war" bit, isn't it, Jim? And for keeping the staff happy and involved. Tell him your ideas for the shop.'

'No, no, that's more than enough about me,' said Jim. 'Tell us what you've been up to, Sid.'

'Oh, no, that can wait,' said Sid dismissively. 'It's not much, and I'll only have to tell it all over again to Mum. One thing's bothering me about this Fowl Club of yours, though, Jim. The name.'

'What about it?'

'Well, it's not very catchy, is it? In fact, it's most unfortunate. How about . . . "The Feather Club" or . . . I dunno . . . yes, I do!' He clicked his fingers. '"The Cluck-Cluck Club"! Wouldn't that be better?'

Lily burst out laughing. Chicken keeping might have its mucky side, but Sid didn't have to make it sound like a sleazy nightclub. Or, knowing Sid, perhaps he did.

Chapter 8

Gladys, meanwhile, had planned her half-day with
care. Time off from work without some chore to do
for her gran, who was a bit of a moaner and inclined
to take to her bed at the drop of an aspirin, was
too precious to waste. Today, a neighbour was sitting
with her, and, joy of joys, the Gaumont was showing
That Hamilton Woman! again. Gladys had loved it
first time round – a proper two-hankie job – so,
with a bag of penny creams, she was planning a
cosy, if weepy, afternoon in the stalls. Lily might
normally have come with her, but Sid's leave had
put paid to that, and it was only natural she'd want
to spend the time with him. And in truth, Gladys
didn't really need any more company than Laurence

Olivier and Vivien Leigh. The prospect unfurled happily in front of her as she walked towards the cinema. A lovely romantic weepie – and such pretty frocks too . . .

But then, there in front of her, leaning on a lamp post – all that was missing was the ukulele – was—

'Bill! No! No! It can't be! Is it really you?'

'Hello there, Gladys. I'm real enough – pinch me if you like! Pleased to see me, are you?'

In films this was the point where the heroine would have fallen into her loved one's arms, but Gladys was enough of a realist to know that she was no heroine, even in her own life. Though she was sure Bill would be quick and strong enough to catch her, she wasn't at all sure she could manage the graceful, loose-limbed melting that others like, well, Vivien Leigh, say, could achieve. Instead she stared, dumb-struck and open-mouthed.

Bill grinned the gappy, jaggle-toothed grin that made her insides melt.

'That's a "yes", is it?'

Leaving no room for doubt, he stepped forward and wrapped her in a close embrace.

'Oh Bill! I can't believe—' was all Gladys had time to say before the rest of the sentence was lost in a kiss.

When their enthusiastic reunion had finally run its course, Bill tucked a lock of her disarranged hair behind her ear.

'It's good to see you, Glad,' he whispered. 'I've missed you.'

'Not as much as I've missed you!'

It was what they'd said last time they'd met. He'd promised they'd say it every time – and he'd remembered! Gladys gazed at him adoringly. She hadn't seen him since the good news about her forthcoming promotion, but she'd written to him about it, and he'd sent back not a letter but a card, a proper 'Congratulations' card, with a little bellboy in a frogged red uniform on it, carrying a basket of flowers. Gladys had been moved to tears. Not only had he gone to all that trouble to find a card, he'd written inside: 'So proud of you!'. It was still up on the little mantelpiece in her room: in fact, she doubted she'd ever take it down.

'But how did you get leave?' she marvelled. 'And why didn't you let me know?'

Bill folded her arm through his, and, taking the outside of the pavement – such a gentleman! – led her off towards Lyons Corner House. ('No point being in the Navy if you can't push the boat out!')

'There's no hiding it, Glad, I'm on standby now. I could be deployed any day. So any chance I get for leave, I'm going to jump at it. No time to warn you, though. Good job you weren't strolling along with your other boyfriend, eh?'

'Oh, you! But—' she paused. 'How did you know where to find me? How did you guess?'

'No guess needed. You told me you were going to

75

the Gaumont, silly. Don't you remember? In your last letter.'

'So I did!' Gladys leant over, aiming for his cheek, but kissing his ear instead. It didn't matter. 'So you do read my letters, then?'

'All of them, every line!' Bill sounded indignant. 'Why wouldn't I?'

'Well . . .' Along with Gladys's growing confidence had come at least some self-awareness. 'I know I can go on a bit. And often I don't have anything that interesting to say.'

'It's interesting to me,' Bill insisted.

Gladys clutched his arm more tightly. She'd at least had a childhood filled with love. Bill had never had anyone – no hugs, no one to wipe his tears when he fell down, or to make a fuss of his smallest achievements. No one to take an interest in his school work, to buy him a toy of his own, or even a bag of sweets. It was the same when he joined up. Pals, yes, but no letters, no birthday cards, nowhere to go on his leaves. No one to feel special about, no one who felt specially about him, who cared about him as much as they cared about themselves. Well, I do, thought Gladys fiercely. She cared about him more than she cared about herself.

Her insides turned liquid again. It was a good job they'd arrived at Lyons and Bill was holding open the door. Gladys didn't want to blub in front of him. She knew she would when they parted, but for now, all she wanted was for his whole leave to be happy.

'You'll never guess, but Sid's home today, as well!' she informed him as the waitress put their plates down.

'Is he, the crafty beggar?' Bill shook salt enthusiastically over his fish and chips. 'Good job I didn't run into him. He'd only have tried to persuade me to go for a drink!'

Gladys passed him the tartare sauce in its little silver sauceboat. So refined, Lyons.

'I'd have turned him down, though, don't you worry.' Not so worried by the niceties, Bill slopped out a hefty dollop of sauce. 'I know where my priorities lie!'

Gladys looked at him from under her eyelashes. On Beryl it would have been a flirtatious look, but Gladys could no more have been flirtatious than have ridden the winner in the Grand National. On her, it was a shy look of sheer incredulity at her good fortune.

'I still can't get over you being here,' she marvelled. 'This is such a treat. Thank you.'

'And you needn't miss the film,' Bill assured her, tucking in. 'We'll go tonight.'

For himself, he'd have preferred something with a bit of humour or a lot of action, but there were advantages to seeing a romance with Gladys. They both fell silent for a moment, thinking of the pressure of his knee against hers, his arm round her shoulders, and the way he could nuzzle her neck when she clung to him in any especially sad bits.

'Eat up,' he said, waving his fork. 'You know I can't tell you what I've been doing – it's all boring technical stuff anyway. So tell me all about this Mr Whatsisname, the new floor supervisor feller, and these changes he's making.'

So, between mouthfuls – the chips were very good – Gladys did, relaying Jim's idea about starting a Fowl Club and all the eggs it would produce.

'And I thought hens only laid powdered egg now!' grinned Bill. 'So what else? What about inside the store? You said something about keeping the staff happy?'

'Like Mr Churchill says, it's all about keeping going and keeping cheerful.'

'Morale, yeah. Always banging on about it.'

'Yes.' Gladys nodded eagerly. 'So there's going to be sports clubs, football, and netball, and cricket and rounders in the summer – and maybe a sports day, even! There's going to be a doctor once a week, for free.'

'What, for the twisted ankles and groin strains?' asked Bill wryly. 'Go on!'

'And a barber coming in, and a hairdresser.' Gladys, like Lily, had days when she despaired of her hair, though for different reasons – hers was mousy and unbendingly straight – so she was especially pleased

78

about this. 'On Wednesday afternoons,' she added. 'So in our own time – but very cheap.'

'Blimey, I won't recognise you next time! Gladys the Glamour Puss!'

Fearing she might have raised his expectations a little too high, Gladys blushed and looked down.

'I do try to look nice for you, Bill. I mean, if I'd had a bit more notice today . . .'

Bill speedily backtracked.

'And you do! You do already! I didn't mean anything by it . . .' Remorseful, he grabbed her hand. 'Gladys. I truly didn't . . . I didn't mean . . . I love you just the way you are.'

The words had spooled from his mouth before he could reel them back, but as Gladys stared at him, he realised he didn't want to, even if he could.

'There, I've said it,' he added quietly.

Gladys started to tremble. She turned their joined hands over, stroking the fine, almost transparent, hairs on his fingers. 'Do you really?'

'Blimey, give a bloke a chance,' protested Bill, blushing. 'I just said so, didn't I? Want me to spell it out in Morse Code? Or flags?'

'No, of course not!'

Gladys screwed up her courage. She'd wanted to say it for so long, but now the chance had come . . . Still, if Bill had managed it . . .

'I love you too, Bill, I do, I really, really do. So much. I only didn't say, because . . . oh, Bill.'

Leaving one hand in his, she sat back and put the other to her chest.

'Ooh, my heart's hammering! I'm sorry, I don't think I can eat any more. Do you want the rest of my chips?'

At the Collinses' that evening, there was another surprise, though perhaps on a slightly lesser plane.

There was a new delicacy on the table, something that had sat in the larder all day with Dora peeking at it occasionally as if it might explode.

'They call it Spam,' she said, as Lily cut into the thick fritter of bright pink meat on her plate alongside the cauliflower and potatoes.

'Special Processed American Meat,' said Sid, who knew everything, or managed to give that impression. 'We've had it in the NAAFI since last year. But if it's reached Hinton, I'm telling you, it really has arrived.'

'Well,' said Jim, chewing thoughtfully. 'It's a funny texture. Sort of slimy, like a face flannel. But it doesn't taste too bad.'

'And at least it brightens things up,' added Lily.

The colourlessness of the wartime diet was as much a trial to her as its sheer repetitive blandness. Everything looked beige and tasted beige. Never mind moaning about vanished brands of knitting wool or soap, how she longed for a vivid orange or a banana. She'd even have sucked on a lemon.

Dora made no comment. She'd acquired this tin

quite legally, but Ivy, with her many and various 'contacts' about which Dora never enquired ('Don't ask a question to which you don't want to know the answer' was another of her mottoes) had offered her up to three more, and she was seriously wondering, after the family's reaction, whether to take her up on it. Best change the subject.

'Still nothing from Reg in the post,' she observed sadly.

'And it's been a whole month since they left,' objected Lily, looking to Sid for his superior knowledge of shipping.

'They're probably not there yet.' Sid took a swig of tea. 'No news is good news. If they'd run into trouble, we'd have known about it by now.'

Indeed they would: it had been a dreadful winter at sea. Ever since last November, when they'd sunk the *Ark Royal*, the Germans had seemed unstoppable, and January had been one of the worst months for shipping since the start of the war. German U-boats had sunk more ships than there were days in the month – thirty-five in all.

'Where should his ship have got to by now?' asked Jim.

'Should be well past the Cape,' pondered Sid. 'But they may have had to put in somewhere en route. Refuel, take on supplies, some mechanical fault . . .'

'So why didn't he write from there?' demanded Lily. 'He might know we'll be desperate to hear!'

'He might have been a bad boy and not allowed onshore. No, scrub that,' Sid corrected quickly as Dora looked concerned. 'Not very likely with our Reg, is it? But maybe someone else was and they all got confined to barracks, well, had to stay on board.'

'That's not very fair!'

'Nothing's fair in love and war, Lil,' Sid chastised. 'Or, if they were going to be in dock a while, they might have been carted to a camp upcountry. Where the only post's a forked stick or smoke signals!'

Dora sighed. 'We'll have to be patient, then.'

'Yes, you will,' said Sid. 'I dunno why you're getting so excited. What's he going to say when he gets there, anyway – "I can't tell you where I am but there's lots of sand"?'

'And what would your letters say?' Lily felt obliged to defend Reg. '"I can't tell you where I am but there's lots of water"?'

'Come on, Lil! I hope I'm a bit better correspondent than Reg!'

It was true – Reg's letters, short and infrequent, were unlikely ever to give Freda, their post girl, a hernia.

'Well,' said Jim, who was privy to the contents – Sid's letters were generally read out loud – 'I admit your last darts match sounded pretty gripping, but let's be honest, the only thing these two really want to hear about is who you're courting.'

This too, was true. With Sid's good looks he'd

never been short of girlfriends, and it was hard to believe he wasn't 'up with the lark, to bed with the Wrens', as the saying had it.

'Crikey, don't spare my blushes, will you?' Sid, unusually, seemed taken aback by Jim's directness. 'You know me, same as always, taking my chances at village dances.'

'Still no one special, then?' enquired Dora.

Sid might not like being put on the spot, but Lily was delighted. Jim was quite right. It was the question she – and her mum, she knew – had been dying to ask.

Sid opened his mouth to answer, but the back door opened, and a familiar voice called 'Only me.'

Lily looked at Jim and Jim looked at Lily, but instead of the eye-rolling that Beryl's arrival mid-meal (again!) might have caused, their eyes telegraphed concern. It didn't sound like Beryl's usual cheery greeting. Nothing like.

Dora twisted in her chair to call through to the scullery.

'Beryl? Never mind your boots, come on through.' So she was concerned as well. Normally it was strictly boots off at the door. 'What is it? What's happened?'

Chapter 9

Poor Beryl. She was in a heck of a state.

'It can't be,' she blubbered, as, tea abandoned, they all clustered around the chair by the fire where she'd been installed. 'The baby's due in a few weeks, and my Les won't be here to see it come!'

Les had got his posting. He and his unit were being shipped out in a fortnight – and, like Reg, he wasn't entirely sure where. All they knew was 'overseas'.

Jim had quietly disappeared to the scullery, but now re-emerged. He tactfully put a cup of tea down at Beryl's side.

'Well done, Jim.' Dora gave him an approving smile. 'Sugared?'

Jim nodded. 'One. And a bit.'

Sugar was precious, but if ever it could be sacrificed, it was now.

'Never mind sugar.' Sid went to his kitbag, undid it, and produced a half-bottle of rum. 'Put her a nip of this in it. And let's get some sense talked around here.'

They all looked at him.

'Well, not by me! What do I know about marriage and babies? Over to you, Mum!'

As he spoke, he drew up the small rush-topped stool, lifted Beryl's ankles, and placed it gently under her feet. Then, with a look at Jim that said 'Danger! Waterworks alert!' they both retreated to the safety of the dining table.

Dora poured a careful capful of rum into Beryl's tea. She didn't really approve of alcohol, and certainly not in the house, but in the circumstances . . . She stirred Beryl's tea for her and handed her the cup.

'Now look here, Beryl,' she said. 'You know what we do round here when someone's in trouble. We all pull together. We did it last year, when you first found out you were expecting, and we'll do it again. It's a crying shame Les won't be with you, but you won't be on your own.'

Lily nodded vigorously.

'The fact is,' Dora continued, unconsciously echoing what Reg had said to Lily, 'you're not the only one. You're far better placed than some, and far, far better placed than you might have been. You've got a good home, a good husband in Les, and you'll have all the help and support you could wish for from Ivy, I know you will.'

'And me and Mum,' put in Lily. 'Whatever you need. Gladys too, I bet.'

'I know, I know . . .' Beryl wiped her eyes with a sodden hanky. 'You'll think I'm stupid,' she snuffled, 'and I am, it's not like I haven't known it was coming, but I dunno, when it actually happens . . . I was in the phone box speaking to Les, and when he told me, I felt my legs just go from under me!'

Lily reflected that given the size she was, Beryl must have been pretty firmly wedged in the box anyway, so there was little or no chance of her sinking to the floor, but she gave her the benefit of the doubt. If you weren't allowed a bit of poetic licence when you were pregnant, then when were you?

Beryl applied her hanky to her eyes again, sniffed, and tried to collect herself.

'It'd mean a lot to me, Dora,' she quavered, 'if you'd be with me when the baby comes. Ivy'll be there if she can, I know, but with Susan . . .'

'You don't have to ask, Beryl,' Dora replied. 'Take it as read.'

'Thank you,' Beryl said in a small voice. 'You're golden, you really are.'

Beryl's appeal came as no surprise to Lily. For two plain-speakers forced together by circumstance, Beryl and Ivy got on surprisingly well, and Beryl showed an equally surprising patience with Susan. But Ivy knew her daughter-in-law: when it came to childbirth she was unlikely to be the grin-and-bear-it type. Ivy had pointed out that the sight and sound of Beryl in labour could frighten Susan into fits; Les had agreed, and had promptly booked Beryl into the local maternity home.

But Beryl was no fool either. In the short time since Les had told her about his posting, she'd obviously realised that encouraging words and forehead-swabbing, when it came to it, would be much more likely to come from the ever-practical but relatively more compassionate Dora.

'If I could add one thing from the, er, male perspective?'

Sid was shuffling the cards, which had also appeared from his kitbag – he never travelled without them. A pile of matchsticks indicated he'd inveigled Jim into a game of pontoon. They all swivelled to look at him as he laid down the pack.

'There's no other way to put this, Beryl, but frankly Les did his bit last summer. Even if he was here, the maternity home's no place for a bloke! He'd have most likely been down the pub if he'd got any sense.'

Dora shot him a look that would have quelled, if not felled, anyone less robust, but Sid, being Sid, got away with it. Beryl gave a damp smile.

'You're right there,' she admitted. 'He's said as much!'

'Exactly! So when you're screaming in agony bringing

the little one into the world, far better that he's throwing up over the side on the high seas or in some miserable billet suffering as well, don't you think?'

Lily had to hand it to Sid. Whenever she'd tried to make a joke of anything serious, like Reg's posting or Jim's medical, she hadn't convinced even herself, but somehow, annoyingly, he managed it. Beryl even half-laughed.

'Yeah – and serve him right!' she sniffed. 'I mean, he's looking forward to the baby and everything, real excited he is, but even if he was here, it's not like he'd be changing the nappies, is it, or doing the feeds?'

'In my experience, not in a rain of pig's pudding.'

Dora had pronounced, and after that, no one was likely to disagree.

Gradually the evening got its usual rhythm back. Dora swept Sid's cards and matchsticks off the table – she didn't approve of gambling, either, however harmless. Lily re-laid the cork mats and got out the pudding spoons – five of them, because Beryl bravely thought she might manage 'just a bit' of the blanc-mange that was on offer.

With Beryl accepting her second helping (typical!), the conversation turned to naming the baby. That was something that would have to be decided, surely, Lily asked, before Les went away? Or had they already chosen?

Boys' names, it seemed, were still a subject of discussion – Ivy was pushing for Cuthbert, her father's name, and Beryl was resisting – but she and Les had settled on a girl's name – sort of.

'Shirley,' she proclaimed. 'Or maybe Hazel. Or possibly Barbara.'

'What's wrong with Winnie?' asked Sid.

'I don't think so,' said Beryl, wrinkling her nose. 'It's a bit old-fashioned.'

'Not for a girl, a boy!' exclaimed Sid. 'Winston.'

Looking dubious, Beryl tried it out.

'Winston Bulpitt . . . I dunno . . .'

'Rubbish! It's got a right ring to it! A future prime minister if ever I heard one!' declared Sid.

Lily wasn't letting him get away with that.

'And what about Shirley Bulpitt? Or Barbara or . . . what was the other one? Hazel? Women got the vote after the Great War, didn't they, so who knows how far we could go when this one's over?'

Sid laughed.

'Nice try, Sis.'

'Well, if we're good enough to rivet your ships, why not?'

Dora smiled, though Beryl said she wasn't sure she'd want any child of hers getting mixed up in politics. Only Jim said quietly that he thought Lily might have a point.

'Well, I think we got out of that one all right,' Sid said later. 'She was only here an hour, and I'm not that keen on blancmange anyway.'

Lily and Jim weren't the only ones to have noticed

Beryl's knack of turning up at mealtimes – and often outstaying her welcome. Now Sid and Lily were tidying up the scullery after their interrupted meal, while Jim walked Beryl home.

'*You* got out of it, you mean!' said Lily tartly. 'She got you off the hook. You were about to have to own up, so come on, Sid. *Is* there someone special that you're seeing?'

'You don't let up, do you?'

'You never do! It's not fair!' Lily objected. 'You always manage to worm things out of people, winkle out their innermost secrets, and you never give anything away! You're not in the Navy at all. I think you're in Intelligence.'

'I wish!'

'Come *on*,' wheedled Lily. 'I won't tell. Not even Mum, if you don't want me to.'

'Especially not Mum! She can smell orange blossom ten miles off!'

'So there *is* someone!'

Sid let out a big breath.

'I . . . look, OK, there is, but I don't want to say any more. I don't want to jinx it.'

'I knew it!' said Lily. 'I thought you were looking shifty when I asked you at tea.'

'Shifty? Me? Must have been a bit of Spam gone down the wrong way.'

'Rubbish! Who is she? I won't tell anyone, I promise, if you don't want me to.'

'And I won't tell anyone how much you like Jim.'

Crafty devil! Now he'd put her on the spot.

'What? Jim? Me? We're friends, that's all.'

'That's why you were so pleased when he failed his medical, was it?'

'Did I say that?'

'You didn't have to. It jumped out and bit me as soon as I opened your letter, however much you tried to play it down. Oh, I'm sorry, Sis. Come here.'

Lily's blush was lighting up the dim scullery better than the overhead bulb. Her brother gave her a big hug.

'You needn't be embarrassed, Lil. Jim's a smashing bloke. I like him, Mum likes him . . . And with Gladys paired off, and Beryl married . . . well, why not?'

Lily wished she could explain. Sid was right about the medical – look how she'd agonised about it and how relieved she'd felt when Jim had told her the result. She knew she liked – perhaps more than liked – Jim, and she thought he liked her too – as a friend. But did it go any further than that? And would either of them want it to? Lily wasn't entirely sure how she felt about it, let alone how he might.

Something was holding her back.

'Oh, I don't know, Sid,' she said.

She spoke slowly because she was thinking it out as she went. She'd never tried to put it into words before. She'd never dared even to think seriously about it before. It had always been too prickly and awkward and it was easier to think about something else. Now she made a stab at explaining.

'It's all very well talking about Gladys and Bill, but it's different for them. A boyfriend is all Gladys has ever wanted, and now she's got one, well, that's it for her. Bill's her world and she's so happy. I can see that, and I'm happy for her.'

'I know you are,' agreed Sid. 'And it's great for Bill too. He's never had anyone, to, well, love him for himself, I suppose. They're good for each other.'

'Yes. But I don't know . . . this promotion I'm going to get when Beryl leaves, and these responsibilities Jim's been given . . . I don't know, I just feel . . . I think he likes me, and I like him, but we're both still – well, finding out who we are, who we want to be, before we do any of that boy-girl stuff. I think there's things we both want to do, at work and everything. Have to do, maybe. Does that make sense? Any sense?'

She hoped so, because she wasn't sure it made sense even to her. But Sid smiled his most generous smile.

'It makes perfect sense,' he said. 'I'd expect no less from you, Sis. You've got the brains for all of us in this family, that's for sure.'

Sid did say the nicest things sometimes.

'Look, now you know he's not got to join up,' he went on kindly, 'you've got plenty of time. See how it works out for the pair of you at Marlow's and take it from there. If he'd been going away it'd be different. It focusses your mind, you know, when you know you might see someone one day and not the next. You know you can't waste time. You have to grab it while you can.'

There was something about the way he said it that made Lily dare to ask him again.

'Who is she, Sid? What's she like?'

'Now, come on Lily—'

'No, you come on! I've been honest with you. Please tell me. Is she tall, short? Fat, thin? Dark, fair?'

'Steady on!'

'Where's she from? Mum? Dad? Brothers and sisters?'

'For goodness' sake!' protested Sid. 'What next? Hobbies? Pets? All right, she plays the bagpipes and keeps a parakeet!'

'Oh, don't be daft,' tutted Lily. 'But go on – at least tell me her name.'

'Her name? It's . . . all right, it's Anna.'

'Anna. That's nice.'

'Yes.'

Lily tried the name again.

'Anna . . . Well!'

'Now, that's it,' said Sid firmly. 'Please don't ask me any more.'

'I wasn't going to! But I hope it works out for you, Sid. I really do.'

'We'll see,' said Sid. He picked up the jelly mould that Lily had dried. 'Does this still live in the larder?'

'On the right,' said Lily. 'The hook under the pickles.'

Sid went to stow it away.

'Anna,' she repeated as he returned. 'See, that wasn't so difficult, was it?'

Sid had made her promise to tell no one, but as it turned out, Lily had no trouble keeping Sid's romance quiet. She'd sworn not to tell her mum, and Jim wasn't about to quiz her – too busy pondering the next phase of his big ideas for Mr Marlow – 'more far-reaching ones' was all he would reveal.

Normally, Gladys would have demanded every detail of Lily's afternoon, but next day at work she was too full of her surprise visit from Bill. As a result, and, as the wireless operator in Bill might have said himself, she was on 'Transmit', not 'Receive'. All Lily had to do was nod and smile along.

'It was so romantic,' Gladys sighed under cover of their polishing the rails. Her duster moved of its own accord as she gazed into the far distance – or perhaps back into the bright bustle of Lyons or the muggy gloom of the cinema. 'Waiting for me like he did, a proper posh lunch and the pictures too . . . back row . . .'

Lily mentally raised her eyebrows. Back row! Things were moving on apace.

'Lovely,' she managed to insert.

'I only wish I'd known . . .' Gladys mourned. 'I'd

have spent longer on my hair. And you don't want to be seen at Lyons in your uniform clothes, do you, really?' She brightened. 'But at least I had my new jumper for the evening.'

'The green one?'

This was Gladys's pride and joy, a recent acquisition, with a lacy yoke. Gladys sighed once more, remembering how her heart had raced under that very yoke as Bill's embraces had become more passionate.

'He says we've got to make the most of the time we've got,' she said. 'He's going to put in for all the leave he can. He says we've got to stick together, two Little Orphan Annies that we are. And . . .' she lowered her voice and said tremulously, 'he told me . . . he told me he loved me, Lily. And I love him. You know I do. So much.'

Checking that Miss Frobisher wasn't looking, Lily squeezed her friend's hand.

'Oh, Gladys,' she said, 'that's lovely. I'm so happy for you. You two belong together.'

She meant it wholeheartedly. But if that was where it took you, whatever her feelings for Jim, that kind of 'belonging' thing didn't feel right for her. She wasn't sure she wanted to belong to anyone but herself, not just yet anyway.

Chapter 10

Spring that year felt like a long time coming. Day after day, the sun made a heroic effort to haul itself over the horizon, only to hide itself in cloud: Lily felt she was more likely to see Christmas decorations than daffodils. She was desperate to put away her shabby winter coat and wear her new work jacket, which, with a blue corduroy skirt and fawn jumper, were the spoils of a highly successful looting expedition at yet another WVS rummage sale.

The additions to her wardrobe at least counted as three things to be cheerful about. It was a tip she'd read in one of Beryl's magazines: every night, before bed, you were supposed to note down Three Good Things that had happened that day. Lily was trying her best, but some days her jaw positively ached from the effort of keeping her chin up.

With Sid and Bill back with their units, Reg still on the high seas, and Jim scurrying around with Mr Simmonds recruiting players for the cricket team and installing hen houses on the roof, she was reliant on Gladys and Beryl for amusement. But Gladys had entered a new galaxy of starry-eyed-ness over Bill and was apt to drift off in the middle of untangling boys' braces to wonder out loud what he was doing at that very moment. And when Lily visited Beryl, she found her a walking medical dictionary, not to say contraceptive. Indigestion, itching, high blood pressure, eclamptic convulsions, backache, piles . . . Beryl had the lot, or felt she might have. Les, meanwhile, preparing for embarkation with his unit, was having problems of his own. Beryl, never one to spare the details, claimed his arm had swelled up 'like a pig's bladder on a stick' after a day of inoculations.

'Mind, if he thinks he's got it bad, I'll wrestle him for it!' she declared. 'Have you seen my feet?' She extended a marginally rounded ankle. 'Water retention, see! Shocking!'

Ivy rolled her eyes at Lily as they went on winding wool. Her patience was wearing thin.

Finally, at long, long last, a letter arrived from Reg: his ship had docked without incident at Port Said. Lily immediately claimed it as one of her Three Good Things, then looked it up in the atlas. It was in Egypt and you pronounced it Port Sigh-eed. Even though the letter was two weeks old and Reg might already be somewhere more dangerous by now, the only sighs at home were ones of relief.

At least he hadn't been posted out East, where the Japanese 'dose of salts' he'd spoken of was having a thoroughly purgative effect. The Collinses' atlas had been getting quite a bashing, all in all, as Lily, with grim fascination, tried to follow their advance. Not for the first time she wished she'd paid more attention in Geography, her most hated subject, as places she'd had never heard of like Salamaua–Lae, part of New Guinea apparently, fell to the Japanese, followed swiftly by Malaya, Hong Kong, and, most horrifically of all, Singapore.

At the same time, she couldn't help worrying that Les's armful of inoculations meant he might be destined for a posting out that way. But Beryl, fortunately, was concentrating on the here-and-now – not even the baby any more, but Les's pre-embarkation leave.

'Our last chance to be a couple,' she expounded to Lily. 'So he'll come home to say hello to his mum and Susan, of course, but then we're off, just the two of us.'

'Off? Where to?'

'Blackpool,' sighed Beryl happily.

Blackpool had long been a cherished destination for Beryl, though Lily wasn't quite sure why. Weren't the pier attractions shuttered up and the beach off-limits?

Not at all, Beryl assured her. Even out of season there was bound to be something on. They might only be staying in a B & B, but it was just two streets back from the prom, and Les had promised her a slap-up dinner at a posh hotel followed by 'dancing the night away' under the glitter ball in the Tower Ballroom.

Varicose veins and swollen ankles were forgotten, if they'd ever existed, and Ivy's black-market contacts harried witless till someone produced a few yards of satin-backed crepe in a buttery yellow. It smelt musty and had a worrying rusty stain down one side, but Beryl was thrilled.

'So spring-like!' she trilled.

She dabbed it with bicarb and water and hung it out to air in the March winds. Then she brought it over to Dora, with a plea to turn it into 'something to knock Les's socks off'. A pattern was duly bought for as svelte a dress as Beryl's size permitted, with cape sleeves and a bow at the neck.

'I suppose I let myself in for it with her wedding dress,' reflected Dora as she hunched over her trusty Singer, trying to fashion a dart. 'This material's a devil to keep straight!'

'You are a wonder, Mum.'

Lily had watched in awe as the length of material had been sliced into bits and then stitched together into something recognisable as a dress under Dora's fingers. She still hadn't signed up for those sewing classes at Marlow's and knew she never would – they'd be a total waste on her. She was having enough trouble with a stocking stitch scarf for Sid, which already looked as if it had been crocheted, not knitted, and wouldn't keep out a draught, let alone a gale on the foredeck.

Even with the war, Lily thought, it was a good job she'd been born when she had. All those female accomplishments that were deemed necessary in the old days – spinning, weaving, darning, stitching samplers! Hardly! Though she did reflect that she'd never have had any problem back then wondering if she ought to get attached to some young man. No one would have wanted her.

When the dress was finished, Beryl twirled ecstatically in their back room.

'You're nothing short of a genius, Dora,' she said, hugging her. 'I might have to name the baby after you. Shirley Hazel Dora, how does that sound?'

Ivy, who'd dropped in to see the finished result, with perhaps 'just a small piece' of cake on the side, did some more eye-rolling.

Three names! Just like the girl, giving herself airs!

'Never mind that. Any more thoughts about Cuthbert?' she asked pointedly.

The trip to Blackpool was a wild success, to Lily's great relief. As usual, Beryl spared her no detail in the telling – including how she'd managed to fit into her honeymoon nightie – just.

'Not that I had it on for long!' she winked.

Lily smiled tightly and tried to steer the conversation to the safety of the Tower Ballroom and the butter-yellow dress.

'Well, that spent more time on the floor than on me, and all!' chortled Beryl. 'A bit of the other can sometimes bring the baby on, you know.'

'Really?' gulped Lily. She hadn't known, and hadn't wanted to, but she did now.

'No such luck,' mourned Beryl. 'I'm going to have to stick it out. I'll be the size of a battleship by the end of it, I can see.'

At least their few days had sent Les off with a smile on his face, Beryl concluded. He'd had to leave her to come home on her own while he re-joined his unit, then travelled straight to Liverpool to set sail on a re-fitted Canadian Pacific liner. Like Reg, he'd been given no specifics about his destination, but again, through rumour, gossip, nudges and winks, his whole unit knew. He was destined for North Africa as well.

'See! I could tell you all thought I was barmy, but he might run into your brother after all!' Beryl crowed.

Lily was spared any further confidences because at that moment, Mr Simmonds clapped his hands and asked for everyone's attention. The store had closed and they were all gathered in the canteen for Beryl's little leaving party.

'I'm sure we'd all like to wish Miss Salter well in her new role,' he said, before presenting her with the gifts they'd clubbed together to buy – a fleecy pram cover and a linen basket – as well as an envelope containing, Lily knew, a Marlow's gift voucher for further purchases from the store. Whatever Jim might think about him having lost his touch, Mr Marlow wasn't completely daft.

Beryl blushed as Mr Simmonds thanked her for her hard work on Toys and welcomed Gladys in her place. Gladys would be fine, Lily knew, working for Mr Bunting, the Toys buyer, who looked like a cuddly toy himself, and one without a hint of a growl.

Lily's promotion didn't get a mention, and she was glad. She was apprehensive enough about the following Monday, when she would step into her new role. Miss Frobisher had spent the past few weeks testing her without warning on various items of stock ('Know your Merchandise', page three of the sales manual) and how to write out sales dockets (page four). She reminded her that, should friends or relations make the mistake of coming in to say 'hello', then, whether she was serving a customer or not, she was to cold-shoulder them politely, and that the more tricky a customer, the more tact you needed.

Lily had nodded eagerly, desperate to do her best, keen for the new challenge. It only reinforced in her own mind that not having the distraction of a boyfriend was the right thing for her at the moment.

Which left the mystery of Sid's girlfriend . . .

Lily might have managed to keep his secret from

everyone else in Hinton, but it only seemed reasonable when she wrote to Sid to ask how things were going. But though weeks had passed since their conversation in the scullery, he was still giving nothing away.

'What have you and Anna been getting up to?' she regularly asked – but the answer she got was always a disappointingly vague, 'This and that'. Instead, Sid would fill his letters with stuff about the latest exercise he'd taken part in, how Nash had fallen off the log over the stream, and how Sid now called him 'Splash', or how, hitching a lift after a night out, a bunch of them had been picked up by a coal lorry, not realising how filthy it had made them till parade next day. In the end, she grew tired of having to edit out even Sid's minimal replies about Anna when she read his letters out to the rest of the household. She was so frustrated that she was even tempted to confide in Jim that Sid at least had a girlfriend, if not her actual name, just so she could let off steam.

But Jim forestalled her, which was good for her conscience at least, by fretting about the next stage of his ideas for the store. Progress so far had been good: several people had signed up for the Fowl Club and were eagerly awaiting the arrival of the first batch of hens. A cricket team had been hastily scrabbled together, and Mr Simmonds was drawing up a fixture list against the police, the fire brigade, and – this would be the Big One – the store's arch rival, Burrell's. The Red Cross and the local ARP had been delighted to welcome a few more volunteers. All of that, Jim said – the stuff for the war effort and to help with what Mr Simmonds called 'staff retention' – had been the easy bit. Now the real work – the ideas to improve the store, to lure in more customers and to boost profits – could begin.

Jim got permission to stay late at Marlow's, visiting the goods inward and accounts departments. He prowled the stockrooms, poking around in cartons and jotting things down in a notebook. He lurked in Burrell's, and Boots, and Marks and Spencer.

'Know your enemy,' he said cryptically, scribing notes at home when the table was cleared after tea. He'd even got hold of a briefcase, if you please, to keep his notes in, which he kept practically chained to his wrist. Lily managed a peek one day and saw headings like 'Inventory Management' and 'Stock Management' (weren't they the same thing?) and another called 'Stock Control' (ditto). But, just like Sid, he wasn't giving away any details and said he wouldn't till he'd discussed the whole thing with Mr Simmonds and Mr Marlow. And whenever he had a free moment, like now, their half-day, he took himself off to the library to do some 'research'.

Lily invited herself along. The transparent pretext was that they might have the latest Agatha Christie, which, coincidentally, was *The Body in the Library*. They both knew it wouldn't be there, but Lily trotted alongside him anyway.

'I wish Sid'd come home,' she lamented, trying to keep up. Lily was quite tall herself, but her legs couldn't match his cheetah-like loping. 'But he won't get any more leave for ages. Can you slow down a bit, Jim?'

'They close in an hour.'

'Did you hear what I said? About Sid.'

'Of course I did.' His pace didn't slacken. 'But why now? Why so keen? He was only home a few weeks ago.'

She couldn't tell him the real reason, of course.

'I don't need a reason, do I?' she stalled. 'He's my brother. I just . . . miss him.'

It wasn't a lie.

'So go and see him.'

'All the way to Hayling Island? It'd take days . . . I'd have to stay overnight!'

'What about this training course of his? That's coming up soon, isn't it?'

'Yes, and in Scotland!' panted Lily from two paces behind. 'Even further!'

'I know that.' They'd reached the library now and Jim waited for her to catch up. 'But it won't be a direct train. He'll have to change somewhere in the Midlands . . . I don't know, Birmingham? Rugby? Northampton? You could get there and back in a day.'

'Jim! That's . . . Why didn't I think of that? You're brilliant!'

'Tell that to Mr Marlow, will you?' Jim started up the steps. 'When I give him the next lot of ideas.'

I won't need to, thought Lily loyally as she pattered up behind him. But she didn't say it: he'd only contradict her. Tact and quiet dignity, she thought. She was learning.

They didn't have the latest Agatha Christie, of course. They didn't even have any old ones, but it didn't matter, because Lily had a new plan for the evening – she wanted to write to Sid. She dashed to the post box as the blackout went up, and was rewarded: within a couple of days, she had her reply.

Sid had had his orders. He and his fellow trainees would be arriving at Snow Hill Station in Birmingham a week on Monday in the late afternoon. As far as he knew, he'd have a couple of hours spare before his connection. Lily would have to take a chance that his first train wasn't delayed, or that the plans didn't change entirely at the last minute, as often happened, but if she wanted to take the risk . . .

'It'd be great to see you, Sis,' he wrote. 'There's a big clock at Snow Hill. Meet me under that. And don't go talking to any strange men – especially not sailors – I know what they're like!'

A meeting with Sid in the offing and her first week as a salesgirl about to start – that easily ticked off two Good Things for the day, thought Lily. Assuming of course, that her first week as a salesgirl would be a Good Thing . . .

Chapter 11

However much she trusted Miss Frobisher to make her transition from junior to junior-cum-third sales as painless as she could, it didn't stop Lily's teeth from chattering like castanets when she presented herself on the sales floor on the first day in her new role.

She'd made a superhuman effort to look smart. She was wearing her better blouse, the one with the fancy revers, and the newer of her two uniform skirts – black barathea, just like Miss Frobisher's suit, not that that had influenced her one jot as, gulping, she'd handed over precious coupons and real money for it. As her hair was famous for taking the smallest opportunity to misbehave, she'd borrowed one of her mum's scarves to stop it from frizzing in case the morning was even slightly damp. Finally, she'd scrubbed her nails till they hurt: her fingertips were still throbbing when she held them out for inspection.

Miss Frobisher nodded them away. But she could tell.

'There's no need to be nervous, Lily,' she said. 'You're ready for this, and you'll make a success of it, I know. I'm expecting great things from you, but . . . There's no need to look like that! Not all at once!'

She shooed Lily off to her usual duties – it still fell to her to polish the rails and un-shroud the baby clothes – though now without Gladys for company. She glanced across to Toys. Mr Bunting was walking Gladys around the stock, Gladys nodding vigorously. Lily hoped she was paying attention for once, and not thinking about Bill.

Nothing happened till about ten o'clock. Miss Thomas was helping a customer whose son needed a new cricket sweater; Miss Temple was stuck with a fussy woman over a heap of boys' shorts. After the long winter, everyone was willing the good weather to arrive. Otherwise the department was quiet. Lily was just wondering whether she might even be sent off for a short morning break, as sometimes happened, when she saw a customer advancing, one of Miss Frobisher's.

Miss Frobisher stepped forward, propelling Lily, puppet-like, along with her.

'Would you mind, Mrs Mortimer, if Miss Collins observed?' she asked, after the usual 'Good morning, and how may we help you today?' rigmarole. 'She's still in training.'

It was a bit of luck, thought Lily. Mrs Mortimer was a dear, a county type, hearty but good-natured, who'd bought all her own children's clothes at Marlow's, and now shopped for her grandchildren. There were six of them counting the newest arrival, a little boy born to her daughter-in-law five weeks ago. She was all smiles.

'Of course not! We all have to learn sometime. What's your name, my dear?'

Lily managed something she hoped was a smile.

'Lil— Collins. Miss Collins.'

'I'm only after scratch mitts for little Bertie, I'm afraid,' said Mrs Mortimer, naming the newest arrival. 'Not the most exciting purchase—'

'But necessary,' said Miss Frobisher, and Lily leapt at once to the drawer where they were kept.

Mrs Mortimer, after minimal deliberation – possibly because there was only one sort on offer – took three pairs.

'He's a little devil,' she said, shaking her head. 'So active, hardly sleeps, ravenous the whole time – his poor mother, she's feeding him herself – and his nurse simply can't keep his nails short enough.'

Miss Frobisher clucked sympathetically as Lily made to pop the mittens back in their packets.

'Perhaps you'd like to record this in your sales book, Miss Collins?' she asked.

What? Write? Miss Frobisher might as well have asked her to ride a unicycle and juggle at the same time. But there was no getting out of it, and, fingers fluttering as much as her heart, Lily took Miss Frobisher's pen. Date. Customer's name and address. Item sold. Cost per item. Number of items . . . Coupons per item. Total number of coupons. Total cost of item. Now do the sum. Do it again to check. Write it in.

Lily had made Jim test her night after night. Three guineas plus 2/11 plus 4/6 . . . 11/6 times three, 5/11 times four . . . but oh, dear, madam's changed her mind – take one of the 5/11s away . . . If a pair of bootees is half a coupon and a baby dress two, how many coupons does Mrs X need to buy three dresses and five pairs? Quick, quick, come on!

The pen hovered. The calculation couldn't have been easier, but she couldn't make a mistake, not on her very first sale, not on the very first page, not in triplicate on her first sheet of carbon! Quick, quick, come on! she thought, and, with a glance at Miss Frobisher, wrote her answers in the ruled columns and added them up.

Miss Frobisher, looking over her shoulder, said nothing. She must have got it right – Miss Frobisher would have stopped her otherwise.

'Will that be cash or account, please, Mrs Mortimer?'

Though you had to ask ('assume nothing'), she knew the answer already. Miss Frobisher never dealt with cash customers.

All that remained was to carefully cut, not tear, the relevant coupons from the book – the baby's own – that Mrs Mortimer handed over, and place them in the tube with the top three copies of the sales docket. Thank goodness there were no coins to count or to drop on the floor!

With the tube whizzing on its way, Lily slid the mittens back into their packets. There was no other wrapping allowed, but everyone was used to this by now, and Mrs Mortimer tucked her purchase in her large pigskin handbag.

'Good luck, my dear,' she said to Lily, taking her receipted bill when the tube came clanking back from the cash office. 'I hope that wasn't too terrifying!'

'Not at all, Mrs Mortimer. Thank you for your patience,' stuttered Lily.

'Time is one thing I have plenty of,' beamed Mrs Mortimer. 'And so do you, to become a real asset, I'm sure.'

'Until next time, Mrs Mortimer,' said Miss Frobisher, stepping out from behind the counter to escort her to the lift. 'Do bring the baby in to see us, won't you, when your daughter-in-law's up to it? And you might like to know . . . I'm hoping for some charming little Liberty romper suits for summer. Let his little legs see the sun, when it arrives!'

Trembling, Lily closed the black Rexine cover of her sales book, first having logged the sale, as a double-check, on the grid at the back. It was over! And Mrs Mortimer couldn't have been kinder. It had been terrifying having Miss Frobisher watching over her – but comforting too.

She glanced over to Toys, wondering how Gladys was getting on, and saw her heading towards a display of model aeroplanes with Mr Bunting and a fellow in a Polish airman's uniform. That should be interesting, thought Lily, but was pleased that Gladys's new boss was obviously being understanding too.

'Well. Not so bad, was it?' Miss Frobisher had swished back beside her. 'Oh, and here's Mrs Elliot. Same procedure, I think. I'll explain, and you can take over.'

No respite, then!

But Miss Frobisher had already moved off again.

'Mrs Elliot, good morning – and how's little Clara? Well, not so little any more . . . Miss Collins is in training, I hope you won't mind if she observes . . .'

And so the day passed, and the next. Gradually Lily became braver about writing out dockets, and by the end of the week she'd shadowed Miss Thomas and Miss Temple as well and had been allowed to serve a couple of customers on her own. She was even getting more confident about handling cash, and about suggesting the so-called 'add-on' items that could boost the value of a sale, if not in her own department, then somewhere in the store – a matching ribbon from Haberdashery, or a pair of slippers from Children's Shoes.

Lily didn't have time to miss Gladys, who was equally happy under Mr Bunting's tutelage. She hadn't recorded as many sales as Lily, but selling toys was a different business, she explained. Customers were often looking for a gift: they came in to browse, for advice or suggestions. If they had something specific in mind, it was frequently not available, so an alternative had to be suggested. Often they had to go away to have a think. Mr Bunting was a gentle and undemanding boss: heresy to Lily, but Gladys said she actually preferred him to Miss Frobisher.

'Satisfied with your new salesgirl?' Mr Simmonds asked Miss Frobisher as they made their way to the management floor for the monthly buyers' meeting.

'Very,' Miss Frobisher replied. 'But I knew I would be.'

He held the door open for her as they left the stone stairs for the carpeted corridor.

'You'll be putting her forward for Employee of the Month next. You think a lot of her, don't you?'

'She's got potential,' said Miss Frobisher coolly. 'But I shan't be letting her get a swelled head, don't worry.'

She had no intention of sharing what she could really see in Lily – a younger version of herself. She'd been just the same when she'd started at Marlow's – bright, keen, taking it all in. She'd also been determined to rise to a more senior level before entertaining any thought of marriage or children. She could only hope Lily would be as sensible.

The only thing clouding Lily's enjoyment of her new role was her need to put in a request for time off so soon after starting it, even though the day she was due to meet Sid was a Monday, which was never a busy day, and, thanks to the timing of his train, she'd only need a half-day anyway. But when she explained to Miss Frobisher that this could be her last chance to see her brother for ages, she was understanding, as Lily had prayed she might be.

Her own husband, after all, was serving overseas – that was all anyone knew, though Lily and Gladys had convinced themselves that he had to be some kind of undercover agent. In their minds he'd been given a false identity and was doing something highly dangerous – possibly, they'd decided, for no other reason than it sounded exotic, in Marrakech. There was no basis whatsoever for their supposition, but Lily justified it to herself in two ways. Firstly, no one had ever heard of him getting any leave. Secondly, surely someone like Miss Frobisher wouldn't be married to anyone doing a common-or-garden trooper's job?

'It's very irregular,' Miss Frobisher said now, taking

Lily's leave request form from her. 'But then nothing about you has been exactly regular since you started, has it, Miss Collins?'

Lily's new status entitled her to be addressed by her surname like the other salesgirls, who were 'Miss' even if, like Miss Frobisher, they were actually married. Miss Frobisher had a young son too, who was looked after by a neighbour while she came to work. Otherwise, Lily and Gladys had concluded, with her glacially glamorous good looks, she'd surely have been recruited as a spy herself. If Lily was honest, she had to admit that she had a bit of a crush on Miss Frobisher.

'It's only because you've made a good start,' her boss continued. 'Mrs Pope can be a very difficult customer.'

'But she didn't buy anything!'

Even though this was Mrs Pope's usual behaviour, Lily had been sorely disappointed. She'd shown the dreadful woman, with her camel coat and her crushed cowpat of a hat, every baby vest they had.

Mrs Pope had rejected the crossover vests with their little ribbon ties as 'too fiddly', while those with envelope necks were 'too confining'. But when Lily had suggested buying a bigger size to get around that – and to extend the vest's useful life – her idea had been dismissed because the garment would then 'ruck up'. Mrs Pope had then gone back to the crossover vests, the ones she'd objected to in the first place, before rejecting them all over again when she looked at the price. By the end of the encounter Lily could have knotted together every vest she'd got out of its packet to show her and used them to throttle the woman.

'She'll be back,' said Miss Frobisher confidently.

'Really? Mrs Pope?'

'She won't find anything different – or better value, given the quality – anywhere else.'

'I did try to tell her that. Tactfully, of course.'

'So I heard.'

'It was only what I'd learned from you and the others, Miss Frobisher. "Buy the best you can afford".'

'Quite so.' As she spoke, Miss Frobisher signed the form for Lily's leave with her usual panache and handed it back. 'There you are. Enjoy yourself.'

Lily hugged the form to herself all the way to the staff office, where she handed it over to be stamped and put in her file. As she watched the clerk cross off half of one of her treasured days' holiday, she prayed that the timings would work out and Sid would be at Snow Hill on time. And that he'd be a bit more forthcoming about this girlfriend of his. If he'd been serious about grabbing your chance while you could, who knew? The mysterious Anna could become her future sister-in-law.

Chapter 12

'When you called these ideas "far-reaching", I didn't imagine you meant wiping Marlow's off the map!'

Jim had presented his further ideas, typed up by one of the management secretaries and placed in a manila folder, on the preceding Friday. Cedric Marlow had promised to read them over the weekend, and on Monday afternoon, in the middle of ordering some show cards for the forthcoming Household event, Jim had been summoned to hear the verdict.

He felt his palms moisten.

'I'm sorry, sir, I didn't mean . . . that's the last thing I meant! Everything in there is intended to keep the store right at the centre of things in Hinton!'

'Oh yes? By changing our name?'

'What?' Jim started in his seat, then realised what Cedric was getting at. 'It's hardly that.'

'Lose the apostrophe?' barked Cedric, usually a softly-spoken and even-tempered man. 'Marlow and Company – hence Marlow's' – he stressed the final syllable – 'to become simply Marlows?'

'It's the modern way, sir.'

'Modern? What about Woolworth's? Are they not modern enough for you?'

'With respect, sir, do we want to be thought of in the same breath as Woolworth's? Boots might be a better example—'

'Boots! A dispensing chemist?'

'They're a lot more than that, sir, to be fair, but all right – think of Selfridges, then. Or Harrods. You wouldn't mind being compared to them, surely?'

Jim hadn't heard a 'harrumph' like it since he'd been in Hinton. It was a sound that took him back to the plough horses in his home village stamping and snorting on a winter's morning.

But Cedric was off again.

'And as for this . . . escalators!'

'Well, not until after the war, obviously. But I have timed quite carefully how long customers spend waiting for the store lifts. And the time it takes to get them from one floor to another. It's on a separate sheet,' Jim added helpfully as Cedric ruffled the flimsy pages. 'Now, at Harrods—'

'Will you stop quoting Harrods at me!'

'All I was going to say, sir, is that they've had an escalator for over forty years. Selfridges has them, too. They even have them on cruise ships, I believe. And in cinemas in America.'

'Cinemas? Cruise ships? America? What have they got to do with . . . now I've heard it all!'

'My point is that they're becoming universal, sir. We've come a long way since the first Harrods customers to use them had to be given a tot of brandy or smelling salts at the top.'

'And is that in your costings?' snapped Cedric.

Jim mentally thumbed through the sales manual. Maybe if he thought of his Uncle Cedric as a particularly tricky customer . . . Random phrases came back to him. 'Never argue with or contradict a customer . . .', 'be aware of their feelings . . .', 'a sense of humour may help . . .'

'No. But perhaps we might run to a glass of Vimto.'

'You think this is funny?'

Mistake, thought Jim. Perhaps the sense of humour was meant to kick in later, recounting the story to your family over tea, or to friends in the pub.

'I'm sorry, sir. I didn't mean to be flippant. But you did ask for innovative ideas.'

'And I didn't mean you to tear down the store that my father founded and that I've built up – A.J. Marlow and Company – Marlow's – and start again! Has Mr Simmonds seen your . . . proposals?'

The hesitation, Jim felt, was because Cedric had been about to say 'your preposterous proposals'. It was no good. He'd blown it.

'Yes, sir, he has.'

'Then I want a word with him! You may go! But send him up, please, straight away!'

'So . . .' Sid began. 'Here we are in sunny Birmingham!'

It had all worked like a dream. A year ago, Lily would no more have thought of taking a train by herself than of driving one, but at Hinton station she'd bought her third-class ticket and found a compartment quite confidently, and though Snow Hill had seemed enormous when the train had puffed in under the huge blacked-out glass roof, the platforms seething with troops and civilians, you couldn't miss the clock. Sid was already there. Both their trains without delay or cancellation – it had to be a record.

Lily had expected the WVS tea bar, or at most the station's refreshment room, but Sid scorned that idea. Instead he swept her out to a fancy bar-cum-café where Lily found herself clutching a glass of lemonade and trying to look as if she did this sort of thing every day. As he was in a sense still on duty, Sid contented himself with a shandy and ordered them a round of sandwiches each.

'Well?' he asked, taking a sip of his drink. 'Why so keen to see me? What's new? Not another promotion!'

'I don't need a reason to see my brother, do I?'

Lily shot back. 'And no, don't be daft! I've got enough to learn as it is.'

While they ate, Lily filled him in on how she'd found her first weeks of selling, the nasty customers and the nice ones, how she'd only had to do one crossing-out in her sales book, and how she'd learnt to wrap the money in the sales docket to stop it clanking around in the overhead tube.

But she hadn't come all this way to talk about herself, so when she'd rattled through that, she was keen to get on to what had really brought her all this way.

'What about you?' she asked. 'It'll be tough, won't it, being away from Anna? This training lasts a couple of months, you said.'

Sid shrugged.

'Not much I can do about it, is there?'

'You'll write to each other, though?'

'I'm not sure there'll be a post box where I'm going, out in the wilds.'

'Poor you, and poor Anna,' said Lily. 'That's going to be hard.' Then she had an inspiration. 'Oh, but Sid, show me! You must have a photograph!'

Sid hesitated.

'A photo? No. Sorry, Sis. I haven't.'

That was odd. Lily knew from Gladys that the first thing boy and girlfriends did was to exchange photographs – and keep them close. Gladys was never without her crumpled passport-sized snap of Bill, and she had a whole gallery pinned to the wall by her bed.

It's funny how one thing seeming strange makes you realise another, and it suddenly struck Lily what had been strangest of all. He'd never called Anna anything but Anna.

This was Sid, who could never resist messing with people's names. He called her 'Lily Languish' or 'Diamond Lil'. He'd christened Bill, whose surname was Webb, 'Cobby', as in cobweb. Jim was 'Jimbo', Nash was 'Splash'. He was even the one who'd come up with 'Bacon' and 'Sausage' as names for the hens.

But Anna was always Anna. Why not . . . oh, she couldn't think of anything truly Sid-like, but not even 'Annie by Gaslight', or to joke that she had 'Queen Anne' legs? But when she asked him, Sid seemed nonplussed.

'What? Why would I call her Annie . . . or Anne? That's not her name, is it? What is this, the third degree?'

He was sounding almost defensive, but Lily couldn't let it go.

'I'm sorry, Sid . . . I can't pin it down, but there's something odd about this Anna. Who is she? What's the big secret?'

Jim didn't hear any more from the management floor all afternoon, and Peter Simmonds wasn't around either. All Jim's doubts returned. Had he misread

Peter Simmonds's seeming support? Had he been encouraged to stick his neck out only to have his head chopped off? When all the lights beneath the first-floor clock were illuminated, meaning the last customer had left the store and staff were free to go, he collected his coat and trudged miserably towards home. He wondered how Lily was getting on. He hoped she'd had a better afternoon than he had.

'Jim!'

Jim turned and saw Robert Marlow hurrying after him – Cedric's son and his cousin, not that they'd ever been close, or even known each other, until Jim had come to Hinton. They hadn't had much to do with each other when Jim had started at Marlow's, and when they did, it was only because Jim had discovered that Robert was masterminding a delivery racket for favoured customers. When the scheme was exposed, Robert had cunningly shifted the blame on to Jim and let him take the rap. Things had finally got straightened out, and Robert had conveniently left to work for a stockbroking firm run by Sir Douglas Brimble and was courting the boss's daughter, Evelyn. And they say cheats never prosper, thought Jim, with only a trace of bile.

'Robert,' he said evenly. He still wasn't sure how he felt about him.

'Haven't seen you for ages!' It was as if the whole delivery business had never happened. 'Got time for a drink?'

It was the last thing Jim wanted to do, and the last person he wanted to do it with, but on the other hand, he didn't much want to face the eager questioning from Lily, when she got home from Birmingham, about how his interview with Cedric had gone.

Ten minutes later he was clinking his glass of shandy – it was a good day for brewers and lemonade-manufacturers in the Midlands – against Robert's whisky, not in a pub, naturally, as it was at Robert's invitation, but in the lounge bar of the White Lion Hotel.

'I just popped in to see Dad,' Robert volunteered with a wide grin. 'Came in on the end of a discussion between him and Simmonds.'

'Oh yes?'

So that was the plan. Jim was the butterfly and Robert was going to pull off his wings, one filament at a time.

'I gather the old man asked you to come up with some ideas,' Robert continued. 'Well, I can imagine how they were received!'

That's right, rub it in, thought Jim, watching the bubbles rise and burst in his glass.

'But,' Robert went on, 'I can tell you Simmonds was arguing your case pretty forcefully. And, for what it's worth, I think you're absolutely right.'

Jim felt his feeble wings flutter back into life.

'You do?'

'I know what you're up against,' Robert

sympathised. 'I came up with tons of suggestions when I was working for Dad – cut off at the knees every time.'

'I see!'

'No, you don't. Look, Jim, they weren't anything dodgy like that delivery business – that was just plain daft, I realise that now, and I'm as sorry as hell you got mixed up in it.' It was nowhere near enough for the trouble the whole thing had caused, but Jim knew it was as close to an apology as a man like Robert was ever going to concede. He gave a little nod of acknowledgement – water, bridges and all that – and let Robert continue. 'Escalators, now – I put that idea forward years ago, before the war began.'

Jim considered. There was no point in Robert lying about it. He couldn't claim credit for Jim's ideas: he didn't even work at Marlow's any more; there was nothing in it for him. Maybe, then, just possibly, he was telling the truth.

'Dad's a dinosaur,' Robert went on. 'Been around too long. He's so stuck in the past, he won't look to the future.'

'To be fair,' said Jim, 'it's pretty hard work negotiating the present right now.'

'I know,' said Robert. 'But I can tell you what I've learnt from Sir Douglas. Firms that start planning for the future now are the ones that are going to be in the best position when this war's over. This idea of yours for a "Bargain Basement"—'

'Huh! We didn't even get to that!'

'Dad and Simmonds were discussing it when I barged in. It's terrific! Not yet, but once we don't need the space down there for the air-raid shelter . . . Dad can't see it, of course.'

'No. I did worry he'd think it cheapens what Marlow's stands for.'

'So we stand by and let Burrell's do it instead? That was the point Simmonds was making. He was weighing in right behind you, Jim. And trying to make Dad see that while some things would have to wait till after the war, you could get on with some of them now.'

'Like losing the apostrophe?'

'Don't,' Robert groaned. 'I've tried and tried. You'll never get anywhere with that one.'

'So what do I do now?'

'Keep your head down, but keep working on him, bit by bit, on some of the other ideas. And wait for him to see sense.'

'What makes you think he will?'

'Because he's got to. He's got to let younger chaps come through. Deep down he knows it. That store's been his life, and he's having awful trouble letting go. But you mustn't let it get to you.'

Now Robert had said it, Jim could see that it was true. He'd seen it before with farmers at home in Bidbury. Their sons had begged for tractors to replace horse-drawn ploughs, for drugs to treat sick animals instead of the old herbal remedies or just plain hope. And he knew what the old boys quoted in reply:

'*Be not the first by whom the new is tried.*'

And how their sons bitterly finished the rhyme:

'*Nor yet the last to cast the old aside.*'

'Thanks, Robert,' Jim said now. 'Thanks for that.'

'You're welcome. God knows, I owe you, Jim.'

It was another approximation of an apology and Jim acknowledged it with a tilt of his glass. Both men drank, and it felt as though a pact had been sealed.

'There you are, hiding in a corner!' trilled an approaching voice.

It was Evelyn Brimble. Jim had met her once before, in the street, when he and Lily had been returning from collecting the first lot of hens, the ones for Dora, a fact Evelyn obviously remembered when she saw him.

'It's Jim, isn't it?' she smiled. 'Hens! How are they doing?'

'Very well, thank you,' replied Jim.

He and Robert had stood up as she arrived, but she waved Jim back to his seat, kissing Robert and flopping down herself in a miasma of scent and a slither of skirt-lining and stockings.

'I am exhausted!' she said, smoothing her mulberry-coloured suit. 'I've been helping Mummy with her parcels for POWs. Poor wretches, they deserve them, of course, but my poor hands! I've been breaking open cartons of chocolate and cigarettes all afternoon!

And it was so draughty in that church hall I'll have a stiff neck tomorrow.'

Jim gaped. Only someone as privileged as Evelyn could even begin to compare her privations with the experiences of the poor souls incarcerated in God-only-knew-what conditions. He opened his mouth to say so, or something like it, but Robert had leapt in. He seemed to find her outburst completely reasonable.

'You poor darling,' he said. 'Let me get you a drink.'

'Mm, gin and bitters, please,' said Evelyn. And then: 'We're not eating here, are we, Robert? My escalope was completely tasteless last time.'

'We'll go wherever you like, Evelyn,' Robert replied meekly. 'I'll get you that drink.'

'And some nuts, or olives or something, if they have them!' Evelyn called after him.

She turned her wide blue eyes on Jim and smiled her most enticing smile.

'So how are you, Jim?' she asked. 'Tell me all about life at my favourite shop!'

'We've just been talking about it, actually . . .'

But somehow Jim didn't think Evelyn would be interested in his plans for a Bargain Basement. He couldn't see her shopping down there, not in a million years. Even a dinosaur like Cedric Marlow would be long dead.

Chapter 13

In Birmingham, an awkward silence had fallen between brother and sister. Lily stared at Sid, waiting. Sid stared at the mural on the café wall – for no apparent reason, an Alpine scene.

'So,' he said finally. 'You want to know about Anna.'

'Yes. What's wrong with that?'

'Nothing.'

Sid took a sip of his drink. He put down his glass very slowly and carefully, then looked directly at her.

'If you want the truth, and I can see you're not going to rest till you get it, here it is. There is no Anna.'

'What?'

'I made her up,' said Sid. 'I had to. I thought it

129

would stop you from going on,' he added, as Lily stared at him, bemused. 'Fat chance!'

'But why? Why would you do that? Why didn't you just say there was no one special?'

'Because there is.'

'Oh. So what's the problem? Why didn't you tell me her real name?'

Sid sighed.

'I really don't want to do this,' he said, 'but here goes.' Still he hesitated, while Lily looked at him, still baffled. Then he said, 'All right. Here it is. Anna is Anthony.'

'What?'

'The person in my life . . . the person I care about. It's never been girls for me, Lil. I— I'm— I have feelings for men.'

Lily had to hang on to the edge of the table. She saw the plate that had held her sandwich, its red-and-gold rim. The table top, their half-drunk glasses, the few scattered crumbs. They were real enough. Did that make what Sid was telling her real as well? She supposed it did. It wasn't one of his jokes. But she really wished it had been. She met his eyes.

'Don't look at me like that.'

'I'm not looking at you like anything, Sid. I'm just . . . looking at you.'

'Yeah? Waiting for me to sprout devil horns and a tail?'

'What? No!'

'I'm sorry. I didn't mean . . .' His eyes were full. 'I'm sorry, Lil. But you would ask!'

It was awful, just awful, after that. Lily was at a complete and utter loss.

Sid, her lovely, lovely Sid – not being . . . she couldn't say it, she hated even to think it, but not being . . . no, not 'not normal'. Not like other people, that was it.

'How did you . . . how long have you been feeling like this? When did you know?'

Sid made a face.

'I've always known, I suppose, from – well, the time I was about your age. Younger, even.'

'My age? But Sid – you had all those girlfriends!'

There'd been so many of them. Jean and Marjorie . . . Kath, Muriel, Rose . . .

'I didn't want to believe it. I thought it couldn't be. I couldn't see how it could, how if it was, how I could ever have a life.' Sid looked at her, willing her to understand. 'I tried, Lil, I really did. I like girls, of course I do, you know I do, I can have a laugh and a joke, kid them along . . .'

Lily did know. She'd seen him do it, teasing Renée across the road and Freda the post girl.

'I took them out, I did all the right things, bought them presents, held their hands, kissed them . . . but I couldn't feel anything. Nothing at all. So I dropped them, nicely, just said I didn't want to get serious, before they could suspect.'

And she had tutted and teased him about it, and Reg had joked about him sowing wild oats and playing the field. Poor Sid. All that time, knowing it was a lie, knowing what he really felt and having to hide it.

'Well?' asked Sid. 'That can't be it. Is that all you want to ask?'

'I don't know what else to ask,' wavered Lily. 'I don't know anything about . . . that kind of thing.'

'No,' he said. 'And I don't want you to. Because I know what you'll do. You'll go to the library and try and find out. To understand. But I beg you, Lil, don't do that.'

'Why?'

Sid pushed his hands through his hair.

'Because if you go looking it up, all you'll find out is how the Bible says it's a sin, when it doesn't, actually – well, it depends how you read it. Then there'll be plenty of stuff about how it's disgusting and wicked and perverted. And then you'll find stuff about "cures" – and I don't just mean cold showers and physical exercise.' He gave a short laugh. 'God knows there's enough of those in the Navy. If that worked we'd all be married men tomorrow.'

'Can it be cured?'

'No! That's the point! It's not a disease, Lily. It's how I am. It's who I am.'

'Oh, Sid.' Lily could hardly get the words out. 'But – what about – haven't I read . . . in the paper . . .'

'What, "From Our Crime Correspondent"? Yes, you will have done. Blokes had up for "gross indecency". In Civvy Street it's prison. In the services . . . if the Navy found out – well, God only knows what they'd do to me.'

Lily burst into tears.

She wasn't sure how she got home that night. She and Sid had walked back to the station in almost total silence. She hardly even registered what they were passing – the badly filled-in craters in the road, the broken pavements, the bomb damage that had left buildings looking like hollowed-out Hallowe'en lanterns and just as hideous. When they got back to Snow Hill, the concourse was even more crowded than before – soldiers, sailors, airmen, civilians, all milling around trying to buy tickets or get information from the harassed porters, ticket collectors and guards.

Lily was lucky: her train was due to leave on time. Sid faced a delay of four hours.

'Another night sleeping with my head on my kitbag,' he grimaced. 'Still, there'll be enough of that in training.'

'What is it you'll be doing?' asked Lily automatically, though she knew he couldn't, or shouldn't, tell her.

Sid shrugged.

'You know I can't say. But there'll be plenty of

sleeping rough and running across the moors and splashing through ice-cold streams in the pitch-dark.'

'Burns,' said Lily, automatically again.

'What?'

'Burns. That's what they call streams, isn't it, up in Scotland?'

'Like I've always said, you're the brains of the family.' People were pushing past them; the frantic activity was making her head spin. Sid took her arm to steady her and kept hold of it. 'Look, Sis, I'm sorry about all this. I know you don't know what to think about what I've told you. And I'm sorry I had to, I really am. You shouldn't have to know this kind of stuff at your age. But you weren't going to let it go, were you?'

'I know. I know it's my fault. I made you tell me. And I'm glad you have. I think.'

'It's a lot to take in. It's not what any of us would have wanted. But I can't help it. I didn't plan for it to be like this, but it's how things are. It's how I want to live my life, if I get through this war, so it's best you know.'

'I have to go, Sid. I daren't miss my train.'

'Lily—' It wasn't just her name, it was a plea. 'Not yet. Give me a hug. Or am I off-limits now? I don't . . . I don't disgust you, do I?'

Lily stared at him, throat tight, eyes brimming. She desperately wanted to say what he wanted to hear – that what he'd told her didn't change anything, that he was still her brother, she loved him just the same, but he spoke first.

'I'm sorry,' he said. His own eyes looked full too. 'I'm so sorry to have disappointed you.'

Lily found her voice.

'You haven't disappointed me, Sid,' she said, meaning it. 'You never could. Nor disgust me. I'm . . . I suppose I'm in shock, that's all. Look, I really have to go. I'll write.'

'OK. I'm sure there will be a post box.'

'Of course there will. And come here. Oh, Sid!'

She flung herself at him, her dearest brother, one of the dearest people in the world to her. She held him tightly, then pulled away and looked at him, so tall, so handsome with his wavy blond hair, his clear blue eyes, his naval blouse against his tanned skin.

'I love you, Sid. I always will, whatever.'

'Thanks, Sis,' he said. 'Knowing that means the world to me.'

She'd meant it, and Sid might be reassured, but Lily knew one of the few certainties left to her in the world had gone for ever. It wasn't till she was on the train home that she realised that in her bemusement, she hadn't asked him a thing about Anthony.

When Lily came down next morning, jaded and dull after an exhausting day, a draining journey and a restless night, Jim was whistling like a kettle.

135

'You're very cheerful,' she said, forcing an enthusiasm she was a long way from feeling.

'Never let the obvious go unstated, eh?' he said brightly. 'You don't look so brisk.'

Lily sat down heavily on the kitchen chair.

'Thanks! Long day, long journey.'

'Never mind. Today's Special coming up.'

'Which is?'

'Toast.'

'Like every day, then?'

'No, because it's made with my own fair hand.' Jim started hacking at the loaf. 'Toast always tastes better when you haven't had to make it yourself, don't you think?'

Lily had rather bigger things to think about, but she didn't say.

'Well?' asked Jim, placing two giant slabs under the grill and lighting it. 'How was it? How was Sid?'

'Oh, no, you first,' insisted Lily.

Though Marlow's seemed like another world and another life, she'd remembered why Jim might have something to smile about – his session with Cedric yesterday, and thank goodness for it. In all her tossing and turning she hadn't yet come up with a convincing enough cover story to hide the truth of her conversation with Sid.

'Your ideas went down well, I take it?'

'Hardly! He dismissed most of them out of hand. I thought I'd completely blown it.'

'So?'

Jim plucked two plates from the rack.

'Uncle Cedric hates them. But Robert thinks they're terrific,' he said smugly.

'Robert Marlow? What's he got to do with it?'

Jim explained about the drink, and the encouragement he'd received.

'He was scathing about his dad,' Jim confided. 'A back number, that's what he called him, totally out of date. But Simmonds is right behind me, and Robert even said he'd put in a good word if he got the chance.'

'You're sure about that, are you?' asked Lily. She wouldn't have trusted Robert as far as she could fling him.

Jim went to the larder to fetch the dripping.

'I know I haven't had much reason – any reason – to trust him in the past. But . . . well, I think maybe, mad as it sounds, he was a bit jealous of me. Now we're not working in the same place and he's got his own sphere . . . He's much happier not working alongside his father. And I think he may even be sort of grateful to me for filling the gap.'

Lily could see it made a kind of sense.

'Well, that's wonderful, Jim. Well done!'

He deserved it, after all. He'd put enough effort into his top-secret 'document' even though she'd mocked him for it. Perhaps he might even share some of these 'big ideas' with her now.

'And I tell you what's even better,' Jim went on, 'he's completely under the thumb.'

'Robert is? Whose?'

'Evelyn Brimble. He took me to the White Lion – they'd obviously arranged to meet there. She turns up, and he's like a performing seal. Yes, Evelyn, no Evelyn, look, Evelyn, if I balance this ball on my nose will you throw me a fish?'

'Really? No!'

'Oh, yes. If they stay together – and he showed every sign of wanting to – she is really going to give him the run-around.'

Lily felt some of the hard, heavy weight she'd been carrying in her chest since yesterday start to lighten a little and she gave a smile.

'I shouldn't be . . . it's a bit mean – but I'm so pleased!'

'Quite. "The mills of God grind slowly, but they grind exceeding small", as your mother might say – aargh, the toast! Why didn't you remind me?'

He leapt away, cursing, to clatter it from the grill.

'Marvellous,' said Lily. 'So the Special's off, is it?'

'Slightly singed, that's all,' said Jim, wafting away the smoke. 'In a posh restaurant, you'd pay extra to have something like this *flambéed* at your table. Now pour us some tea and tell me about *your* day.'

But the smell of burning had brought Dora downstairs. She immediately wanted to know about Sid too, of course, but, grateful that the inferno hadn't been any worse, she was for once fairly easy to buy off with quick assurances that he looked well, though he wasn't looking forward to his course. Lily then quickly switched to the bomb damage in Birmingham, the shredded-looking buildings and the pitiful ribs of factories that she'd seen, and in the general tutting and head-shaking, more searching questions never came.

Chapter 14

But if Lily thought she'd got away with it, Jim hadn't forgotten, and on the walk to work, his interrogation resumed.

'So?' he demanded. 'Did you get what you wanted?'

'I don't know what you mean,' Lily stalled.

'Oh come on!' he said, exasperated. 'It was glaringly obvious you only went to pump the poor bloke about his girlfriend! He never got to answer that time at tea, because Beryl turned up, but I reckon Sid's got someone. You've been bullying him about it in your letters, but he wasn't giving enough away, and you wanted to pin him down.'

Unbelievable! He could read her like a book. No,

not even a book – like an ancient manuscript – hieroglyphics, even. But what Lily had learnt from books – and what so often caught out Agatha Christie's numerous suspects – was that when you had something to hide, the best thing to do was to stick as closely as possible to the truth.

'Well, I was disappointed,' she said. 'There's nothing to tell about a girlfriend.'

'I don't believe that for one moment.' Jim looked at her narrowly, like someone squinting into the sun. 'There is someone, and there's either something he's not telling you, or there's something you're not telling me. What is it? Is she an older woman or something? Married? Engaged? Divorced? Oh Lord, she's not pregnant, is she?'

'No!'

Lily stalked ahead. For once, she was the one setting the pace. If only he'd known how unlikely it was that Sid would get a girl pregnant – ever!

'What is it then?' Jim easily caught her up. 'Is she posh? Titled, even? No? She's a Wren, is she? Or a local Hayling girl? Or – or – no, I know – she's black! Indian? Chinese?'

Lily stopped and turned on him.

'Now you're just being ridiculous! How is Sid going to meet a Chinese girl?'

'You may not have noticed, Lily, but the whole world is at war. There are displaced people all over.'

'He's been on Hayling Island, not Hong Kong!

Look, he took me to a café place, we had a long chat, then I caught my train back. But I've got nothing to tell you about any girlfriend. Now, leave it, Jim. Please. And tell me about these amazing ideas that are going to transform Marlow's.'

Jim knew when she meant it, so he left it, though Lily could tell he was still curious, and over the weeks that followed, keeping Sid's secret put a distance between them, there was no doubt about it.

Lily wrote to Sid straight away at the address he'd given her in Scotland, to prove she really had meant what she said, and that nothing had changed between them. In her heart, though, she knew it wasn't true. Before she went to sleep every night, she prayed for Sid, though with no firm idea of what exactly she was praying for.

He'd sounded sure about how he felt, but was he really? Maybe he just hadn't met the right girl yet. But in thinking that, was she as bad as the people who said that people like him could be 'cured'? Unhappy, frustrated, and against his advice, but as he'd known she would, she tried to find out what sort of 'cures' were recommended. There was nothing in their old *Pears' Cyclopaedia* at home, and when she went to the library, she didn't dare ask the librarian for guidance as she blundered around the shelves. She didn't even really know what she was looking for, and when she did finally find a reference in a medical dictionary, and the recommended 'chemical cure', she had to bundle the book back on the shelf and leave in a hurry, feeling sick.

It didn't help that she heard nothing back from Sid for ages. Two letters arrived simultaneously from Reg, and the obligatory snap of him in shirt and shorts, standing by a camel. 'Local transport!' he'd written on the back. Dora proudly put it on the mantelpiece, but the only communication Lily really wanted was from her other brother, and when that finally came, it was addressed to Dora.

As usual Sid didn't say exactly what he was doing, just that 'they're working us hard', so he didn't have time to miss the absence of cinemas or dance halls or even pubs. Reading between the lines, and knowing what she knew, Lily couldn't help trying to imagine herself in Sid's head, cold, miserable and separated from this Anthony he cared so much about. In the library, she'd read about some writer called Oscar Wilde, and the terrible things he'd endured in prison and afterwards. She couldn't help seeing Sid's incarceration in a camp in the wilds of Scotland as a faint foretaste of what he might have to suffer if what he was – a homosexual – there, she'd said it – ever came to light. It was a miserable, hollow time.

If anyone abhorred a vacuum more than nature, it was Beryl, and she had no trouble in filling it – literally, because, as Jim pointed out with some distaste, she seemed to be going around with an Anderson shelter strapped to her front. She was certainly very large, a fact she bemoaned daily, and even more so when the baby's due date came and went.

'Hello? Can you hear me?' she demanded of her stomach one evening at Lily's when she was a week overdue. 'Look, you've had your fun. I know you're in there, time's up now!'

Click, click, went Dora's needles. She was working on a bed jacket for Beryl.

'Babies come in their own good time,' she said, counting stitches. 'Surely the midwife told you that?'

'Eight days over?' cried Beryl. 'That's pretty poor timekeeping if you ask me! You'd be out on your ear at Marlow's if you went over by ten minutes, isn't that right, Lily?'

Lily could only agree. She was as keen as anyone for the baby to come. It would be a welcome distraction.

But he or she was in no hurry, and it was a few more days before there were any developments. It was a Monday evening, and yet again, Beryl had spent it at the Collinses'. Ivy's patience had worn to threads. She'd told Beryl straight that her moaning was getting her down, and it was getting to Susan too. She'd scribbled all over her favourite *Milly Molly Mandy* book in a temper and had taken to trying to push Beryl out of the best armchair.

A 'Fuel Flash' for housewives had just come on the wireless when Beryl suddenly pressed her belly.

'Oof! Ooh!'

Lily and Dora paused in the wool they were winding, and Jim looked up from the newspaper. German bombing raids had started up again, this time not aimed at industrial towns, but at beautiful cities like Exeter and Bath whose historic buildings were being destroyed.

'*Oof!* That got me!' said Beryl.

'Indigestion,' said Jim firmly. 'You would polish off that leftover junket.'

'And you'd know, would you?' snapped Beryl. 'Typical man! I'm telling you, this was different.'

'Was it? How different?' Dora laid aside her wool and indicated Lily should do the same.

'Proper griping. No, worse. Like someone scissoring my insides.'

Lily winced.

'And like . . . all round me somehow. Oh, Dora. Do you think it's the baby?'

After willing it to happen for weeks, Beryl now looked terrified. As well she might, thought Lily. It sounded horrific.

'There's a fair chance, don't you think?' Dora might have been calmly speculating on the likelihood of rain.

'Let's get you out of here!' Lily gulped. She didn't want Beryl having it right here, on the floor!

'Ambulance,' nodded Beryl, leaning back with her eyes closed.

'Nonsense!' Dora stood up. 'The walk'll do you good.'

'Walk?'

'Bring the baby on, and take your mind off the pain,' said Dora briskly. 'Two birds. Come on, up you get.'

As Beryl, breathing heavily and blinking in panic, was hauled to her feet, Dora issued more orders.

'Now, Lily, you run over to Ivy's, tell her to get to the maternity home with Beryl's little bag. Then you stay with Susan. You'll have to get her to bed, and most likely stay over. Don't look like that, there's nothing else for it. But me or Ivy'll come in the morning, don't worry, so you can get to work. And Jim—'

Jim had returned to his paper but looked up.

'I'll hold the fort here, no problem. Do the hens.'

'Do the hens? You're coming with us!'

'Me?'

Lily smirked at the horror – no, terror – on his face.

'Yes, you! If she gets a strong pain, she'll need someone on either side of her till it passes.'

Beryl gave a little whimper.

'*Ooh*! There it is again! *Owww* . . . Dora, I don't like it!'

'Who said anything about liking it? You'll have a beautiful baby at the end of it, that's all that matters.'

'*Ooh*, I could curse Les, I really could!' cried Beryl, bending over. 'Why isn't he here instead of sunning himself in blooming Africa?'

Les had managed to get word back to Beryl that he'd arrived safely, but since then there'd been no further intelligence, not a scrap. It wasn't the moment to point out that he was more likely to be dealing with sandstorms, scorpions and boiled-over radiators, not to mention snipers and landmines, under the African sun. Beryl wasn't listening.

'Dora . . .' she whimpered. 'I'm frightened!'

'You should have thought of that nine months ago,' said Dora crisply. 'Lily, fetch me my shoes!'

It was a testing evening all round. Susan was definitely unsettled, and Lily had to read her *Little Grey Rabbit's Birthday* no less than three times to get her off to sleep. At two in the morning Susan woke up crying; she'd wet the bed, so that had to be stripped and changed, as did she, under great protest. Next morning, they were both tired and crabby. But when Lily heard what Beryl had been through, she realised that her night had been the equivalent of sleeping peacefully under a down quilt in a four-poster bed at the Ritz.

'She's had it! At last!' Ivy wheezed as she came through the door.

Lily had managed to get Susan up, though not washed, dressed, or fed, and she now fell on her mother with slobbering kisses while Ivy launched into a detailed description of the birth – far too detailed for Lily's ears. Beryl, it seemed, had laboured all evening and into the night, and at the very end, when she was all but exhausted, the doctors had discovered that the baby was facing the wrong way and had had to turn him. Lily clenched her teeth and felt her insides do the same, as Ivy, by now clattering about the kitchen assembling breakfast, airily interspersed gory accounts of 'forceps' and 'blood loss' with questions about how Susan had slept and if Lily fancied marg or dripping on her toast. Lily declined both, saying she'd have breakfast at home, and asked the only things that mattered to her and which Ivy had managed to omit.

'But Beryl's all right, is she? And is it a boy or a girl?'

'Bless you, didn't I say?' Ivy had marshalled Susan into a chair and was tying a tea towel around her neck for a bib. 'A little boy. Well, I say little . . . nine pounds two ounces! Quite the little prize fighter!'

'A boy! That's wonderful! We must let Les know!'

'I'll send a wire as soon as I can get to the Post Office. Let's hope he's still at the last address he gave us. They move them about so, don't they?'

'I'm sure they'll send it on. News like that . . . Oh, Ivy, that's wonderful! You're a grandmother! Congratulations! And Susan, you're an auntie!'

Susan looked up blankly and poked her finger in the margarine.

'Can I go and see Beryl?' Lily went on. 'And the baby? After work?'

'I'm sure she'd love you to.' Ivy held a cup of milk to Susan's mouth. 'I'll pop in again this afternoon and take this one with me. I'm hoping when she meets the babby she'll stop some of her nonsense! Won't you, miss?' She smoothed her daughter's hair with stern affection.

Lily carried the news of the baby's safe arrival to Marlow's, though she spared her colleagues the gruesome account she'd had from Ivy. Gladys clasped her hands and went all gooey; Jim mourned that if only Cedric Marlow would give the go-ahead to his suggestion of a staff newsletter, Beryl could have been headline news.

He and Peter Simmonds were still lobbying Cedric to move on at least some of the ideas in Jim's famous 'document'. They'd belatedly realised that everything he'd agreed to in the beginning – the sports clubs and the First Aid demonstrations – had been things that didn't cost anything. Now they were pushing ideas which might involve some outlay – even for a few miserable sheets of foolscap every month – Mr Marlow was proving harder to persuade.

'Right now it's a case of an irresistible force meeting an immoveable object,' sighed Jim as they left at the end of the day. 'A bit like you and me.'

'I don't know what you mean!'

'Er, Sid and this girl of his?'

He still wasn't letting it drop. Trust him!

'A very flattering comparison, I'm sure. Which am I?' retorted Lily. 'In fact, don't answer that! And anyway, never mind that now. I'm going to see Beryl. Are you coming?'

'You are joking!' Jim looked horrified. 'By the time your mum and I got her there last night, she'd squeezed my arm so tight, she'd practically cut off the circulation. I'm surprised they didn't admit me as well!'

'Typical man! Always have to be the centre of attention!'

'Oh, I see,' smiled Jim. 'It's all women together now, and men the evil oppressors. No, I won't come, thanks all the same, but give Beryl my love. Oh, and I got her these.'

From his coat pocket he magicked a quarter-pound box of Milk Tray.

Lily gasped. 'Jim! Where did you get those? And how?'

'Aha. A little shop I know. I heard a customer mention they'd got some in.'

Lily took the box and caressed it. She didn't dare ask how much they'd cost.

'I thought these had disappeared for good! Oh, Jim – they're not off the back of a lorry?'

'The chap said they were legit. Anyway, it's too late now. Maybe they've been sitting in a warehouse somewhere . . . I just hope they taste OK. You can say they're from both of us if you like.'

'That's sweet of you, Jim. I haven't got her anything!'

Jim smiled.

'You and your mum were her only friends in the world when she needed them. That's worth a lot more than a few chocs.'

Chapter 15

'Never again! Never, never, never! I tell you, Lily, don't talk to me about the war! I feel like I've been through a minefield, run over by a tank, and sat on some barbed wire!'

'Yes, all right, Beryl—'

'I mean, think about it. It makes no sense, does it? A great hulking baby coming out of down there?'

Beryl was sitting up in bed in the maternity ward in the pink bed jacket confected by Dora. She was pale, of course – Ivy hadn't exaggerated the blood loss, as Lily had had to hear all over again – but she'd brushed her hair and Vaselined her lips in anticipation of her evening visitors. It was good to know that while it might have battered her body, it'd take more than a long labour to dent Beryl's usual spirit – or pride in her appearance. Before she could resume her diatribe or go into any more gynaecological details, however, Lily jumped in.

'But where is he, the baby? I thought he'd be with you.'

'Oh, no, they keep them in the nursery down the corridor,' explained Beryl. She'd opened Jim's chocolates while they'd been talking, and her finger circled the selection, deciding which one to choose. 'They'll bring him in for a feed when he wakes up.'

Lily felt sure that if she ever had a baby she wouldn't want to let him or her out of her sight, however traumatic the experience. Beryl, however, seemed perfectly relaxed about the situation. She popped a coffee cream into her mouth and offered Lily the box. Lily would have loved one – the hazelnut whirls were her favourite – but thought she'd better decline.

'No, no, thank you, they're for you. Build your strength up,' she said. 'But I do hope I get to see him before I go!'

'Oh, you will, night and day I'm supposed to feed him. He's nearly due. Mm. That chocolate's heavenly. Tell Jim thank you.'

'I will. I'm sorry I haven't got you anything.'

'Don't be daft!' said Beryl. 'You made the baby that little, er . . .'

What was it? Lily had finally managed to craft some sort of tiny T-shaped thing in plain knitting stitch, with much help from Dora with the casting on and off, and shaping some sort of neckline.

'That thing! You don't ever have to put him in it, Beryl. You can use it as a pan-holder if you like.'

Beryl laughed.

'He'll wear it, don't you worry! Go on, have one!' She held out the box. Lily cracked and accepted.

'But you haven't told me, and Ivy didn't say.' She spoke indistinctly through a melting mouthful. 'I felt so stupid, they all asked me at work – has he got a name? Did you and Les ever decide? Or did he leave it up to you?'

Beryl beamed proudly. 'He's called Robert.'

'Robert?'

Really? After the girls' names Beryl had mentioned, and her firm rejection of Cuthbert, not to mention Winston, Lily had expected her to go for something more modern, less traditional. Unless . . . no . . . that was ridiculous! How could she even think it? Impossible! But . . . her face must have shown her confusion. She'd always been hopeless at hiding her feelings, and Beryl gave a little gasp.

'Oh come off it! Lily! You're not serious?'

'What?'

'I can see it in your face! You think I had it away with Robert Marlow! You think he's the father, not Les!'

The women in the beds on either side put down their magazines and looked across. This was better entertainment than hectoring articles about using up leftovers and adverts for laxatives.

'No— I—'

'Yes, you do! Lily, for goodness' sake! What do you take me for – *ooh* – *ow*! Don't make me laugh, it hurts!'

'I'm sorry, I'm sorry!' cried Lily – for both Beryl's twinges and her suspicion. 'It's just – well, admit it Beryl, you were always so . . . so forward with him at the shop . . . flirting with him, almost! And well, I wouldn't put it past someone like him to have taken advantage!'

'Oh my Lord, bless her! Hear that?' Beryl appealed to her neighbours as, denied their drama, they lowered their heads again and pretended they hadn't been listening. 'Look, Lily,' Beryl went on in a lower voice, 'Cedric Marlow might have married an ordinary girl from the shop floor, but Robert's nothing like his dad. He's on the make, that one, even if he did think he was cock of the walk and turned out to be a feather duster. He'd never get himself involved with a girl like me, not in a million! Anyway, you told me yourself, he's courting that Evelyn Brimble, he's been sweet on her for ages.'

'Yes, I know, but . . .' Lily wondered what she did know any more. Her world had been so rocked by what Sid had told her, she'd begun to think anything was possible. 'I'm sorry. I know you love Les. It was just . . . just a thought. A silly one, obviously.'

She felt ashamed now, and the taste of it vied with the delicious chocolate on her tongue.

'I *do* love Les, you know,' Beryl was serious for once. 'I know it might have seemed like I married him 'cos I had to, but the way he stepped up when he found out I was expecting, and the way he's looked after me since – the more it goes on, the more I appreciate him. He's a good 'un, Lily.'

'I know.'

'I've got no illusions. He might never set the world on fire, Les, but he's a good man and he'll never leave me or treat me bad, like my dad did my mum.' She shook her head almost wonderingly. 'He worships the ground I walk on, to tell you the truth, and I know he'll be the same with the baby. That's worth much more than a bit of swank.'

Lily nodded. She'd never felt in so much agreement or sympathy with Beryl.

'And as for Robert, I just like the name! That's all right with you, is it?'

'Yes, of course it is. He's your baby. You can call him whatever you like.'

'Thanks very much! But Robert Marlow . . . no, I tell you, I'm flattered!' grinned Beryl. 'Best laugh I've had in ages! Wait till I tell Les he's got a rival – and who it is! He'd better look smart when he gets home, hadn't he?'

'Yes, all right, very funny, you have a laugh at my expense,' conceded Lily, but mention of Les made her remember what Ivy had promised. 'Ivy's sent him a telegram,' she volunteered. 'Did she tell you?'

'Yes, one to his last PO Box, and one to Staff HQ in case he's got moved on.' Beryl was serious for a moment. 'I wish he was here, Lily, I really do. I want to see them together, him and the baby. I want to see Les holding him, like he should be.' She smoothed the bedcover over her stomach. She still looked pregnant, Lily thought, but perhaps that was normal. 'And I'd like him here for me, as well. But I know I'm lucky, really. She's been very good to me, Ivy has. And your mum. They were fantastic last night. I couldn't have done it without them.'

Lily smiled.

'We're all going to help you, Beryl,' she said. 'We'll be here even if Les can't be. We'll help you with Robert.'

'It's Robert Leslie, by the way,' said Beryl contentedly. 'To be known as Bobby.'

'That's nice.'

'Yeah, Susan couldn't stop saying it! Over and over! Scored a hit there, at least!'

A trolley trundled up with Beryl's supper on it, and a minute later ('Wouldn't you just know it?') a nurse arrived with a squalling, winkle-faced thing in her arms. So this was Bobby! Lily stood up to have a good look, but his face was mostly screwed up into one huge open maw, and the rest of him cocooned like an Egyptian mummy, so she wasn't able to do the obligatory marvelling about long eyelashes and tiny fingernails that she'd heard other people do as they clucked over babies. The nurse began to unwrap the bundle, and Beryl started unbuttoning her nightdress. Lily thought it was time to go.

'Thanks for the chocs,' said Beryl. 'Oh, and take the paper. Ivy brought it with her, but I'm never going to have time to read it, am I? Not with this little monster.'

But there was no resentment in her voice, and as she took the baby into her arms her smile had a quality that Lily hadn't seen in her before. Beryl was a mother now. She might seem like the same old Beryl, and in many ways she still was, but she was also a totally different person. She'd left Lily and Gladys far behind.

It wasn't often that Lily read the *Hinton Chronicle* – the 'Hinton Oracle' as Jim called it, or in a particularly slow news week, the 'Hinton Chronic'. He still hadn't got over the fact that on the day after Pearl Harbor, the paper's front page had been evenly divided between that cataclysmic event and the apparently equally gripping story that 'Hinton Man Stole Undies from Washing Line'. For that very reason, he couldn't resist buying it most days, but Lily preferred to get her news – if she could bear to listen to it – from the BBC.

Tonight, though, with her mum at her knitting

group, and letters to Sid and Reg about the baby's arrival written and posted, Lily sat at the table with the paper Beryl had pressed on her. She was determined not to go to bed till Jim was back from his ARP duties – she knew he'd laugh about how she'd put her foot in it with Beryl about Robert Marlow, and she wanted him to hear about it from her, not Beryl.

Lily flicked through the pages. In its usual fashion, the *Chronicle* had printed national, local and international news and the utterly trivial side by side. There was nothing quite to match Jim's favourite headline, though the boy who'd used his grandfather's wooden leg to wallop another for imitating the old man's limp ran it close with 'Grandad's Mocker Gets a Sock'. Lily was about to turn over when her eye was caught by a small paragraph in 'Stop Press'.

'Local Woman Caught in "Reprisal" Raid'.

Lily pressed her hand to her mouth. No. No. No . . .

It was Jim who found her, curled up on her bed in the dark.

'Lily?'

He came gingerly across towards her. She'd rushed upstairs in such a state, hardly knowing what she was doing, that she hadn't bothered with the blackout: the inky sky was the only illumination in the room. The bed sagged as he perched on the end.

'I wondered what had happened. The light left on downstairs, a half-drunk cup of tea . . . then I saw.'

'In the paper . . .' Lily's voice was tiny, cracked. 'It's Violet.'

'I know,' said Jim. 'A bloke at the ARP hut was reading it. I was dreading telling you.'

'Oh Jim!' All Lily's shock and pain burst out. 'But she was only our age! And she only went to Bath to look after her aunt! It's so unfair!'

'Yes. It is. Desperately.'

Lily started to cry again in little snatches; she couldn't help it. She was aware of Jim sitting there, obviously not knowing quite what to do. He'd never been in her room before, not in the dark, not like this, not with only the two of them in the house. She sensed him half stretch out his arm towards her, then draw it back. He sat and let her cry.

'Lily,' he said gently after a bit. 'Come on. That's enough now. Dry your eyes.'

Obediently Lily fumbled with her hanky, but the sodden ball was wetter than her tears. Jim reached in his pocket for his own.

'Here. Have mine.'

She couldn't do that! She shook her head on the pillow.

'I need to blow my nose,' she said thickly.

'Well, do. That's what hankies are for. Take it.'

Lily sniffed and rolled onto her back. Sighing, she sat up, her knees bent. Feeling about a hundred years old, she took the hanky without looking at him and noisily applied it.

'There,' he said, when she'd finished. 'Better?'

'Not really.' His hanky was as wet as hers now. 'Oh, Jim . . . I can't bear it. Why Violet? What had she ever done to anyone? And her poor mother . . .'

The thought set her off again.

Jim didn't say any more, but edged up the bed and put his arms around her. Lily flopped forwards and rested her head heavily on his shoulder. Bit by bit the tears that had been a flood started to come in waves, and then little ripples that ran through them both.

There they stayed, quietly swaying from time to time, till they heard the latch on the back gate click. Dora was home. They both understood. Jim rapidly stood up and Lily slid off the bed.

'Blackout,' she said.

'I must do mine too. Then I'll go and explain to your mum, if you like. Tell her about Violet. And say you've gone to bed?'

'Oh, yes please! I'm too tired to explain it all tonight.'

'Of course you are.'

They stood facing each other.

'But Jim . . . don't go yet. I have to . . . I'd like to go and see Mrs Tunnicliffe. Violet's mother.'

'That would be kind.'

'I don't know where she lives.'

'We can find out.'

'Yes. I suppose we can.'

'And – if you want me to . . . I'll come with you, shall I?'

'Oh, yes please!' said Lily again. Her eyes shone in the half-light. 'Thank you, Jim. And thank you . . . for just now.'

'What, the hanky? Don't be silly. It's only what anyone would have done.'

That wasn't what she'd meant, and he knew it; she knew he did.

'I'm so glad you came in first,' she said. 'I'm so glad it was you.'

Jim went downstairs, thinking it out as he went. He needed to explain to Dora, but he wasn't sure where to begin. He couldn't tell her the whole story. She had no idea how Lily had first come into contact with Violet Tunnicliffe and her mother, and Lily never wanted her to.

Chapter 16

It had been Lily's very first day at the store when the air-raid warnings had sounded mid-afternoon. As they'd done so many times before during the worst of the Blitz, the staff had shepherded customers to the basement shelter, where everyone clustered together on benches around the walls. Trapped into conversation by Beryl, Lily had been sitting opposite Violet and her mother, but had hardly noticed them till Violet had suddenly got an attack of nerves and had become hysterical. Everyone had fluffed around ineffectually, but Lily, acting almost without thinking, had stepped forward and smartly slapped her face. It had worked, and brought Violet to her senses, but in the stunned silence afterwards, Lily realised that it was a huge transgression for an employee, let alone one who'd only just started. Whatever the reason, or the outcome, she'd assaulted a customer, one thing that funnily enough didn't feature in the staff manual.

Miss Frobisher had certainly not been impressed, and the matter had gone up to the staff office. Lily, mortified, had fully expected the sack, but Mrs Tunnicliffe, Violet's mother, had rung Cedric Marlow, no less, to thank Lily for her swift action, which she said had averted a worse crisis – Violet had been known to scream herself into fits.

At first disbelieving, then just grateful that she'd kept her job, Lily had kept the incident from her family. She'd escaped with her life, but she didn't want Dora to know how close she'd come to disgracing herself. She'd thought that was the end of it, but she'd run into Violet again just before Les and Beryl's wedding. Violet, delighted to see her again, had insisted on Lily borrowing, and then keeping, a dress that she'd worn as a bridesmaid herself. This was where Jim felt it was safe to begin the story.

'You remember the girl who turned up at the wedding?' he said, as Dora kept an eye on the milk she was boiling for cocoa.

'The one who sorted Lily out with her bridesmaid dress? You said she was a customer.'

'That's right.'

On the day, Jim had managed to deflect Dora's

suspicion that Lily had been 'pushing herself forward' with customers by telling her the truth, more or less – that Violet had taken a liking to Lily and had offered the dress simply as a kindness.

They both watched as the milk started to catch at the sides of the pan.

'Well, the thing is, I'm afraid she's been killed. She was staying in Bath, and the house took a direct hit in the raid at the weekend.'

'Oh, no! Oh, that poor lass! She wasn't much older than Lily!'

'Eighteen. The awful thing is, she was terrified of air raids. I mean, who isn't, but she had it really bad. Needed bromides and such like. She'd had some treatment and she was supposed to be better, and her mother sent her down there for a change, I suppose – and to keep her aunt company.'

'Well, why wouldn't she?' Dora snatched the seething milk off the heat just before it erupted. 'Who ever thought a place like Bath would be a target?'

'I know. It's supposed to be because we bombed Lübeck.'

'Pah!' The milk foamed into the cups. 'As if Hitler needs an excuse, the things he's put us though, and the Russians, and the Poles, and his own people!'

Dora clattered the empty pan back on the stove and stirred the cocoa viciously.

'No, well . . . as usual it's the innocent on both sides who pay. And Violet was one of them. But it was in the paper, you see, and Lily read it, and – well, she's pretty upset.'

'So upset she won't come down?' Dora laid aside the spoon and looked at him shrewdly. 'Whatever you say, Jim, Lily must have had something more to do with this Violet, or known her better, somehow, than you're letting on. You and she don't want to tell me what or how, and I'm supposed to take it on trust.'

'Yes,' said Jim evenly. 'That's about the size of it. But you needn't worry, Mrs Collins, please. It's nothing bad, I can assure you.'

'It's hard, you know, being a mother,' said Dora abruptly. Jim was startled. It was unheard of for Dora to reveal anything remotely personal. 'Beryl's about to find out. You start off knowing everything about your children – what they eat, how they sleep, when they go to the toilet. You're in charge of it all, and it's hard. It's hard work. But you bring them up to walk and talk, and that's all very well for a bit – it's lovely in fact. They're the world to you, and you're the centre of theirs. But they grow up. They walk away from you and stop talking – to you, anyway. And even though you know it's got to happen, and it's only right that it does, that's hard too.'

Jim nodded slowly. It made him think of his own mother, and not without guilt. He knew she missed him sorely.

'Shall I go up?' asked Dora. 'See if she wants anything?'

166

'To be honest, Mrs Collins, she's probably asleep by now. I think she's worn herself out with crying.'

Dora tutted.

'I'll leave it then. Least said.' She moved to the sink, ran water into the milk pan and started to scrub it out. 'Now drink your cocoa while it's hot.'

Jim's kindness continued next morning. He made Lily's tea in her favourite cup, the one with the roses and worn gilt rim, and when she shook her head at his offer of toast, parcelled up a slice of bread and dripping and made her tuck it in her pocket in case she fancied it later.

On the walk to work, he asked about Beryl and the baby. But Lily's visit to the maternity home had been all but obliterated by the news about Violet, and when she could answer only dully, he understood at once. He didn't try to jolly her along, but let her walk in silence.

After clocking in, before they parted to go to their separate cloakrooms, he patted her awkwardly on the arm.

'At least it's half-day closing,' he said. 'So not long to go.'

Lily nodded. Her eyes still felt sore and dry from all the crying and she felt them start to smart again at the thought of the mornings and afternoons Violet would never see.

A porter whistled them out of the way as he

trundled along with a sack truck, and Jim pulled Lily against the scuffed wall.

'I'll find out where the Tunnicliffes live,' he said. 'Leave it to me.'

'Thank you.' Lily's voice was hardly above a whisper.

Hinton had got off lightly even at the height of the Blitz, but she'd seen enough bomb damage in the newspapers and on newsreels, and for herself in Birmingham recently, to be able to imagine exactly how Violet had died. All night, as if it had been happening to her, Lily had felt the terror Violet must have experienced at the squeal and thud of the bombs, the shuddering aftershock, the tearing timbers and the cascade of bricks and plaster. Then there'd have been the dust, the burst water main, the escaping gas, the fires . . . It was true what they said. This was the first war in which ordinary people, the ones at home, were suffering as much as the troops. No wonder they called it the Home Front.

The store was quiet that day, and Lily found that the daily routine of polishing and tidying, folding and smoothing, soothed her and she was grateful to be occupied. Mid-morning, she was looking through a catalogue of pre-war babywear that Miss Thomas had found in a drawer, and marvelling at the lavish range on offer, when Jim hissed her over to his department.

'Sorted,' he said. 'I simply asked in accounts. The address is Juniper Hill.'

The prosperous part of town. That made sense.

'We could go this afternoon,' he offered, keeping one eye out on Lily's behalf in case Mr Simmonds was on the prowl. 'If it's not too soon for you.'

'Oh.' Lily blinked. 'Yes, I suppose we could.'

'We may as well. Or you'll only sit about and mope.'

Lily nodded. He was right. As usual.

April had been its usual impish self. As soon as you thought it was safe to put your winter things away, back came the cold and the wind, but the past week had been almost cloudless – beautiful, yes, but a gift to the bombers. Every silver lining had its own cloud.

Nothing in the weather could deter the birds, though, at their busiest time of year, and the further Jim and Lily got from the tight-packed streets around Lily's home into more spacious and tree-lined roads, the more visible and persistent they became. They were everywhere, chirping, cheeping, darting about, fussing with bits of twig and foliage. Jim knew all about birds and their calls, and kept grabbing Lily's arm and pointing, crying 'Chaffinch!' or 'Thrush!' But the birds were too quick for her, and by the time Lily looked, the fleeting thing had gone.

Apart from Jim's observations, they didn't talk much on the way. Lily was thinking about Violet. She'd known her so briefly, but Violet had made such a big impression and had been such a big influence on her, one way and another. She remembered how stunned she'd been by her offer of the dress, and how she'd tried to refuse. Violet had sweetly but stubbornly insisted. Watered silk in a deep periwinkle blue, it was the most beautiful thing Lily had ever worn, and probably ever would.

'This is it.'

Jim had stopped by the entrance to a gravelled drive with pillars at either side.

'Sizeable place. As we might have guessed.'

A five-barred gate stood open. The house was of grey stone, early Victorian, double-fronted like the doll's houses in Marlow's Toy department, but unlike them, clearly more than one room deep. There were bay windows on each storey, and, poking from the roof, three dormers – the servants' quarters, presumably. There was a huge monkey puzzle tree in the middle of the front lawn, with daffodils and narcissi around it. On the steps of the house Lily could see primroses in pots. The blinds were, as she'd expected, drawn.

'I hope she's in,' said Jim. 'There's no car or anything. I'll wait here.'

Lily hesitated. She knew what happened in her own neighbourhood when anyone died. Everyone 'rallied round' – neighbours were in and out of each other's houses with tea and sympathy, and the widow or widower didn't have a minute to themselves. But she wasn't sure if the same applied to people like the

Tunnicliffes. Their lives were different. They were stiffer and more formal, weren't they? For all she knew, the done thing was to keep a discreet distance, send a deckle-edged card, and present yourself at the funeral looking solemn. Maybe turning up like this was a serious breach of etiquette – again.

'Well?'

'I'm not sure I should have come.'

'If you think I've wasted shoe leather walking you over here to have you chicken out, you can think again!' retorted Jim. Then he added more kindly, 'Look, I don't mean to rush you, Lily. I can understand why you're nervous, but this is the right thing to do. You want to pay your respects and you've every right. You'll feel better for it, I know you will. Now go on.'

His hand rested momentarily on her shoulder and gave it a little squeeze. It reminded her of last night and being held against his shoulder in the dark. It gave her a quivery feeling on top of the butterflies she already had, but Jim smiled encouragingly. Forcing both feelings down, she gave a watery smile, walked up the drive, and pulled at the bell.

For a long time, nothing happened. At first, Lily was grateful: it gave her time to think through what she was going to say. Then it went on for so long that she thought there must, after all, be no one there. Half disappointed, half relieved, she was about to give up when she heard footsteps and the door was opened by a maid.

'Is Mrs Tunnicliffe in, please?' she said, finding her voice.

The woman hesitated.

'Is she expecting you? She's not really seeing anyone.'

A door opened towards the back of the hall: Mrs Tunnicliffe.

'Who is it, Cissie?' Her heels tapped on the tiled floor as she approached.

Lily remembered her from the shelter – the only time she'd seen her – as dark-haired, slim and elegant. She still was, in a black panelled dress with a pearl brooch, but she looked smaller and older than Lily remembered. Or maybe that was just the effect of the last few days.

'I don't suppose you remember me, Mrs Tunnicliffe,' she stammered. 'My name's Lily Collins. I work at Marlow's. That's where we've met. Um . . . in the downstairs shelter. Last year.'

'Of course,' said Mrs Tunnicliffe. 'I remember perfectly. Come in.'

She led Lily down the hall into the sort of room Lily had read about so many times in books. Comfortable without being exactly cosy – to Lily's eye, it was too big for that – if she'd had to sum it up in one word, she supposed she'd have called it 'cultured'. Chairs and a sofa covered in a chintz printed with flowers and birds. A big upholstered footstool heaped with magazines and books, new ones, still in their wrappers, and a baby grand piano covered with silver-framed photographs. A marble fireplace with a padded fender and brass firedogs; polished side tables with dried rose petals in porcelain bowls. French doors with long side windows over-looked a terrace that Lily knew without needing to see would have three wide, urn-flanked steps down to an undulating lawn. There would be basket chairs under a cedar tree, and, in happier times, jugs of lemonade, croquet mallets and balls. Now there were cards of condolence on the mantelpiece and a pile of unopened letters.

'I'll ring for some tea,' said Mrs Tunnicliffe, gesturing to Lily to sit down.

'Oh! No! Please! I don't want to put you to any trouble!' said Lily quickly. 'I shan't stay. But I had to come. I had to come and say – I'm so very sorry about Violet.'

Mrs Tunnicliffe gave a sad smile.

'I thought you might, you know. Violet was so pleased to have run into you again. And about the bridesmaid's dress.'

So Violet had told her! That was a relief. It was one of the things Lily had been wrestling with.

'I wanted to explain about that,' she said. 'I only accepted it in the first place because it was a loan, but Violet insisted I keep it. Of course I'll return it now.'

'No, no, you mustn't! I wouldn't hear of it!'

'Really? But . . . don't you . . . Are you sure?'

'Absolutely. Violet wanted you to have it, and you shall. She talked a lot about you, Lily. She was a . . . she was rather fragile, you know, and she admired you a lot. Envied you. Your spirit.'

Lily shook her head. She found it incredible that someone like Violet, so well-born, so well-educated, with so many advantages, could have found anything to envy in her – especially her spirit, which had so often – like the first time they'd come into contact – literally! – landed her in trouble.

'Well, I admired her,' she said. 'When I met her again, she seemed to have managed to get over some of her . . . anxieties. Got more of a hold of herself.'

'Did you think so?' Mrs Tunnicliffe sounded wistful. 'She'd be pleased about that. She did have some treatment. But any improvement was only down to medication, you know.'

'Medication?'

'For her nerves.'

'I see.'

Lily was learning a lot – more than she wanted to – about medication. First in relation to the way Sid was, and now Violet . . . it seemed there was nothing that medication couldn't supposedly cure. On the surface at least.

'Violet was never strong, physically or mentally,' Mrs Tunnicliffe went on. 'But Bath was starting to do her good. She was even talking about getting a little job. She'd seen one advertised, a couple of after-noons in a dress shop.'

'That would have been perfect!'

'Yes, well, it might have worked out, if she'd been able to stick it.'

Lily remembered what Violet had said about the courses she might have done – cookery or floristry had been mentioned. Maybe she'd actually started them and not been able to stick those either?

'She certainly loved pretty things,' her mother continued. 'And I was able to indulge her. She was my baby, you see. My husband died when Violet was young. And my boys are quite a lot older.'

She nodded towards the piano where two hand-some young men stood proud in their gleaming frames.

'My elder son's at the Admiralty and the younger works for the Ministry of Information. He's going to drive me to Bath tomorrow. To make the arrangements.'

'Oh! I didn't know Violet had brothers, but I'm so glad – glad for you, I mean. That you're not on your own,' said Lily impulsively. Then, feeling she might have overstepped the mark, she added: 'My father died too, and I'm one of three. And the youngest. With two older brothers.'

'There you are. You and Violet had all that in common. Even if you never talked about it, maybe you somehow recognised that in each other. Perhaps that's why you chimed with each other.'

A silence fell between them. There didn't seem to be any more to say. Cones of sunlight fell on the pale carpet, and outside, birds that even Lily could identify as wood pigeons were carolling gently.

'I mustn't keep you,' she said, standing up. 'But thank you for seeing me, Mrs Tunnicliffe. And thank you of course for letting me keep the dress. I shall treasure it. And I know the loss to me doesn't come near what you must be feeling, but I'm so sorry, like I said. And I did want to come and say it in person.'

Mrs Tunnicliffe stood up too and held out her hand.

'I appreciate it, I really do. It was good of you, Lily. And brave. But, as I said, you have spirit.'

'I nearly didn't make it,' Lily confessed. 'I got stuck at the gate. Jim gave me a push.'

'Jim?' Mrs Tunnicliffe faltered, then gave a little half-laugh. 'Ah, Violet mentioned a young man. He was taking photographs at the wedding. She said he looked very nice.'

'Yes,' said Lily. 'He is.' But the spirited bit of her added, 'When he isn't being thoroughly annoying!'

Chapter 17

When she got back to the road, Jim was lounging against the wall reading an Aldous Huxley. He stuffed the book in his pocket.

'How was it?'

'It was odd,' said Lily. 'She was sad, you could see that, but not crying, thank goodness, I couldn't have stood that. She was just sort of quiet and accepting. Dignified, I suppose.'

'That's how her sort behave, isn't it?' answered Jim. 'Playing fields of Eton. No weeping and wailing. Stiff upper lip and all that.'

'I suppose so,' Lily agreed. 'But – oh, I don't know.'

It was all very well talking about showing your feelings or not, but Lily wished she knew what hers were. Everything was so muddled in her head. Violet hadn't really been better, just kept under control with drugs. Lily had still fallen for it, though maybe that was excusable; she'd only met Violet a couple of times. But what about Sid, who she'd lived alongside for years without suspecting anything was wrong, or how much he might be suffering? All that time he'd been acting a part, and she hadn't seen through it. Was she especially dim? Or did she only see what she wanted to see?

Jim was looking at her sidelong, waiting for more.

'I don't know,' she said again. 'It's just that every-thing seems so . . . upside down. Apparently, Violet was never really better, just dulled down with pills or something. And – wait for this – she envied me – me! My "spirit"!'

'Hah! They must have had her on horse pills!'

'It's not funny, Jim. I'm trying to be serious here.'

Jim held up his hands in submission.

'All right, I'm sorry. Look, if you're saying every-thing's askew, well, yes, of course it is. Look around you. We're at war.'

'I don't mean in the world. Well, I do – but I suppose I mean more . . . in my world.'

Oh, this was hopeless! Susan could have done a better job of expressing herself. Lily tried again.

'I know it's selfish and silly. And I know so many people – so many – are having it so much worse. I do know that. And I know I should count my blessings and feel grateful – and I do, I promise I do. I count my Three Good Things every day. But it all seems so pointless. The only really good things would be Reg home safe, and Sid, and Bill as well, for Gladys – and Les of course, to see his son. I just want a few things to feel certain. Is that too much to ask?'

'Much too much!' exclaimed Jim. 'Anyone who tells you anything'll ever be certain again right now would have to be an idiot or a fantasist. But it's got to end sometime, this war, and it will, and we will win it, and I can tell you, when we do—'

'Things'll go back to normal?'

'Not if normal means like before, no! Quite the reverse – at least I hope so.'

Marvellous! Just the opposite of what she wanted to hear!

'Nothing's going to be the same in this country,' insisted Jim. 'But in a good way. They said after the First War that things wouldn't fall back into their old patterns, but there were still enough of the old guard left to make sure they did. But it won't be the same after this one. People like Uncle Cedric, even Mrs Tunnicliffe – they're decent enough people, don't get me wrong, I don't mean them in particular, but their sort – they've had their chance and the game's up. They've mucked it up for the rest of us, and now for themselves. It's going to be different, Lily. Initiative and this "spirit" of yours that Violet could see – they're going to count for something.' He paused. 'I thought you were up for that – you and your woman prime minister!'

Lily looked at him in his floppy old shirt and khaki trousers with his book sticking out of the pocket. His face was open and eager and his brown eyes shone. When he'd first said things wouldn't go back to normal, she'd felt nothing but cold dread, but now it was a thrill of excitement and possibility. His conviction had infected her, as it so often had on smaller things, like building the henhouse, or even his absolute certainty that he could coax another cup of tea from the pot. Now, though, he was talking about things that might really matter.

'So. Nothing certain any more. All change – and I'd better get used to it?'

'What's ever certain in this life?' replied Jim. 'All we can ever know is that the sun will go down and the sun will come up, and this time next week it'll be Wednesday again.'

Lily smiled.

'Maybe. So I'd better hang onto my hat!'

'Well,' said Jim reflectively. 'You don't very often wear a hat, do you? Only that funny beret thing when it's really cold. But . . . well, you can always hang onto me.'

It was a strange thing, thought Lily in the weeks that followed. Violet Tunnicliffe might not have lived a very spectacular life – she'd tiptoed, rather than tap-danced through it. She might well have been anxious, under-confident, highly strung. But her short life had made a big difference to Lily's, and in death, she had had an even more profound effect. In dying in the way she had, so suddenly and so shockingly, she had closed the gap that, since Sid had confided, had existed between Lily and Jim.

Lily still kept Sid's secret to herself, though. If she could have told anyone, that person would have been Jim – he surely would have helped her to answer some of the questions that still swirled in her mind, and to damp down some of her worst fears. But she'd promised Sid – it wasn't for sharing. The other thing, though, that she'd sworn blind to Sid just a couple of months ago, and which had been true at the time, that she wasn't ready for a boyfriend – that she started to question.

She thought about it a lot. She tried not to let her thoughts wander at work – she was too keen to impress Miss Frobisher for that – but she mulled it over when she was watering the veg or wiping up, or, like now, doing the ironing for her mum.

She'd started to see Jim differently these days. Still not soppily, or anything – not all hearts and humming-birds. She had to be honest – he was hardly a handsome romantic hero straight from central casting – more strip of wind than *Gone with the Wind*, more Clark Kent than Clark Gable. But what did handsome matter? Nothing, to Lily.

181

Jim was clever and funny. Even more importantly, he was good and kind, and modest and thoughtful – hugely underrated qualities, Lily had always thought. And yes, he could be annoying – maddening, sometimes, in the way he put her on the spot over the things she said, teased her rotten, and read her thoughts, even the most embarrassing ones. But she was hardly a perfect romantic heroine herself, with her unruly blonde curls that never lay flat, and a nose that turned up a bit too much at the end, not to mention her impulsiveness and untidiness and the way she could be, she had to admit, pretty mardy sometimes. He seemed to take it all in his stride, and to accept her just as she was, no pretence, no false front. She didn't have to try to be smart or sassy, let alone seductive with him – not that she'd have known how. She could simply be herself. And most of all . . . he'd been so sweet about Violet, so understanding, just . . . there. And it had felt so comforting to be held by him.

Lily had always thought that friendship with a boy and having one as a boyfriend were two completely different things. The way she'd seen it was that a boy asked you out, and you went on 'dates' with him. Gradually you got to know each other and could see if you got on. Getting to know Jim as she had, over time, though, had turned that on its head. She'd started off knowing of him as a colleague, and then as another brother, almost, around the house . . . But now . . . could it work the other way around? Could you be friends first and then move on to something else? Could it be more of a progression?

But then . . . what about the risk? Wasn't the easy, jokey but caring friendship they had now too precious to throw away by trying to turn it into something more? Lily wasn't usually over-cautious – if you didn't try something, how did you know? But if . . . if . . . if it didn't work out, if they tried and it was a disaster, what then? It would be awful. And anyway . . . Lily sighed and got up on a chair to unplug the iron from the socket of the ceiling light. She had no idea what Jim thought about her, really. She thought he liked her, but was it anything more – or was it all one-sided?

She knew what her mum would say: the same thing Dora said when ticking Lily off about waiting for the iron to cool down before she coiled the flex.

'Give it time!'

Lily supposed she'd have to.

What time brought them was, firstly, the advance of summer. The war news still wasn't good; Britain had started its own reprisals on Germany, a big bombing campaign, and planes thrummed over and around in the night, sometimes prompting treks to the dank, dark Anderson shelter, sometimes just leaving them wakeful under the covers. The Marlow's employees who'd signed up for fire watching were on red alert on the store roof; some of the hens in the Fowl Club went off lay.

At home, digging determinedly for victory, Jim, Lily and Dora got busy with the veg beds. The rhubarb was looking good, and the turnips, though the spring cabbage had suffered in the frost. Jim was going to sow winter cabbage, and peas, and even had hopes for Brussels sprouts.

At work, Lily and Gladys were firmly established in their new roles, and Cedric Marlow was starting to move on some of Jim's ideas – though it would never be fast enough for him.

He'd had to accept that with metal and treads going for caterpillar tracks for tanks, escalators were not something the store would see in the near future. And as for losing the apostrophe!

'He makes the dinosaurs look positively frisky,' Jim complained as he dug over a seedbed. 'Got stuck in a glacier in the Ice Age.'

Bit by bit, though, the ice cracked and creaked. Irresistible force? Immoveable object? Gravity might eventually move glaciers, but what got Cedric Marlow moving was, Jim suspected, a combination of Peter Simmonds's persistence and perhaps a little gentle persuasion from Robert. Because a couple of weeks later, under duress, Mr Marlow finally gave the go-ahead to Jim's idea for a staff newsletter.

Jim and Lily spent many happy hours debating what it should be called. It was also a safe subject to talk about in letters, though Jim rejected Sid's – surely not serious? – suggestions of *The Bugle* or *The Trumpet* as 'too overblown'. Eventually a shortlist emerged – the choice was between *The Marlow's Mouthpiece* ('A bit shouty?'), *The Marlow's Mercury*, a classical reference Jim informed her, ('No one else'll get it, but Uncle Cedric'll love it') and Lily's favourite, *The Marlow's Messenger*.

Waiting for Mr Marlow's decision was worse than waiting for Beryl's baby, but finally the verdict arrived from on high – it was to be *The Messenger*!

Jim was cock-a-hoop, and Lily was thrilled for him. Now the search was on for the story to lead the first edition (Ed: J. Goodridge). There'd be no stopping him now!

Almost as exciting was a clutch of letters that arrived all at once. Sid had settled in up in Scotland and seemed a bit more forthcoming about his life there.

'*The grog ration helps with the muscles at the end of the day and the lads are a good bunch*,' he wrote, even though he'd previously complained that the Navy's rum ration was heavily watered down. '*Still miss a pal I made on Hayling, though*,' he added, and Lily knew he was telling her that Anthony was still in his thoughts.

Reg's air mails were cheerful, too, though he, and the vehicles he had to maintain, suffered in the hot wind that blew the sand into fantastic shapes – '*and into every nook and cranny – and I don't mean just the engines!'* He'd made good friends with a New Zealand — a Kiwi, he called him — and there were Australian, Canadian and South African troops as well. The letters were initialled in the corner — checked by his captain before sending.

Les's superior officer had a harder job. Les wrote as he found, and his letters, when they came, since they were even more infrequent than Reg's, arrived with thick black lines scored through them. Beryl brought them over to share — she was just as regular a visitor as before, though now accompanied by baby Bobby, and, in the evenings, when Ivy went out to her cleaning job, trailing Susan too.

She turned up one Sunday afternoon in June. Jim and Lily were, as usual, in the backyard, making the most of the sunshine after being cooped up in the shop all week. The spindly runner beans were starting to creep up the canes, and, hopeful of a good crop, Dora had arranged a swap with another Red Cross volunteer who was anticipating an equally bumper crop of gooseberries. Lily wasn't wild about gooseberries, but you had to take what you could get.

Beryl parked the pram in a sunny spot, put the hood up to shield the baby's eyes, and handed the latest letter to Lily to read out. Les, it seemed, had had a scoop of his own. He'd been featured in the *Union Jack* Forces' newspaper — for his prowess at darts. The same letter also asked Beryl to send his snooker cue.

'Snooker! Darts!' exclaimed Jim incredulously.

He was sowing carrots; late, but it was a ploy to avoid carrot fly, he'd explained. 'Where is he, remind me, North Africa or Butlin's?'

'As long as he's safe,' said Beryl, jiggling the pram handle to get Bobby off. It was a heavy old-fashioned thing that Ivy had borrowed from a neighbour, but it was good and solid for rocking baby Bobby to sleep, which luckily he liked a lot of. Beryl had pretty soon given up on feeding him herself ('What a perform-ance! And the agony – and he hasn't even got teeth!'), but she could get baby milk from the clinic, and there'd be cod liver oil and orange juice when he was old enough.

'She does her bit,' Ivy had confided in Dora once Beryl was home from the hospital. 'I've made sure of that. I still do the cooking and the cleaning, but she does all the babby's washing, nappies and all, and tidies up after him, no complaint, I'll give her that. And he's a boon with Susan, little Bobby. She can't get enough of him.'

Lily had seen it for herself: Susan would sit content-edly for hours beside the crib or the pram, staring fixedly at Bobby.

'My baby!' she'd say. 'See my baby!' She also endlessly sang him her favourite rhymes – 'Singa songa sisspuns' and 'Baa baa black cheep'. The baby obligingly closed his eyes and went to sleep, though whether through lulling or sheer boredom was anyone's guess.

Ivy's telegrams about the birth had reached Les, and he'd wired back ecstatically, saying he'd be wetting the baby's head and no mistake. He'd also managed to send back two little leather camels – one for the baby and one for Susan. Beryl had attached Bobby's to the pram hood with a bit of string, and though it had a funny smell, and Dora fretted ('You don't know where it's been or who's handled it!'), it worked like a charm and was another thing that seemed to hypnotise him to sleep.

Once Bobby had dropped off, Beryl came to join Lily on the low wall around one of the veg beds. Jim had gone inside to mull over a report he was writing for the *Messenger* on the First Aid, Fire Fighting and Fire Watching refresher training that Mr Simmonds had been running.

Beryl kicked off her shoes and wiggled her toes, which were painted a pearly pink – Beryl wasn't about to 'let herself go'. Lily admired the colour and learnt it was Monte Carlo Pink. Lily knew Black Market Pink would have been more accurate, but she didn't say.

'And how are you?' Beryl asked. 'You got over that Violet business yet?'

Lily lifted her shoulders minutely.

'I suppose so. I still think about her. We've been so lucky so far. Everyone we care about is safe.'

They both instinctively reached out to touch the wooden fence for luck.

'I've been thinking about her too, you know,' said Beryl as they settled back.

'Have you? Why?'

'I've been thinking about weddings,' Beryl replied. 'And I've had an idea. I love Bobby to bits, don't get me wrong, he's my world, with Les away. But I'm not going to be just a mum for ever. They can't make me do war work now I've got him, but I can't go back into shop work, with the hours, or any kind of job I can think of. So I've had to come up with one I can do from home.'

'Go on.' Lily was intrigued.

'There's less nice material and clothes about now than there was even when me and Les got married. So I'm going to hire out my wedding dress. And I wondered – you can say no if you like – but if you'd consider letting me hire out your bridesmaid's dress to go with it.'

'Oh!'

'You don't have to give me an answer now,' Beryl continued. 'But it seems such a waste. You said yourself you'll never wear it again even if you got it shortened, which'd ruin the look of it, anyway. So why not use it to make someone else's day – and make a bit out of it as well. I'd give you a cut, of course, fifty–fifty.'

'I see!'

'And I'd give your mum something too – I wouldn't have a wedding dress to rent out if it wasn't for her.'

Lily considered. She thought about Violet, and the job in the dress shop she'd wanted, and the pretty things she'd apparently loved. She thought about Violet's kindness and gentleness, and the dress itself, hanging on the back of her bedroom door covered in an old sheet that was beyond even sides-to-middling. Beryl was right – it did seem a waste, and a shame for all that Violet had given her to come to nothing just because Violet's life had. Violet had thought Lily had initiative and spirit – well, this would show initiative, and Violet's own spirit could live on.

'Think about it, anyway,' offered Beryl.

'I don't need to.' Lily had decided. 'I think Violet would be thrilled to think her dress could give other people pleasure.'

'That's brilliant! Thank you!' Beryl hugged her. 'I've got a name for it – "Beryl's Brides" – sounds good, doesn't it? I'll get some cards up in newsagents as soon as! Hey, and maybe Jim can do me a little piece in his famous newsletter. I am ex-staff, after all!'

'She's got her head screwed on, that girl,' said Dora admiringly when Beryl had gone. 'We all thought it was Les doing her the favour, marrying her when she was in trouble. But she could be the best thing that ever happened to that lad. She'll make something of herself, and of them, you mark my words.'

Chapter 18

With the shenanigans and secrecy around Sid, and then the ballyhoo around Beryl and the baby, Lily felt she'd been neglecting Gladys. Thrilled as they both were by their new roles in sales, they posed one major disadvantage: the friends had been parted. They could no longer exchange a few words under the guise of dusting fitments or have long chats in the stockroom. Lily had often wilted under the relentless weight of Gladys's non-stop chatter, but now she missed it. She couldn't always co-ordinate her dinner breaks with Gladys, or with Jim, for that matter – he often spent his free time, even at work, scribing stuff for his newsletter or locked in conversation with Mr Simmonds anyway. Talk about 'with power comes responsibility'!

But she was pleased for Jim – pleased for and about him. His enhanced role at Marlow's had taken the sting out of his being judged unsuitable for the Army – and seemed to have removed at a stroke all thoughts of leaving. She also wondered if, behind the scenes, Cedric Marlow had guessed how disappointed Jim must have been and had offered him more responsibility as a consolation – and might even be testing him for an even bigger role in future now Robert had left.

Back down among the workers, Lily and Gladys still had one thing in common – they were about to be judged too. Their probation period in their new roles was up, which meant a review of their performance so far with their respective buyers.

'Don't tell me, you got "very good" in every single one of your proficiencies,' sighed Gladys.

The girls had agreed to meet after work for a 'debriefing'. Whether you liked it or not, the war had crept into even the way you thought and spoke.

It was another gentle, generously sunny June evening. They'd splashed out on a bag of broken biscuits and a bottle of lemonade, and were sitting on a bench outside the library in the shade of a plane tree.

'You are joking!' Lily nearly choked on her biscuit. 'Two "very good", one "good", and two "requires improvement"! The cheek of it!'

'Two! Never! What were they?'

Gladys's faith in Lily's superior ability was, as ever, touching.

'Can't you guess? "Appearance", for one – well, it's my hair, isn't it? Fair enough, I suppose, though I do try! But to be marked down on "quiet dignity" . . .'

'How come? Did Miss Frobisher say why?'

'She didn't have to,' said Lily. 'It was the other week. There was a jam on the stairs, someone had dropped a box of socks. I was already cutting it fine coming back from break, so I had to step on it to get back to the department . . .'

Gladys hissed in a breath. Running on the sales floor was strictly forbidden.

'Well, if I hadn't,' said Lily indignantly, 'I'd only have got a "requires improvement" for "time-keeping"!' She delved in the bag, ever hopeful of a fragment of custard cream. 'Can't win, can you? What about you?'

'Oh, two "requires improvement", two "satisfac-tory", and a "very good" in "politeness",' said Gladys, debating half a Rich Tea versus the same of Digestive. 'Mr Bunting – he's so nice, I do like working for him. But he still said I could be more . . . what was the word? Ass . . . something . . . when it came to selling.'

'Assertive?' asked Lily. 'But not pushy, I know. It's a fine line.'

There was one thing Lily didn't tell Gladys in case it sounded like showing off. Miss Frobisher had said that her marks, which had had to be agreed with

Mr Simmonds, didn't fully reflect what she thought – which was that Lily had great potential.

'That being the case, I feel it would be helpful for you to get some experience on other departments.'

Lily had gaped.

'Because I mustn't be selfish,' Miss Frobisher had continued. 'If there's somewhere else in the store where you could blossom, it's part of my job as a manager to make sure you're given the opportunity.'

What she didn't add was that she'd had to stick her neck out with Peter Simmonds to get him to agree, and she'd only got his agreement at the cost of Lily not being replaced while she went off on what Miss Frobisher called these 'placements'.

Lily had gaped again.

'Well, if you really think I'm up to it, Miss Frobisher . . . What other departments were you thinking of?'

Not Fine China and Glass, please, bull in a china shop wasn't in it! Not one of the men's departments, surely, like Ties and Neckwear, or Pipes, Cigars and Tobacco? Terrifying! And not Shoes and Footwear, all that running back and forth and climbing to the top of ladders to get the boxes?

'Shoes, for one,' Miss Frobisher had replied. 'Excellent training you'd get under Mr Howlett. And somewhere on Accessories, maybe. I can't say I see you in Fashions, Lily, but yes, Accessories, perhaps.'

'Whatever you think,' Lily had answered meekly. 'I'm grateful for the chance.'

'You see!' said Gladys now, when Lily told her the edited version – that she was going to be sent off to do holiday cover as and when other departments needed it. 'You're going to go far, Lily!'

'I don't know about that.'

'You are! I won't, and I don't want to.' She peered in the bag. 'It's only crumbs now. Have you had enough?' Lily nodded and Gladys shook out the bag to the patrolling pigeons, who pounced in a clatter of wings. 'All I want to do is marry Bill and have babies.'

Lily smiled.

'Like Beryl?'

'No, not like Beryl,' said Gladys firmly. 'I just want to keep house and look after my little ones when I have them. I can't understand her, setting up a business when Bobby's still so little.'

Lily had told her about Beryl's new enterprise. 'Beryl's Brides' had yet to acquire its first customer, but Beryl had drawn up what she called a contract in an exercise book and got Lily and Dora to sign it.

'So we all know where we stand,' she'd said. 'Who owns what, who does what, who pays for what, who gets what out of it. I don't want us falling out.'

Lily had been dumbfounded; even Jim had been impressed.

'We're not all the same, Gladys,' said Lily now. 'You've just said so about you and me!'

'See? See how clever you are, turning it back on me? You're so quick, the way you jump on things people say.' She squeezed Lily's arm. 'Your mum's going to be so proud of you, Lily. And there's Jim getting on so well . . . I'm happy just jogging along.' She smoothed the biscuit bag out on her knee and folded it carefully into squares. 'But even so . . . I wouldn't mind doing something at work. Making some kind of a mark. Not for me. But something to make Bill really proud of me.'

'He's proud of you already, I'm sure,' said Lily loyally.

'Even more proud then,' replied Gladys. She stood up, and the pigeons, startled, skittered off. 'Even more.'

The war ground on. Sid and Bill were frustrated still to be tied up in training when they wanted to be 'fighting men', as Bill put it to Gladys.

'*I've had enough of this*,' he wrote in a letter that a pal on leave had smuggled out and posted for him. '*Drills and pointless parades and polishing kit, practices and exercises and mock-ups! I want to be up and at 'em!*'

News from North Africa wasn't that encouraging either, and letters were even fewer and further between. No one knew if Les had received his snooker cue, let alone if he was still having enough of a swan to make use of it. Reg did write to say he was suffering from prickly heat, but he still wanted socks, and thick ones, as his new boots were too big and gave him blisters if his feet slipped up and down.

Lily was about to have her own footwear-related problem. Just a couple of days after her appraisal, Miss Frobisher called her over and announced that the sort of opportunity she'd been talking about had arisen. One of the salesgirls on Shoes was taking her annual holiday, and Mr Howlett needed cover.

'It's only for a week initially,' Lily explained to Dora that evening. The runner beans were swarming up the canes now, flowering frantically red. 'And it'll be back to junior work, really. But I'm going down tomorrow to have it all explained.'

'They must think something of you, Lily,' her mum said. She smiled, but her eyes looked tired; she'd been on her feet at the WVS tea bar all afternoon. 'And I do too. You said when you started there you'd try your best, and you have. I'm proud of you, I really am. It'll be something to tell Sid and Reg, won't it?'

'You can tell them, Mum.' Lily knew how hard it was to find anything to write that was cheering. It seemed so lame to have to fall back on what the weather had been doing, or the hens, or the veg. 'And you go and sit down. I'll do the watering.'

'Will you, love?' That was a rare endearment, and Lily hugged it to herself. 'In that case, I'll go and get those letters done now.'

Miss Frobisher could spare Lily because it wasn't exactly a busy time, certainly not on Childrenswear. July brought the Summer Sale, which meant trying to whip up excitement over the increasingly limited stock. In August, they helped out on Schoolwear, kitting children out for the new term. But now, on a sleepy June day, the first floor was quiet. With Lily downstairs learning the Shoe department ropes under Mr Howlett, Gladys was enjoying a pleasantly drowsy end of the afternoon, drifting about the Toy department straightening the displays and mentally drafting her next letter to Bill. She was suddenly aware that she had a shadow.

'Hello!' she said, turning, and as she'd been taught: 'May I help you?'

'I'm bored.'

Beside her was a boy of about eight in flannel shorts and shirt. He had curly auburn hair and freckles, and two very scabby knees above his long socks and sandals.

'I'm sorry to hear that,' said Gladys, looking around for his mother – or any adult who might be his parent or relative. There was no one. 'You're not on your own, are you?'

'I might as well be,' said the lad. 'Mother's debating about a tea trolley. I ask you!'

'I see,' said Gladys. 'Not of much interest to you.'

'Hardly!' snorted the boy. 'That could never happen, you know,' he went on, pointing to a jigsaw depicting a Luftwaffe plane plunged into the sea, with its crew on a piece of flotsam awaiting rescue, or, ideally, capture. 'If the plane went into the water at that angle in those seas, they'd all have broken their necks.'

'Really? You're very knowledgeable,' said Gladys, as easily impressed as ever. 'You should be advising the Ministry. Or at least the makers of the puzzle.'

'Maybe I'll write to them,' said the lad. 'I've done that before. I wrote to Woolworth's to complain about their sherbet lemons losing their fizz. They sent me a grovelling letter and a quarter pound of them back.'

'That's a good wheeze,' said Gladys, even more impressed.

'Can we do the puzzle anyway?' asked the boy.

'What? Well . . .' Gladys looked around. The department was deserted – not a proper customer in sight. If anyone did appear, Mr Bunting, who was poring over a catalogue, or one of the more senior salespeople, could easily see to them. 'Oh . . . all right then. Why not?'

She carried the jigsaw over to a counter and eased off the lid.

'Right,' said the boy, taking charge. 'First we have to find the corners, and the side pieces. But if as you go along you see any bits that obviously go together – the swastika off the plane for instance – put them to one side.'

If Gladys was good at one thing, it was taking instructions, even from an eight-year-old, and soon two heads were bent industriously to their task. It was only the announcement over the tannoy that broke the spell.

'If anyone has seen a boy aged eight with auburn hair wearing grey shorts and a blue shirt, would they please contact or bring him to the Furniture and Household department immediately. Thank you.'

Gladys shot upright.

'That's you!'

'So it is!' grinned the boy in delight. 'I'm famous!'

At almost the same moment, Mr Simmonds arrived, closely followed by a tall, harassed, but handsome woman in a striped summer dress.

'Charles! What do you mean, wandering off like that!'

'Miss Huskins? What do you think you're doing?'

'That looks like fun! Better than tea trolleys, eh?'

It was Jim, arriving close behind, who posed the question. Charles responded eagerly.

'You bet!' He turned to his mother. 'Sorry, Mother, I didn't think you'd worry.'

The woman sighed.

'It's my own fault. I should have known better than to bring you, and given that I had, better than to take my eyes off you for a second!' She gestured helplessly to Mr Simmonds. 'I'm sorry for the kerfuffle. But I had a moment of panic.'

'Completely understandable, Mrs Jenkins.' She was obviously a regular customer. 'Miss Huskins here should have found out where you were and brought your son straight back to you.'

'I'm jolly glad she didn't, she's been a brick!' Charles exclaimed. 'Don't go telling her off. I never meant to get her into trouble.'

'He's safe, that's the main thing,' concluded Mrs Jenkins. 'Let's say no more about it. Now you stay right by my side while I finish my shopping, Charles, please.'

'Ohhh,' wheedled Charles. 'Can't I stay here and do my jigsaw?'

'I think we might be closed before you finish that,' observed Jim. 'All those choppy waves? Devilish hard to get right.'

'We'll have to buy it then, so I can finish it at home,' pronounced Charles smugly.

His mother shook her head in exasperation.

'He has an answer for everything,' she said despairingly to Mr Simmonds, and then to Charles: 'You deserve punishing, not rewarding! But all right then. Put it on my account, will you please, Miss?'

Gladys, who'd watched the whole scene unfold with her heart in her mouth, swallowed it down to nod and frame a choked 'Yes, Mrs Jenkins.'

'But it's a down-payment, Charles,' his mother continued, 'on the very good marks you are going to get in your end-of-term exams. Is that clear?'

'Absolutely,' said Charles, with a grin at Gladys. 'Thanks, Miss Huskins. I'll let you know if I send that letter!'

Mr Simmonds darted her a suspicious look, but Gladys, grateful for an ally, smiled.

'Please do,' she said to Charles. He wasn't a bad boy, and he'd spoken up for her like a shot. 'I hope to see you again. I'll put all this back in the box and bring the account over for you to sign, Mrs Jenkins.'

Jim marshalled Mrs Jenkins and the boy off towards his department. Mr Simmonds watched Gladys sweep the jigsaw pieces back into the box.

'Next time . . .' he said.

'Yes, Mr Simmonds,' said Gladys. 'I'll know what to do.'

'But actually,' she said to Lily and Jim later as they left the store in soft evening sunshine, 'he should have been thanking me! We got a sale out of it that we wouldn't have had if Charles had stuck by his mother.'

'That's a fair point,' agreed Jim. 'And Simmonds knows it, I'm sure. But he has to do things by the book, doesn't he?'

'I might have known you'd take his side!' Lily had been silent until now, still reeling from her afternoon learning more than she'd ever wanted to know about soles, uppers, linings, heel heights, and width fittings. 'Your new best friend!'

'I'm taking no one's side,' said Jim reasonably. 'I'm just saying. He's a stickler. And he's not my friend. He gave me hell for trying to sub down his report on the cricket match against Burrell's for the next newsletter.'

'Well, it's made me think,' said Gladys.

'Careful!' joked Jim, then winced as Lily's elbow stuck into his ribs.

'What, Gladys?' she asked.

'Well, children get bored silly when their mothers are shopping, unless it's something for them,' Gladys reasoned. 'It's not the first time they've had to announce a lost child over the tannoy, is it?'

This was true.

'So,' she went on, 'instead of having them wander off, why don't we have a special corner for them on the Toy department, where they can . . . I don't know, play with bricks, or do a puzzle, or do colouring if there's ever any paper to spare? I could keep an eye on them . . .'

She tailed off as the other two looked at her.

'All right, it's a stupid idea.'

'Gladys, no, it's not, it's brilliant!' cried Jim.

'Genius!' added Lily.

'I wouldn't go that far.'

Typical Gladys, she'd blushed crimson.

'No, really, I'll put it to Simmonds tomorrow, and he can put it to Mr Marlow,' enthused Jim. 'I'm not giving up on my Bargain Basement, or the other things, but this is something we could do now – another march we could steal on Burrell's!'

'Well, don't whatever you do say it was my idea,

I'd be so embarrassed,' said Gladys. 'Especially after today. It might seem like cheek.'

'Gladys, you're hopeless!' cried Lily. 'Tell her, Jim, she must take the credit.'

'Of course she must,' said Jim. 'No question. I'll start a column in *The Messenger* – "Suggestion of the Month"! I've a good mind to drop Simmonds's rotten old cricket report in favour of it, too!'

In the end, Jim managed to squeeze both in. When *The Marlow's Messenger* came out the following week, there it was – 'Suggestion of the Month' with the sub-heading 'Good thinking, Gladys!'

Displaying uncharacteristic abandon – perhaps the summer sun had gone to his head – Cedric Marlow had approved the idea straight away and had given a fulsome quote.

'"This is something that will offer customers both convenience and more time to shop in a relaxed manner. A 'Play Corner' will be established in the Toy department as soon as is reasonably practicable",' Lily read aloud as she and Gladys pored over the Toy department's copy of the newsletter that Mr Bunting had generously said Gladys could take away. 'That's wonderful, Gladys! Now there's something to tell Bill!'

Gladys glowed.

'I know,' she said. 'My name in print!'

'In lights, practically! You see? You see what you've got to offer? You see how it doesn't matter that everyone's different?'

'You're going to say something clever again, aren't you?'

'You said it yourself,' smiled Lily. 'You made a sale that wouldn't have been made otherwise. And you weren't even trying!'

'That was different. Charles was a child, not a proper customer. I probably couldn't have done it if it had been Mrs Jenkins.'

'Gladys, you really are hopeless! You will not see, will you!' cried Lily. 'That's just it. I know it's hard when there's all that stuff in the sales manual to remember. But it doesn't mean you can't be a normal human being as well. All you have to do is see your customers not as customers but as a child's mother or father and stop being so shy and scared of them and just be natural and your own kind self and – well, you could sell anything!'

Gladys still looked disbelieving, but Mr Bunting had tried to bolster her up too. After all, he wasn't exactly the pushiest of salesmen. He achieved most of his sales through quiet persuasion and kindly benevolence.

'Well done, Miss Huskins,' he'd said. The jigsaw sale had seen her reach her weekly target for the first time since she'd started. 'It just shows. There's more than one way to skin a cat!'

The expression had always made Gladys shiver – it wasn't very nice – and at the time she hadn't quite seen what he'd been getting at, but now that Lily had explained it, she could sort of see what he'd been saying.

'You are going to send Bill the article, aren't you?' Lily demanded, linking her arm through her friend's. 'Because if you don't I will! He's going to be so proud!'

And he was. The letter got through quickly and he replied straight away.

'Gladys, you're a star! That's my girl!'

Chapter 19

The thirteenth of June was a Saturday, not a Friday,
but it might as well have been for the news it brought
from North Africa. There was silence in the Collinses'
household when even the BBC newsreader, profes-
sional as he was, couldn't help sounding subdued.
Though the bulletin only said that British troops were
engaged with the enemy on the British Gazala Line,
everyone knew it meant the start of another huge
push by Rommel to take back Tobruk. Dora listened
with her fingers pressed to her lips. Lily felt more
like sticking her fingers in her ears. War in the desert
meant tanks: Reg was attached as a mechanic to a
Tank Unit. Everyone knew how to read – or hear –
between the lines by now. 'Engaged with' meant fierce

fighting. And not fighting that was going well for the Allies.

Lily knew the news would be received in silence at the Bulpitts' too, because Les's easy ride had come to a screeching halt – his last letter had said he was driving lorries. The men all named their trucks after film stars: Les had wittily called his Loretta after Loretta Young. So much for that: lorries carried things, and whatever they carried – troops, supplies, fuel – they'd be where the action was too.

'That's that, then.'

Jim got up and turned off the radio. This was usually the cue to ask: 'Who's for cocoa?' but this time he didn't. The fear in their throats would have made swallowing impossible.

Dora got up and wordlessly took her writing pad from the sideboard. It was all they could do. Write, and hope.

On Monday evening the news was graver still, with 'reverses and setbacks' reported for the Allies. Beryl arrived, ashen, bringing with her not just Susan and Bobby but an almost unrecognisable Ivy.

Usually Ivy came waddling in, huffing and puffing about the heat, adjusting her corset, taking off the grubby hat she wore on her frazzled perm, and expanding gently into the armchair. Dora would pull up the stool for Ivy's gouty leg, put the kettle on, and the two would settle in for a gossip. Today Ivy was shrunken and silent. She held out her hands helplessly to Dora, and the two women hugged each other in silence.

Jim, Lily and Beryl left them indoors with Susan and the baby and went out to the yard.

'She's gone right to bits,' said Beryl. 'I've never seen her like it. I think it's been too much for her on top of everything else.'

'I suppose with the worry about her husband all the time, as well as Susan . . .' Lily tailed off. Eddie Bulpitt's merchant ship was in danger every single day.

'That's it, isn't it?' agreed Beryl. 'Susan's that delicate with her chest and her heart, she could go any time, and who knows when or if Ivy'll ever see Eddie again? It's not like you're not worried every day – it's always there, like a toothache, but now, with the news . . . and knowing he's bound to be in the thick of it . . . If she lost Les too . . .'

Her voice trembled.

Jim tried his best.

'Look, Beryl, you know Les is in North Africa,' he said kindly. 'But that's all. It's a big place. Units move around. He may not be anywhere near Tobruk.'

'Ivy reckons he is. Says she can feel it in her waters.'

Jim had tried to reassure Dora in the same way, and though Dora was never one to reveal personal details, especially about her waters, Lily knew he hadn't convinced her either.

'And what about you?' said Lily, taking Beryl's hand. 'How are you doing?'

'I haven't slept a wink,' said Beryl flatly. 'I just lie and watch Bobby all night, watch him breathing, bless him. I daren't think about it, what it'd mean for me and him if Les didn't come back or . . . or . . . if he was wounded, or taken prisoner . . .'

Lily understood. She understood perfectly. She might not have been married, she might not be a mother, but she was having the same thoughts about Reg. She'd had them about both her brothers the minute they joined up, and even more so about Jim, when his joining up, let alone fighting, hadn't even been a reality, only a possibility. She felt ashamed of how she'd behaved over that now, but you couldn't help how you felt. Only try to hide it – not that she'd succeeded very well at the time.

Beryl heaved a huge sigh.

'But someone's got to stay strong, haven't they, or try to? It's no good me falling apart. That's not going to help anyone. I've got to, anyway, with Bobby to look after.'

'That's the spirit,' said Jim. 'Good for you. But I don't underestimate what it costs you.'

He'd often been exasperated with Beryl's ways, Lily knew, but she could hear a new respect in his voice.

'Ivy's been so good to me,' said Beryl. 'Now it's my turn.'

Lily squeezed her hand.

'You know you can count on us,' she said. 'We're always here.'

'I do know.' Beryl squeezed Lily's hand back. 'And thank you. But you're going through it too, with Reg.'

'Maybe,' said Jim. 'But look, Beryl, if you need anything . . . if you need a man about the place for any reason . . . goodness knows, I'm no substitute for Les, but you know where I am.'

Lily looked at him gratefully, and Beryl sidelong.

'Well, Mr Goodridge,' she said, fluttering her eyelashes. 'I can't think what you mean!'

Jim coloured scarlet, obviously horrified, and Lily couldn't resist a smile. They might all be worried; they might all be secretly imagining the worst, just to prepare themselves, and then pushing the thought deep down. But in the midst of it all, you were still yourself. And you couldn't keep a personality like Beryl's down for long.

The next few days were hardly easy, all the same. Dora sent letter after letter off to Reg; Sid wrote from Scotland, but they had nothing to tell him in reply. Ivy and Beryl had each written to Les, and Susan had sent a picture of a big yellow sun and a stick man beside it, supposed to be him.

'At least he was still standing,' said Beryl wryly.

It was a good thing they didn't know what was to come, though the news each day gave plenty of sombre clues. By midweek, the Germans claimed to have the upper hand and to have taken 'many thousands' of prisoners. By the weekend, Tobruk itself, that poor, bombed, besieged and broken town, fell to the Axis powers. There was no hiding it; it was a rout.

No one could eat, no one could sleep. Jim tried his best to stay positive, pointing out that every day that didn't bring a letter from Reg didn't bring the dreaded War Office telegram either. At work, though, Lily was struggling.

Before all this had happened, she'd coped well in the first week she'd spent down on Shoes. Too well in fact, because when another of the salesgirls went off on holiday, she was dispatched down there again. This time she was a wreck, fetching lace-ups instead of slip-ons, brown instead of black, evening slippers instead of sandals. And Mr Howlett was no Miss Frobisher.

'It's not good enough, Miss Collins,' he snapped, calling her into the cubbyhole he called his office.

'I know, Mr Howlett. I'm sorry. I'll try to do better.'

'Try? There's no try about it! You'll have to! What does it look like to customers?'

Lily hung her head. She knew better than to give him excuses, but Gladys, bless her, must have said something to Miss Frobisher, because at the end of the day Mr Howlett called her in again.

'Miss Frobisher has explained your situation,' he said coolly. 'But I can't make allowances. When you're at work, you're at work. You must leave your troubles at the door.'

Lily looked at him. He was nearing retirement now, a lifelong bachelor after a broken engagement, Lily had heard, neat, trim and spruce in everything – stature, hair, moustache. Lily wondered if he'd ever lost anyone he cared about – or feared he might have done. There'd been the fiancée, of course, and he must have had parents who'd died – and perhaps siblings. He knew what a battlefield was like as well, because he'd been with the Royal Warwickshire Regiment through the Great War. He must have seen fellow soldiers die, if not friends; comrades, if not exactly loved ones. But maybe instead of making him feel that he was fraying around the edges, like Lily did, it had simply bound him in harder.

Lily tried to do as he'd said – not for his sake, and not even for her own – she didn't care a fig about 'opportunity' or 'going far' now. She did it for her mum and for Miss Frobisher, who still did care, and by sheer force of will, she made herself concentrate.

She knew Gladys was worried about her. She asked every day after Reg, though Lily wished she wouldn't, and worked tirelessly to try to cheer her up. She insisted on buying her a jam tart in the canteen when they found themselves on a break together, and offered to treat her to the pictures to 'take her mind off things'. It was sweet of her, and Lily knew she meant well, but the jam tart lodged lumpily in her throat, and as for the pictures – as if anything could!

Somehow she got through the long week – still no

news of Reg or Les – hanging on by her fingertips for Sunday when she needn't put on a show any more. But when she dragged herself home on Friday evening – Jim had gone straight to one of Mr Simmonds's stirrup-pump practices – she found her mother in the kitchen. The ingredients for tea were on the table, but Dora was just standing there. She hadn't even started preparations.

'He's safe!' was all she got out before Lily fell into her arms and burst into tears.

'There, there,' Dora rubbed her back soothingly, though her voice had a catch in it. 'It's all right. He's sent a wire. It came dinnertime.'

'A wire – oh Mum . . . oh Reg!'

'Just says he's fine and we're not to worry.'

'Fine? Not to worry? It's all right for him! He's known this past fortnight he was alive!' cried Lily, unfairly and ungrammatically.

'I don't suppose he's been having the best time of it either,' Dora chided. 'I'm sure he's let us know the first moment he could.'

'Yes . . . yes, I know . . . I wonder how he managed it?'

Reg must have moved heaven, earth and miles of unforgiving desert to send a wire, possibly even – most unlike him – broken the rules. Then another thing struck her. Dora had been alone in the house that afternoon. Alone when the knock had come on the front door, the one they hardly ever used. Alone with the sick fear rising as she walked down the hall, opened the door, saw the telegram boy in the street.

'But what about you, Mum? Your heart must have stopped.'

Dora didn't tell her that she'd gone cold all over, through and through, and that inside she was still shivering.

'It's the lads who deliver them I feel sorry for,' she said instead. 'Just boys, not even your age, some of them. But I suppose I can say that, since it wasn't the worst news.'

'No. We're the lucky ones.'

This time, anyway.

They peeled apart and Lily wiped her eyes on her cuff. It was her new work jacket, but she didn't care. Nothing mattered as long as Reg was safe.

'I don't suppose . . .' she began.

Dora shook her head.

'They haven't heard from Les. At least, not earlier, when Ivy was round.'

Oh well. It would have been too good to be true. But perhaps Reg's news would give a bit of hope, at least. The desert was a big place, as Jim had said. The entire British force couldn't have been at Tobruk.

'And then, after all that . . .' Dora reached in her apron pocket and brought out an envelope. 'More in the afternoon post.'

Sid's handwriting!

'Read it,' she said. 'It'll cheer you up.'

215

Lily's gunning heart slowed to a stutter. She opened the letter and read it aloud. Sid apologised for the short notice, but said he'd been granted a few days' leave – '*Enough to make it worth the journey home at last! See you Sunday morning, trains permitting. And if you'll have me!*'

'If you'll have me! Listen to him!' said Dora. 'Now I must get on. I'm that late with tea, and Jim'll be home soon, starving, I daresay, and I need to think about what we can have Sunday. I'll have to get down the shops early tomorrow . . . oh, and I must collect those gooseberries . . .'

Lily folded the letter and put it back in the envelope. She could hardly take it all in; it was certainly far too soon for her to be thinking about food.

'I feel so guilty,' she said. 'Two lots of good news for us and nothing for Ivy and Beryl.'

'Watch and wait, wait and hope,' said Dora, pulling a lettuce apart at the sink. 'That's all we could do in the last war, and it's not so different in this.'

'You'd forgotten I was going, hadn't you?' asked Jim, when Lily blinked to see his knapsack in the hall the next evening.

She had to admit she had. Bit by bit she'd relaxed over the past twenty-four hours, but after the anxiety of the past fortnight there were still huge dark patches in her brain that until so recently had been occupied with worry about Reg. Now it was time to let the light in on all the other things that they'd thrown into shadow.

'Remember now?' Jim stooped to stuff a pair of socks into a side pocket. 'My holiday! If you can call helping with the haymaking and pulling thistles out of the wheat a holiday.'

'Is that what you'll be doing? I thought you were only going to help your mum with some jobs?'

Jim's father had been gassed in the Great War and was a semi-invalid. His mother had her hands full looking after him, doing all the work around the house, and taking in laundry on top.

'I am – she's got a list as long as your leg. Re-putty the windows, dig over the veg patch, creosote the shed . . .'

'Where do haymaking and thistles come into it then?'

'That's in my free time! Down the road, you know, at Broad Oak Farm.'

'Oh, there – Ted Povey's place.'

'Well remembered! Yes, you won't know me when I come back. I'll have muscles on muscles.'

'Sid'll be quite jealous.'

'I doubt that, after all his weeks of rough-stuff.' Jim straightened up. 'Meanwhile you'll be an expert on high insteps and fallen arches – if I've got those the right way around?'

Lily pulled a face: she'd been forced to stay on Shoes. The idiot salesgirl – and this one was a girl, not much older than she was – had gone on a hiking holiday to the Lakes. There, stupidly scaling something called Scafell Pike, she'd taken a tumble. The clue was in the name, thought Lily uncharitably, when she was told that the girl had broken her wrist and would have to take further time off.

'Only two more days to go, thank goodness.'

'And you'll have Sid here to help you through those. Then back to Miss Frobisher.'

'Yes.'

It was a shame Jim and Sid would miss each other, but in a way it was a good thing that he'd be away when Sid was home, thought Lily. She and her brother could have plenty of quiet time together, out of the house, without her having to fib to Jim about why they were going off or what they'd been discussing. It would be her first chance to talk to Sid since their meeting in Birmingham and to ask him properly about – well, everything. Who Anthony was, and what he was like, for a start. How things stood between them, and how things would or could proceed. And to try to get a better idea of what the rest of Sid's life was going to be like, because it was obviously going to be nothing like any life that she could have imagined.

Jim went off early the next morning, having lectured them all the previous evening about the hens, the watering, pulling off side shoots on the tomatoes, and keeping on cutting the lettuces. Lily watched him shoulder his knapsack as she stood on the front step.

'I wasn't expecting you to be up.'

'The birds woke me,' said Lily.

It was a lie; she'd wetted her finger and written a '6' on her forehead the night before, which Gladys swore always worked for her. Lily had been disbelieving, but somehow it, or something, had worked.

'Well,' she began, for want of anything else to say, or the inability to think of anything.

She'd genuinely thought she was getting up simply to see him off, but now her throat felt as if someone was stamping on it. This was ridiculous. Jim was going on holiday, and for a week – not off to war for goodness knew how many years, but she hadn't felt this bad even when she'd thought that was going to happen. What had come over her in the last few months? The answer was obvious. She really did care for him. Very much. And she'd miss him.

'Don't work too hard.'

'I'll try not to,' said Jim. 'But I've told you. I'll be coming back for a rest!'

Lily smiled thinly.

'Nonsense. But it's supposed to be a holiday. Make sure you have some fun as well.'

She didn't mean it; they were just words. What she really wanted to say was 'I wish you weren't going' or 'I wish I was coming too!' How stupid. And selfish. Jim's poor mum hadn't seen him for months; she had to manage without him all the time. And if Lily had been going, she'd have missed Sid, and she didn't want to do that. Jim was only going for a few days, and, knapsack or not, to Worcestershire, not the Western Desert. She was being ridiculous, and she felt feeble and thoroughly ashamed of herself, especially when Beryl had still had no news of Les.

Even so, she watched Jim go, right down to the corner, till the last glimmer of early sun on the buckles of his straps disappeared. And even when he'd turned out of sight she listened for the sound of his shoes striking the pavement in the sleeping streets.

Chapter 20

There was no time for moping, because Dora kept her busy, topping and tailing the horrible hairy gooseberries for a tart, and even entrusting her with the pie crust.

'Not so rough! What's that poor bit of pastry ever done to you?' she demanded as Lily thumped the rolling pin down. 'Now give it a half-turn and roll it again. Gently this time . . . what did they teach you at school? That teacher wants sacking!'

But when the tart was cooked, even Dora had to admit it wasn't a bad effort. She'd spent ages making the stuffing for a tiny piece of rolled shoulder of lamb, which was now spitting happily away in the oven and smelling like heaven.

Sid must have smelt the meat cooking, because a

few minutes later he was there, clattering down the entry and through the door, and reeling back in comic alarm as Lily flung herself at him.

'Steady!' he chided. 'You'll have me off my feet!'

Lily let go, but she was puzzled. There might not be room in the kitchen for Sid to whirl her around as he'd done outside Marlow's on his leave in February, but that wouldn't usually have stopped him from trying. Somehow, he didn't seem his usual self.

Dora hurried to take his things and give him her customary critical up-and-down. But Sid didn't give her the chance to start quizzing him – all he wanted to know was if they'd heard from Reg.

Lily was relieved to see him perk up and his face split into its familiar grin when he heard their brother was safe – and that the news had come by telegram.

'Must have a mate in HQ Comms,' he concluded. 'Or maybe this Tank Unit thing's a blind, and he really is changing the spark plugs on the brig's car!'

But after that, and sympathising over the continuing lack of news about Les, and asking where Jim was, Sid seemed to sink down into himself again.

'To be honest, I'm whacked,' he confessed. 'I've been rocking in a train corridor half the night and trying to kip in a luggage rack the rest. No, seriously, I have. I'm sorry, Mum, but I'll have to get my head down for a bit. You two carry on with dinner. I'll have mine later.'

'No, don't be silly! We'll wait,' said Dora bravely,

though Lily could see how disappointed her mum was, fearful that the meat would spoil while she, up so early, was famished.

'If you're sure . . . Look, wake me at two, will you?' said Sid. 'I'll be on better form by then.'

And he was – or was trying to be, Lily could tell. He'd changed into his comfy old trousers and checked shirt, wetted and combed his hair and had a shave, all of which, he said, made him feel one hundred per cent better. But Lily had put on enough brave faces lately for customers to know when someone was covering up, and she didn't think her mum was fooled either. Dora, though, knew better than to pry, so when dinner was cleared away, with Sid turning down seconds – another highly suspicious sign – she said she'd do the washing up and shooed the pair of them out to take a walk.

'Go and put some colour in your cheeks!' she scolded. 'For someone who's been doing all this outdoor activity, Sidney, you look like a ghost!'

It was true – under his tan, Sid looked quite grey. He looked as if he could do with going back to bed, frankly, but he waited uncomplainingly in the yard while Lily fetched her cardigan. They went out of the gate and along the cinder path that ran between the backs of the houses in silence.

'Shall we walk along the cut?' asked Lily when Sid still said nothing. 'Or have you had enough of water lately?'

'Anywhere,' replied Sid.

'Right, that's it.' Lily stopped in a scatter of ashes. 'Sid, for goodness' sake, tell me, what is it? You're not yourself!'

Sid shushed her.

'Let's just get out of here. It's Sunday afternoon, the whole street's probably out the back.'

They trudged on, Lily seriously worried now. Still Sid said nothing. As they went down the steps to the canal path, she could see that the water level was low and the water so thick and green it almost looked as though it had a skin on it. It stank as well. She wished they'd gone to the park instead, but it was too late now. She led the way through the echoey tunnel to an old log under a willow, too rotten even to be taken for firewood.

'Well?' she asked when they'd settled themselves in the mottled shade. 'Please, Sid. Talk to me. Something's not right.'

'No, it's not,' he said. 'Quite a few things aren't.'

He stared straight ahead through the willow fronds. A moorhen hiccupped past. A man on a bicycle. A courting couple. Lily couldn't help feeling that Sid wasn't seeing any of them: he seemed miles away, far out of reach.

'Sid?'

He looked at her, almost startled.

'Sid,' she repeated. 'What is it?'

Sid gave a deep sigh and seemed to make up his mind.

'Look, OK, I'll tell you. I haven't been training for the past month. I've been on light duties. After sick bay, that is.'

'Sick bay? Why? Why didn't you say? What with?'

'It's this blooming foot.' Sid stretched out his leg.

'The one you injured last year?'

Sid had damaged his foot during his basic training and had spent weeks at home recuperating, just as Lily had started work. It had felt like a bonus at the time, having him around, and the foot had mended – or so they'd thought.

'It's never been right since,' he said brusquely. 'But I didn't let on.'

'You idiot, Sid! You went back too soon, I knew you had! The doctor did say give it a couple more weeks . . .'

'Leave off, will you?' Sid groaned. 'You sound just like our mum, and that's not a compliment, by the way. I know I'll be getting it in the neck from her when I tell her, don't think I don't.'

Too right he would!

'Sorry, go on.'

Sid pressed his thumb into the yielding surface of the log, making a crater.

'Well, the course was all about amphibious landings – commando-type stuff. There was a loch with a beach, and we practised time and again. At dawn, at dusk, by night – a lot by night. They'd wake you at two in the morning, ten minutes to get your kit on, off you went – they worked us pretty hard. That was on top of the cross-country runs, route marches, rock climbing . . .'

'Rocks?'

'Not all beaches have dunes, do they? There's cliffs – look at Tobruk.'

In the awful days before they'd heard from Reg, Lily had indeed looked at Tobruk. She'd read all she could about the place. It had been so desperately fought over and had changed hands so many times because it had a natural harbour sheltered by cliffs, perfect for landing supplies and supposedly impregnable. In other words, vital to whoever held it.

'Sid – it sounds awful!'

'Yes, it was – bloody awful some of the time,' he admitted. 'I didn't think it was possible to be so cold or wet or miserable. You needed that grog ration, I can tell you. But at the same time though . . . it was so good as well.'

Lily couldn't quite see how.

'It's hard to explain. I know you and Mum don't feel the same – no one could who's just stuck at home watching and waiting and reading the papers or hearing the news. But after a year of it I'd had enough of watching and waiting. And to think I might be part of something important at last – proper action – something that meant something, that might actually make a difference—'

Something really dangerous, thought Lily.

'If you say so. But your foot . . .'

'Yeah, that.' Sid picked up a stone and dug into the hollow he'd created. 'It was so stupid. I turned my whole foot and ankle out on a run. A rabbit hole or something.'

'And don't tell me, you didn't stop, you ran on.'

'Of course I did!' Sid chucked the stone viciously away. 'I wasn't going to give up for some tiddling thing like that! But by evening it had all swelled up. I couldn't get my sock on, let alone my boot. The MO put me on bed rest, sent me for X-rays and what have you, and the upshot is – it's crocked. Crocked for good.'

'But you seemed to be walking all right just now.'

'Like I say, bed rest and light duties. It's fine as long as I don't strain it.'

'That's all right then.'

'No, it's not all right!' Sid burst out. 'I'm being posted to COPRA!'

After that, he went quiet again. He said he didn't want to talk about it or tell her any more because he'd have to tell their mum, and he didn't want to go through it all twice over. They made the walk home mostly in silence, Sid deep in thought again and Lily left to wonder what on earth COPRA was and what could possibly be so bad about it.

When they got back, Lily made a pot of tea and Dora produced some scones – only plain, since dried fruit was rationed as well now, but there was a pot of bramble jelly from last autumn. They sat at the table. Lily listened mutely as Sid relayed the story of his foot, which had seen him classified as unfit for active service and put on the HBL – Home Base Ledger.

'As a writer!' he ended scornfully.

HMS COPRA, it emerged, was a shore base in Scotland that dealt with pay and conditions for Combined Ops. New postings, changes of posting or of rank – every one meant an assessment or re-assessment of pay.

'So . . .' Sid swirled the dregs of his cup as if he were trying to read the leaves, or maybe not to read them. 'Instead of being in the kind of unit I was aiming for, I'll be stuck at a desk working out their pay and allowances. But they reckon I'll do fine as a writer, 'cos it's pretty much what I was doing before.'

Sid had been a clerk for the Hinton Gas Light and Coke Company. Lily looked at her mother, waiting. She knew it wasn't her place to speak first.

'Well,' said Dora, pulling the corners of the cloth down more neatly over the oilskin underneath. 'I can see you're fed up about it, Sid, so I won't say what you've been expecting, which is that you've brought it all on yourself, going back too soon last year and over-taxing that foot of yours ever since.'

Lily thought she'd better not point out that her mum just had said it. Perhaps Dora meant that she'd say it, but not go on about it, which to her credit, she didn't.

'But I'll say one thing. You might have fancied yourself as a hero, with a row of medals on your chest, and I don't doubt you'd have got them, one way or another. But I can tell you, all too often it's the heroes who don't come back, and I don't want to be one of those mothers that gets their son's medals in the post.'

Lily looked gravely at Sid. His mouth had twisted and he looked away.

'I'll say one more thing and then I'll give over,' Dora continued when he said nothing. 'This war isn't just about you, Sidney. If your foot was going to give out, it's better, don't you think, that it did it now, in training, than on some beach in France or Africa or wherever? When it could have been not just the end for you, but let down the other fellows in your unit? You wouldn't have wanted to put them in danger, would you? You can't deny that would have been a far worse outcome than having to sit at a desk for the rest of the war.'

There was another long pause. Then Sid reached out and covered Dora's hand with his own. When he spoke his voice shook.

'You're right,' he said. 'You're right about all of it. I should stop being so damned pathetic – excuse my language. I know I should count myself lucky. Adolf's not going to come bombing the West Coast of Scotland, is he? Or launch an invasion up there. Looks like I'll make it through, doesn't it?'

'I know it's hard,' said Dora. 'I know it's not what you wanted. But things don't always work out like we want, do they? Let alone how we expect.'

Sid gave a thin smile and looked at Lily. It was his first acknowledgement of the secret they shared, one which their mum was excluded from, but which her words reflected too, if she'd only known. Lily thought it was the saddest smile she'd ever seen.

Sid said he needed an early night, and he still hadn't stirred when Lily left for work next morning. She could understand he needed to catch up on his sleep, but as she had in the past, she couldn't help feeling that there was still something not right – something else on his mind. She couldn't help feeling his dejection over his desk job was only the half of it – and she felt it had to do with Anthony. The uneasiness followed her like her shadow.

She tried all day to take in the salesgirls' commands as they sent her to fulfil customers' requests, but she still brought out two pairs of dress shoes in the wrong sizes and styles, then nearly lost her footing on the wheeled ladder trying to crab it along the shelves when she was already halfway up, which was strictly forbidden. Thank goodness Mr Howlett, off on an exercise with the Home Guard, wasn't there to see. Or her mother, or Sid – she'd be the one with a crocked foot next!

She couldn't wait to get home, promising to convey

Gladys's best wishes – and sympathy – to Sid, though on hearing about HMS COPRA, and knowing that Wrens did most of the clerical jobs, she predicted that Sid would soon perk up once he got there.

'He'll soon change his tune!' she laughed cheerily. 'He'll be in Heaven!'

Well, they do say ignorance is bliss, thought Lily.

When Lily got in, she found Sid at the kitchen table dealing with a frayed flex on a lamp. Dora too had been saving up some jobs. Jim was handy, but had declared electrics were beyond his capabilities – unless, he said, they wanted to save Hitler a job and be blown sky high simply by pressing a switch.

Lily had been racking her brains all day – it had been behind the ladder incident – about how to get Sid out of the house for another talk. He seemed a tiny bit brighter – or maybe that was just because their mum was around getting tea – bubble and squeak with a few specks of leftover lamb that had made their way into the dripping. But with the meal over, it was Sid himself who gave Lily her chance. He suggested the pictures.

'Doesn't matter what's on,' he said. 'Let's go and sit in the circle like a couple of swells. I'll even treat you to a quarter of caramels while they're still around.'

There were fearful rumours swirling that chocolate, sweets and biscuits, the only things that had made the war bearable so far, were going to go on ration.

Lily agreed enthusiastically, though she had no intention of them ever getting as far as the Roxy or the Gaumont. Instead, when they got into town, she coiled her arm cunningly though Sid's and steered him to the bench by the library where she and Gladys had conferred about their probationary reviews and shaken crumbs out to the pigeons.

'What's this?' he queried. 'A kidnap?'

'No, a proper conversation,' said Lily, dusting the bench of a few fallen leaves – it was only the end of June, but it had been so hot.

'What about?'

'Sid!' Lily sat down and dragged her brother down with her. 'You know what about! What else?'

'I don't want to talk about it,' said Sid at once. 'I don't want to talk about him.'

'What? Why?'

'Because I can't,' said Sid. His voice sounded thick. 'I can't start.'

Lily felt her whole body tense – neck, shoulders, thighs and calves. She felt as if a hand was actually gripping her heart. Just as she'd suspected, something was wrong, something much worse than being posted as a pay writer to HMS COPRA.

But what? She didn't have the – what was the word? – the vocabulary – or the knowledge or the experience she needed. Had Sid and Anthony had a row? Had Anthony thrown him over? Found someone else? Those were the sort of things that happened between boy and girlfriends. Was it the same between – well, boyfriend and boyfriend?

'Sid, please,' she implored. 'I know something's wrong. Please – don't you trust me?'

He reached out and touched her hand.

'Of course I do. It's just . . . I've hardly taken it in myself. I can't. I only heard on the train down.'

'What? What did you hear?'

'It's Tony. He's dead.'

Chapter 21

They sat there all evening. Bit by bit, with aching pauses while he bit his lip and stared into the cool green leaves above while he collected himself, Sid told her everything, right from the beginning. How he'd met Tony completely by chance, because he was in the Fleet Air Arm and Sid had only been sent to where they were based with a message. How he'd asked for directions to the CO's office, and Tony had pointed it out, and they'd exchanged a few words.

'Not much more than name, rank and serial number really,' he remembered with a flicker of a smile. 'But there was something there. We both knew it.'

Tony had said he'd better get on, but he'd also pointed out the NAAFI – if Sid would be stopping for a drink and bite to eat? And Sid, who'd have to wait for a reply to the message anyway, had said he might well be. And then when he'd gone into the canteen, looking around, lost, Anthony had waved from a table and recommended the corned beef hash . . .

Lily listened in wonder. It was all so ordinary, and exactly what might have happened between a boy and girl. Maybe that was it, that was all she needed to know. It made what Sid was seem so much more understandable, more everyday, and not so strange any more. It was still wildly dangerous, of course, and against the law, and that would be a constant worry, for him and for her – but if it was how Sid had been made, and if he could still be happy . . . and with Anthony he obviously had been.

'We couldn't meet that often,' Sid went on. 'Trying to wangle us both getting leave at the same time . . . But we did get some time on our own. We actually managed a whole weekend. Went to the New Forest. Stayed at a country pub, went for great long hikes, talked . . . never stopped talking. We had a laugh . . . got to know each other. And he . . . well, he was just a great bloke, Lily. You'd have liked him so much. Clever and funny and quite a thinker, too. He thought things through. He knew what he was up against, opting for pilot training.'

Everyone knew. The first thing you were told when you trained as a pilot was to write your will.

235

'So you had, what, a few weeks, a couple of months? Then what? You had to go to Scotland?'

Sid nodded.

'He was going to be posted any minute as it was. Nothing we could do about it. We did write, of course, and if we could fix a time, he'd try to phone.'

'How did you manage that?'

'I'd lurk by the phone box in the village, and he'd call from a pub near his base. I had some wasted trips, I can tell you, when he couldn't get out of camp. But when it worked, it was great, 'cos we couldn't say what we wanted in letters.'

'No. Of course not.'

The censor's pen would have run dry.

'And then he told me he'd got his posting. Coastal Command. And my heart's been in my mouth ever since.'

That was something else everyone knew. The life was intense, the hours were insane, the danger was immeasurable. The rewards were there, sometimes, but at huge cost. Life expectancy for a pilot was between six and twelve weeks.

'He was chipper about it, of course,' Sid went on. 'Really excited, thought he could beat the odds. And some of them do. Some of them have to, or we'd all be saluting Adolf by now.'

'But that must have made it even harder to stay in touch. Or get any news?'

Sid nodded.

'I wasn't expecting much. I knew he'd try his best, but what with his ops, night after night, day after day, the way they push them, and the way I knew he'd push himself, and the way they were flogging us up in Scotland . . . There'd be no more phone calls, and I wasn't surprised not to get a letter, either. When little did I know . . .'

Yesterday he'd dug his fingers into the log. Today he fed them one by one into the slats in the bench. A breeze had picked up; the shade above and around them was no longer still. Lily pulled her cardigan tighter.

'And you heard on the train? How come?'

'Another complete fluke. A Fleet pilot got on at Crewe with his girl. They crammed in next to me, standing, and he asked for a light. We got chatting, I said I knew someone in the Fleet Air Arm . . . turned out this bloke had trained with Tony. They all follow each other's careers . . . word gets round. And he told me. Tony's plane ditched in the North Sea a month ago. Anti-aircraft fire. Blew up mid-air.'

'Oh, Sid. Oh, no.'

'So you see why I've been going around like one o'clock half struck.'

'Of course. Oh, Sid . . . It must have been awful for you: me and Mum so happy about Reg . . . and blabbering on about stuff at home, the hens, and Mr Howlett, and asking you things the minute you came through the door . . . awful.'

'You weren't to know.'

'But . . .' Lily realised she was blabbering again and stopped herself. 'When you must have just wanted to be on your own.'

'Fat chance of that, eh?' said Sid resignedly. 'And when you dragged me off for that walk . . . My head was so muzzy. I couldn't think straight; I couldn't get my thoughts in any kind of order. And when you kept going on . . . my blessed foot was a blessing in disguise as an excuse.'

'Oh Sid, I'm so sorry!' Lily burst out. 'It was only . . . it is only . . . because I care!'

'I know. I know you do. I knew what you really wanted to ask, but I couldn't have told you then. I couldn't have formed the words. I was still so . . . numb with it. Felt sick when I thought about it, sick when I didn't, when I remembered him alive. So alive.'

Lily felt a shiver run though her, and it wasn't just because it was properly chilly now. The breeze was getting into its stride: the flag on the library, which had been hanging inanimate, had stirred into life. Sid tutted and put his arm round her shoulders. He pulled her close and chafed her upper arm. He felt warm and strong and, thank God, alive, so alive.

She leant into him gratefully. The last time she'd been held like this it had been Jim's arms around her, and she remembered how good that had felt. She hoped Sid and Tony had known something like that closeness too. From what Sid had said, but hadn't said, about their weekend, she felt sure that they had.

'Sorry, Sis,' he said now. 'This is no good. You're getting cold. We'd better go.'

'No. I'm fine. Let's stay.'

She didn't want to go home yet, to her mum's enquiries about the film they hadn't seen, to cocoa and the news. She half-turned to face him.

'Do you think it would have come to anything? You and Tony?'

Sid let out a long breath.

'I'd like to think so, I really would. People say some stupid things, don't they, about meeting someone you could love. How they're twin souls, or two halves of the same person and that. I can't go in for that sort of guff. I think how you know it's right is when you meet someone who immediately gets who you are. You don't need to explain anything to them. They just know. Without being told.'

Lily knew exactly what he meant.

'Would you like to see a photo?' Sid asked suddenly.

'Oh yes! If you have one! Yes, please!'

Sid reached in his shirt pocket and brought out a small snap.

'He sent it when he got his wings. Of course he couldn't write anything on the back. We had to pretend we were just pals.'

Poor Sid. Always the secrecy, the dread of being found out. Lily took the photo. It was the standard one they all had taken – in a stiff new uniform, eager, beaming, proud.

'Oh Sid! You're right. He does look . . . lovely.'

He was terribly good-looking, of course – she would have expected no less. Dark hair, deep-set eyes, dark too, from what she could tell, but with a mischievous spark in them, and a curving, confident smile.

'He looks happy too, and I bet that was down to meeting you, Sid.'

'Very flattering, Sis, but—'

'I'm sure it was. I'm sure you made him happy, even if it wasn't for nearly long enough.'

'I hope so.'

'I'm sure. No one who knows you could be unhappy being with you.'

'You're a good girl, Lily.' Sid took back the photo and replaced it in his pocket – next to his heart, thought Lily. Then he pulled her close again. She rested her head on his shoulder and he rested his head on top of hers. 'I'm sorry to dump all this on you.'

'I'm so glad you have,' she said fervently. 'I'm so glad I made you tell me in the first place. What if I hadn't and you had no one to talk to at all!'

'True.'

Lily half-turned again and clutched his hands in hers.

'I may not understand all of this, Sid – or any of it, really – about how you must be feeling, except it must be the worst feeling in the world. And I'm sure you can't think about anything else at the moment, or anyone. But you will be happy again, Sid, not now, maybe not for a long while. But eventually. You've got to be. No one deserves it more than you.'

Sid didn't say anything, and Lily's heart ached for him. She knew it was far too soon for him to believe it yet, and she wasn't sure if she'd said it to reassure him or because she needed to believe it herself.

Awful as it was, Lily was happier, much happier, that it was finally out in the open between them, or if not happy, then relieved. She hoped Sid felt a little bit lighter too, for having shared it. They didn't pretend to Dora that they'd been to the pictures when they hadn't, just said it had been too nice an evening to be inside, so they'd sat on a bench and talked.

'Very wise,' said their mother.

Dora knew full well there was something going on with Sid. She'd have preferred to know what, but if Sid had talked to Lily, and she felt he had, that was something. At least her children got on. You heard such awful things about family feuds and pointless rivalries: even in times like these families found things to fall out about.

Sid made a supreme effort for the rest of the evening. He knew his mum wasn't really fooled, and that Lily knew it was an act, but he put in a medal-winning, mentioned-in-dispatches performance all the same, getting out the atlas and showing them where he'd be based.

'Here,' he said, pointing to a dot on the map. 'Largs. At the seaside, kiosks on the prom, crazy golf, Kiss Me Quick hats, the lot. Well, it used to be. It's a bit different now.'

'There must be some of it left?' asked Lily, remembering Beryl's tales of her honeymoon in Blackpool.

'Not much. It was two Italian families that made it what it was – owned half the restaurants and ice cream parlours in the town. They've been interned, of course, and the big complex they built – called The Moorings, funnily enough – well, that's where COPRA's based. In the café and ballroom.'

'It doesn't sound so bad,' observed Dora.

'No,' said Sid. 'It isn't. I'm darn lucky, really. And I'm just going to buckle down and get on with it.'

Dora gave him a smile of pride and encouragement mixed. 'That's my boy', it said.

'I can see it takes away a lot of worry for you, Mum,' said Sid. 'And you'll have to come and see me, won't you?'

Dora looked aghast. Leave Hinton? She'd never been further than the county boundary, and that was on a Sunday School trip. She'd been sick on the coach.

'I don't know about that,' she demurred. 'It's an awful long way. And I've got all my commitments here.'

It was the response Sid had expected.

242

'Sorry, Mum, I was forgetting,' he teased. 'Can't afford to interrupt the vital sock and balaclava production line, can we?'

Bless him, he really was trying his best to be the Sid they knew. He turned to Lily.

'If Mum can't be spared, what about you, Lily? Fancy some sea air to put some colour in your cheeks? If Marlow's can manage without Jim for a week, do you think they can spare you?'

Jim!

Sid's bombshells one after the other, high explosive followed by incendiary, and Lily's anxiety for him before, during and after, had all but wiped Jim from her mind. Only now, as Sid and Dora headed for the kitchen and the ritual cocoa, Sid expounding about his three weeks of writer training in Leeds, and then an exam, did she wonder how Jim was. Was he successfully working his way through his mother's list? Was he out in the hayfield now, after a day of creosoting and puttying, turning over the hay in the dusk and pitching it onto a cart? It wasn't exactly a seaside holiday like Sid had described. He'd hardly send a postcard, so it was impossible to know.

So far, she simply hadn't had a moment to miss him, but now Lily felt an empty ache inside. She wanted Jim back. She needed him. She needed to see him with his head on one side, his clever, narrow face, and his brown eyes taking it all in. If anyone could make sense of Sid's situation, he could. But then – of course, he didn't know. He didn't know the truth about Sid. And he didn't know about Anthony, alive or dead.

Lily hated secrets. She wasn't comfortable with the fact that there was still a part of her friendship with Violet that she'd had to keep from her mum, and she felt guilty that she knew so much more about Sid and his life than Dora did. It simply didn't feel right, even if she and Sid were protecting their mother from something she'd be better off not knowing, or not at the moment, anyway.

But Jim was different. He already knew all about Violet, of course, and he knew something was up with Sid. How could she possibly not tell him? She'd be keeping from him part of herself – an important part. And just when – oh, all right, she'd have to admit it – just when she was starting to hope they might become more than friends.

Chapter 22

Before any of that, though, there was another day on Shoes and Footwear to be got through. Mr Howlett was back, sporting a sticking-plaster over one eye, though whether the result of a mock-battle or a mutiny (he was second-in-command of the local platoon) he didn't say, and no one dared ask. Whatever it was, it hadn't improved his temper or terseness, and Lily made sure she didn't, as it were, put a foot wrong.

At the end of the day, though, he surprised her by thanking her for her help over the past couple of weeks and even said he'd be making a favourable report to Miss Frobisher. Lily ran home as lightly as if she'd been wearing a pair of the satin dancing slippers she'd brought out for a customer earlier on.

The more Lily had thought about Sid's story, the more she thought Jim would have to know. Apart from the fact that she didn't want to keep it from him, Jim wasn't bound to Sid by a blood tie, let alone a mother's emotions. He was better educated, better read – he might not even be that shocked. But she'd have to get Sid's permission.

Sid was in the yard when she got back, polishing his belt buckle and buttons: he'd be leaving after tea. Lily could hear her mother banging pans in the kitchen, so she knew it was safe to talk as long as they kept their voices down.

'Sid . . .' she began as she watched the hens scratch and peck. You'd think they'd have realised by now that no worm was going to break through the blue bricks of the yard, but Jim said that wasn't the point. It was just what hens did.

'It's all right. You can tell him.'

'How did you know I was—'

Sid paused in his polishing and gave her a shrewd glance.

'Look, whatever you say, I know you and Jim are . . . have been getting close. He lives here, you work together . . . I know you, Lily. you're not going to be able to keep it in. And why should you?'

Lily was so relieved she didn't even challenge him about herself and Jim. She couldn't have denied it, anyway.

'You really don't mind?'

'You need to tell someone, Sis. It's a big thing to keep to yourself.'

'Oh, thank you!' Lily reached out and touched his wrist. 'Thank you. And when I do . . . can I tell him everything? Even . . .' She lowered her voice, 'About Anthony? Naming him, I mean?'

Sid held his belt buckle up to the light, turning it this way and that.

'I've had a bit longer to think about it now,' he said. 'About him, I mean. I took myself off, told Mum I was going to meet a mate. But I just went to the pub on my own, sat there with one drink, hardly touched it. But it gave me a bit of time and space to myself. There's not a lot of that in the services.'

Lily could well imagine. When Beryl, pregnant, had flown to them in a panic, Lily had had to give up her bedroom and move into her mother's. It had only been for a couple of nights, but she'd been desperate to get back her privacy, which she knew she was lucky to have anyway. Sid and Reg had shared a room since childhood, but that was nothing compared with sleeping in a dormitory with a dozen others.

Satisfied with his efforts, Sid lowered the belt buckle and resumed.

'I sat there and thought back over every minute I'd had with him, everything we'd ever said or done. I could see him as clear as day. I wouldn't have been surprised if he'd pushed open the door, walked in, and ordered a pint, he was that real to me. And I suddenly remembered the last thing he'd ever said to me.'

'What?'

'Be lucky.'

Lily's heart thumped.

'Did you say it back?'

'No.'

'I'm glad.'

'Me too. It felt too much like tempting Fate – and I'd feel even worse about it now.'

He bent to re-cap the tin of polish. Lily looked at the strong sweep of his back, the dextrous fingers, the defenceless nape of his neck.

'What *did* you say?'

Sid straightened.

'I told him I loved him,' he said simply.

'Did he . . .'

'He'd already said it, that weekend we had. But I was too . . . I don't know, too shy, too overcome, to say it back at the time. But I'm so glad I did at the end.'

'Yes. Oh, yes.'

'So tell Jim everything, Lily. I'm not ashamed. About me. About Tony.'

He looked at her with what was almost compassion.

'And . . . you might want to tell him how you feel as well. Don't try and tell me you don't. I know I said before you and Jim had got plenty of time but what I think now is . . . there's no point holding anything back. This war . . . there's no end in sight, and anything could happen. You might not get the chance to say it again.'

Sid left later that evening – another night, he joked, of kipping in the luggage rack. On the surface he seemed completely restored to his usual self, assuring his mum a few days of home cooking was all he'd needed, though Lily knew that under the final heaped plateful Dora had put in front of him, his pain was still deep and real.

Lily made sure to hug him extra tightly and tell him that she loved him. But she didn't tell him to 'be lucky', even in getting a berth on the train – it would have felt like sacrilege. Those words belonged to him and Tony – she wanted Sid to remember them coming from him.

Dora knew her boy was still not quite right, but still she said nothing. Like Lily, she'd concluded that he was brooding about something more than a shore-based posting. Dora was never a woman afraid to speak her mind, but she also observed the rule that it was better not to ask a question to which you didn't want to hear the answer. From his demeanour, she doubted Sid would have given her one anyway, or at least, not the truth, and she didn't want to put him in the position of having to lie. What was the point? It was either a case of 'this too will pass' or in the fullness of time, it would all come out.

In her reckoning there were only a few things in life that really mattered: your family, your friends, your health. Your work, perhaps, if you had it. Well, there was nothing wrong in the family, nothing that the war ending tomorrow wouldn't cure, anyhow. Sid's health and his work were connected, as he'd explained, and they'd aired those. That only left friends – relationships, in other words – and Dora had decided that that must be where the trouble lay. But she took some comfort in the fact that whatever had been troubling Sid when he'd first arrived seemed to have been at least partially soothed. He was looking a bit less drawn: he must have talked it through with Lily. She hugged him tightly too and told him to take care.

'What, of stabbing myself with a pen nib? Getting writer's cramp?' he grinned. 'Relax, Mum. Save your worrying for Reg. It's not over in North Africa yet, not by a long way.'

When Lily and her mum had waved him off, the news at nine o'clock confirmed it. Rommel, bucked by his success at Tobruk, was attacking relentlessly, trying to push the Allies further and further east. The worry about Reg, which had only just subsided, reared up again – while Beryl and Ivy still hadn't had a word from Les. On top of that, after an eight-month siege, the Russian port of Sebastopol seemed about to fall to the Nazis. Dora switched off the wireless and headed for the kitchen to make the cocoa without comment.

Lily wondered if Jim was listening to the news by the inglenook in his parents' cottage, the dog at his feet, or if he was still out in the fields. Maybe neither. Maybe he was at the village pub, clashing tankards and singing old country songs with the other farm labourers. That was what country folk did after a long day's work – wasn't it? – at least if Thomas Hardy was anything to go by.

Lily sighed. She'd have to wait to find out. In the meantime, she could work out how to put everything she had to say to Jim. Not least if she'd dare to go as far as Sid had suggested and tell him how she felt.

The next day was Wednesday, the blissful half-day at work, made even more blissful for Lily by the fact that she was back on her beloved Childrenswear.

'Not a moment too soon, with the Summer Sale starting next week,' was Miss Frobisher's welcome. 'I'm afraid the stockroom is not quite as you left it. Miss Temple and Miss Thomas have been a little overwhelmed.'

Eileen Frobisher had realised from the start what a good worker Lily was – instinctive, too. She anticipated rather than having to be told. Before the salesladies had even given the signal, she'd bring out the next size or a different style for a wavering customer.

She wasn't going to go so far as to say it had been hard coping without her; it didn't do to give someone who was still learning the notion that they could go up a size in hats. But Mr Howlett's report had been more than favourable – and he didn't bestow praise lightly. Miss Frobisher felt vindicated in her experiment, and in the case she'd argued to Mr Simmonds, even if letting Lily go off elsewhere meant more work for her remaining staff.

'So did you enjoy the experience?' Miss Frobisher led the way to the stockroom. The Summer Sale was nothing like the glory days before the war, or even before coupons, but there'd still be some offers to tempt shoppers – basically, whatever they could get.

Remembering how she'd suffered over Reg, Lily's first instinct was, 'You must be joking!' But despite her lack of concentration at times, she knew she'd learnt a lot, not just about shoes, but some different and persuasive ways of selling. The customers had been a different breed down on Shoes and Footwear, and the staff were too; slicker, somehow. Their silky persuasiveness wasn't something Lily wanted to imitate, or felt she could, but she could see that it worked for them. More than one way to skin a cat, indeed. So that, more or less, was what she replied.

'Good,' smiled Miss Frobisher. 'That's what I hoped you'd say. And your brother reported in safely in the end, I gather.'

'Yes, thank you, Miss Frobisher. Just last Friday.'

Had it only been Friday? With everything Sid had told her since, it seemed like a lifetime ago. Gladys, who seemed to have appointed herself Lily's mouthpiece, must have passed on the happy tidings.

'Well, here we are.'

They'd reached the stockroom, and Miss Frobisher led the way to their section. Not as Lily had left it? It looked as though someone had lobbed in a grenade. The rails and shelves were all jostled, and there was a heap of stuff on a trestle with a taped notice saying 'Sale', which obviously needed sorting and re-repricing. A couple of cartons of bought-in stock were spilling their contents on the floor. Miss Frobisher nodded towards them.

'You know what to do?'

'Unpack, unfold, hang, save the wrapping.'

'Quite. And the markdowns on the table . . . the reductions are on this clipboard, see? With the general tidying as well it'll take you till dinnertime, I should think. But I know I can leave you to get on with it.'

That was another advantage of Lily Collins.

'I should get it done well before then, Miss Frobisher,' Lily assured her. 'Then I'll come straight down. I noticed some of the lower drawers behind the counter were—'

She stopped. She didn't want to criticise Miss Temple and Miss Thomas, but at their age, both of them were pretty creaky. She knew how their knees cracked when they had to stoop, and how they had to grip the counter to lever themselves up again. They must have been slinging the Cellophaned vests and knickers back any old how once the customer had gone, rather than getting down to put them back in their regulation piles.

'You'll want to hang the Sale signs, won't you?' she asked instead. 'I've had plenty of practice leaping up and down ladders lately.'

Miss Frobisher swallowed a smile. Who exactly was in charge here? But initiative and taking responsibility were not to be discouraged. Oh, what the heck?

'We've missed you, Lily,' she said. 'Welcome back.'

After all the anxiety of the past couple of weeks – with Reg, with Sid, with Jim away, with the hateful time on Shoes – Miss Frobisher's words were like salve on Lily's soul. She hugged them to herself all morning as she worked.

Chapter 23

Gladys had missed her too. They'd missed each other, which was why they'd agreed to have a proper catch-up on their afternoon off.

Lily wanted to hear all about Bill, but she knew Gladys would also want to hear more about Sid. Though she'd already told her the headline news about HMS COPRA, while she worked busily in the stockroom she also practised a highly-censored version of the rest of their time together that avoided the main revelation but still contained enough of Sid (and his Sid-isms) to feel believable.

As they retrieved their things in the cloakroom at one o'clock, Gladys had a suggestion.

'I vote for tea and a bun, a good chinwag, then let's go over and see Beryl.'

'To see if there's any news of Les?'

'That, of course – and to take her this.'

From her locker she flourished a tiny cardigan wrapped in a scrap of tissue paper. It was only plain stocking stitch, nothing fancy, but it had a V-neck and buttonholes – a work of art compared with Lily's cobwebby effort.

'Gladys! That's beautiful! Did you make it?'

Gladys shrugged modestly.

'Well, even I can't write to Bill more than once a day, and I've done him that many bobble hats and scarves – I just thought I'd have a change. See what I could work on finer needles.'

Lily gave her a long look, but didn't say anything: she felt sure Gladys was thinking ahead to the babies she was hoping to have with Bill one day.

'Well, it's a triumph. Beryl'll be thrilled. Now let's get a shake on, or Lyons'll be out of Soup of the Day.'

'Lyons? Are we celebrating?'

It was a step up from their usual haunt, a modest café in a side street, but they were salesgirls now, with a small pay rise to show for it – why shouldn't they splash out? That was Lily's reasoning, and Gladys, as always, went along with it happily.

Over lunch – at Lyons, the midday meal was definitely lunch, not dinner – Lily duly gave the rehearsed rundown on Sid. Then she turned the spotlight on her friend.

'Your turn. Tell me the latest.'

Gladys had plenty to tell – Bill's rumoured posting to HMS *Faulknor* looked unlikely now; he was still in Portsmouth waiting to hear where he was being sent instead.

'But he's definitely going to sea?'

Gladys nodded mournfully.

'But I can't complain. We've had a good run. But – oh, Lily. I don't know how I'll get on without hearing from him for weeks, maybe months on end.'

'It will be hard on you. Both of you.'

'It's a poor show, he says, for a wireless operator. But he can hardly use the machines to send me a message.'

She ran her finger around the rim of her cup. Lily reached across and squeezed her free hand.

'Do you think he'll . . . I don't know . . . make some declaration before he goes?'

Gladys raised her head, eyes shining like a couple of searchlights in the night sky.

'Oh, Lily, if only! That is—'

'You want a sign, don't you?' said Lily sympathetically. 'You want a ring.'

'Is that so awful?' pleaded Gladys. 'It's been nine months since we first met – nine months, three weeks and four days to be exact.'

Lily's heart swelled with love for her friend. It was

a wonder Gladys didn't know to the precise hour and minute – though she probably did.

'Other people get engaged, married even, much quicker than that when their boyfriend's being posted – plenty even when they're not!' said Gladys plaintively. 'Loads of people we know – that stuck-up piece on Cosmetics . . . nice, shy Brenda on Books . . . even Miss Bradwell on Schoolwear, and she's got to be nearly forty!'

'Miss Bradwell's thirty-four,' offered Lily. 'I know, because—'

'Whatever, I don't want to be waiting till I'm her age!' Gladys wailed. 'And look at Beryl and Les! They were married in weeks!'

'Beryl was pregnant,' Lily pointed out. 'I hope you're not thinking of that as a way out! Or in. Or whatever.'

'No! I'd never . . . I want to do things the right way round. Oh, it's no good talking about it. It's up to him, isn't it?'

Well, there was a question, thought Lily. Does it have to be? Sid thought she ought to tell Jim how she felt. And she wanted to. But would she dare?

Bobby in her arms, Beryl opened the door to them looking frazzled: the baby wouldn't settle, and she didn't know why.

'I've changed him and winded him, given him some gripe water, in case,' she explained. 'He's been like it a couple of days now. I don't think he's ill, he doesn't feel hot or anything – though he's doing his best to get himself that way.' She pushed a lock of hair off her forehead with the back of her hand. 'He's getting me all hot and bothered too.'

'Let me have a go.'

Gladys handed Lily her bag and gas mask and held out her arms for the baby, a wriggling bundle of whinge.

'What's up with you, young man?' she queried. 'Giving your mummy a hard time?'

With a skill – and confidence – Lily had never suspected, Gladys applied the baby to her shoulder and began to rub his back rhythmically in circles, swaying slightly and murmuring against his little head, 'There, there . . . there, there. You're all right . . . you're all right . . .'

Magically, within seconds, he had calmed and started making little chuntering noises. Gladys carried on, nonetheless.

'Will you look at that!' said Beryl, too grateful to be envious. 'You've got a gift there, Gladys.'

'She's got a proper gift for you, as well,' said Lily loyally. 'Well, for the baby.'

'Come on through.' Beryl led them into the back room, Gladys carrying the baby without stopping in her soothing. Then they all pulled up short.

If Lily had thought the stockroom was bad, this was worse. It looked as though not just a grenade but a whole ammunition dump had gone up.

'I can't keep on top of things,' Beryl explained, seeing their look. 'It's Ivy.'

'What about her?'

Beryl gave a huge sigh.

'We didn't do so badly at first. I mean, she was in shreds over Les, but I kept her going. It was a struggle, but we managed. But the longer it's gone on, the more we hear about what's going on out there, and still no news . . .'

She bit her lip.

'You can't help imagining, can you? All sorts goes through my head, and it's going through Ivy's too, I know, day after day, night after night . . . So now she gets up in the morning, gets Susan up, then they both sit around staring into space. I'm doing everything – or trying to.'

'Beryl! You should have said!' protested Lily. 'We said we'd help, didn't we?'

'I didn't like to impose,' said Beryl.

That was a first, and Lily's face showed it.

'I know, I know. I'm not usually backward in coming forward. But you had your own worries. But when you heard Reg was OK, and still we heard nothing – well, it's like Ivy's properly given up.'

'Oh, Beryl,' said Lily. 'Where is she now?'

Beryl hung her head.

'At The Grapes.'

'The pub?' Lily exclaimed. 'What, with Susan?'

'Says it's the only thing keeping her going.'

Gladys had put Bobby down in his pram and was rocking the handle gently to ease him over the transition, but she flashed Lily a look of alarm. Beryl saw.

'I can't stop her, can I?' she said defensively. 'She's always liked a drop if there was any going, look at the wedding, but she's never sought it out and she'd never have it in the house. But now . . .'

'Beryl, we can't have this,' said Gladys. Lily had never heard her so firm. 'Not for her, not for Susan – or for you and Bobby. It could be what's making him like he is. They pick up on things, babies.'

'Well, that's not the end of it,' admitted Beryl. 'You know this black-market stuff she gets? Well, she came back Saturday with a half-bottle of brandy, another on Sunday. And it's all gone. I can't have her taking to drink,' she added desperately. 'I saw enough of it with my dad. And if she gets caught with stuff off the back of a lorry . . .'

The prospect was terrifying. Even though Ivy was at the bottom of the chain – receiving, not selling – the police could, and did, make examples of people like her.

'Well, we've got to sort her out,' said Lily. 'We'll help tidy up, won't we, Gladys, and then I'll send Mum round. If anyone can talk some sense into Ivy, she can.'

'Oh yes, yes please!' cried Beryl. 'Please do! Ivy really looks up to your mum. If she gives her what for—'

Lily had been thinking more carrot than stick, but she didn't say. Dora would handle it in her own inimitable way.

'And,' she added, 'she'll make you some tea. I don't suppose you've been eating?'

'I can't remember the last proper meal,' Beryl confessed. 'But there's nothing in the house.'

'Mum can bring something over. Don't worry, Beryl. You concentrate on yourself – and the baby.'

Beryl, beyond herself, burst into tears. Lily made her sit down, while Gladys, as practical as ever, plucked a muslin square off the clothes horse for Beryl to wipe her eyes.

'I don't deserve you two, I don't really!' she sniffed when she'd recovered a bit. 'I wouldn't mind, but I'm trying to get this dress business going!'

'Beryl!' Lily exclaimed. 'You can't think about that now!'

'I've got no option, I'd already put the cards up, hadn't I? I'm not going to turn people away. What would it look like?'

'So you've had some replies?'

'Yes, I had a couple of girls round at the weekend. I kept them in the front, of course – I could hardly bring them through here with Ivy reeking of drink and Susan sticking her finger in the jam and drawing on the cloth. Who'd want to hire a dress for their big day from a place like that?'

No one, evidently.

'So what were they like?' asked Gladys. 'Do you think they'll come to anything?'

'Well . . .' Beryl considered. 'One of them, if she was a 36-inch bust then I'm Scarlett O'Hara! She was a 38 at least – and rolls of fat round the middle – my dress wouldn't go near her. But the other one, nice girl, came with her mum, and they both seemed quite keen. On the wedding dress, that is. I did show them the bridesmaid's, Lily, gave them all the patter . . .'

'I'm not worried about that,' said Lily quickly, and meaning it. 'Anything you make on that's a bonus.'

'Anyway, they said they'd have a think and let me know. When's Jim back, by the way?'

'Jim? Why? Do they need a photographer? Or want to borrow a suit?'

'No! This girl's marrying someone in the Black Watch, he'll be in a kilt, most like. No, I need to talk to Jim about business.'

'Business?'

'He's the one in the know, isn't he, about records and accounts and such? All that snooping around he did for his ideas for Mr Marlow?'

'I don't know about snooping—'

'That's what you called it at the time!'

'I did not!'

'You did, actually,' Gladys put in.

'Well . . . I may have done,' Lily admitted, remembering how stupidly jealous she'd been of the famous 'document' and the amount of Jim's time it had seemed to be taking up.

'Anyway,' Beryl went on, 'the point is, I need his help. It's not that I haven't tried. I got a book out – *Accounting Made Simple*. Huh! Might as well have been *Chinese for Beginners*!'

'Jim can explain.' It was Gladys, loyal as always. 'He's ever so clever like that.'

'Well, the answer's Sunday,' said Lily. 'That's when he's back.'

'Right. I want to do it all properly, see, proper double-entry profit-and-loss accounts or whatever you call them. So I can show you and your mum, and you can see I'm not on the fiddle.'

'As if we'd think that! You wrote us up that contract. And anyway, we're friends.'

'Yes, we are. That's why it's even more important.'

Bobby was sound asleep now, so while Beryl and Gladys started setting the room to rights, Lily made a pot of tea. As they sat and drank it, Gladys went back to what she'd said earlier at Lyons.

'I can't get over you and this dress hire lark when Bobby's still so little.'

'Bless her, she doesn't get it, does she?' Beryl appealed to Lily. 'It's not for me, Gladys, nappies and gripe water all day, and nothing else. That's not who I am.' She set her cup back on its saucer. 'But you – you've got a real knack with babies. Look how you got Bobby off.'

264

'And she's been knitting,' Lily added. 'Go on, show her.'

Gladys retrieved the miniature cardigan from her bag, and Beryl marvelled, just as Lily had done.

'You're an angel! Thank you!' She leant over and kissed Gladys's cheek. 'Thank you very much.' Then she sat back and said shrewdly, 'But you're getting your hand in for your own as well, aren't you?'

Trust Beryl to say what Lily had tactfully not. Gladys, naturally, tried to deny it, but Beryl was back to her usual self – direct and to the point.

'I know you, mind,' she said. 'You'll want to do things in the right order. Engaged, married, then babies. Well, tell him to get on with it!'

'Beryl! I can't!'

'Of course you can. You make sure you get that ring on your finger before he goes off on his posting.'

'How?'

'It's obvious!' Beryl looked sly. 'Offer him an inducement!'

Gladys looked vacant, and Beryl rolled her eyes.

'Stop making him sleep on the settee at your gran's, for a start! You do know about the birds and the bees, do you?'

'Hang on, that's hardly doing things the right way round, is it?' put in Lily.

Beryl tutted impatiently.

'She doesn't have to end up like me, up the stick

before I walked up the aisle. Bill can take care of all that!'

Gladys had turned puce.

'Beryl . . . you don't understand. It's not that we don't want to, and we have talked about it – and Bill promises he'd take care of the – well, you know . . . so there wouldn't be any chance of . . . you know . . . But as if we could, with my gran in the next room . . . and anyway—'

'Oh, for heaven's sake, listen to yourself!' Beryl exclaimed, so loud that Bobby gave a startled little cry in his sleep. She lowered her voice. 'You know full well she's half-deaf and snores louder than a goods train! You're both over the age, what's holding you up? How long have you and Bill known each other?'

Nine months, three weeks, and four days, thought Lily, while Gladys gabbled further embarrassed excuses, and Beryl accused her – and Bill – of shilly-shallying. ('I don't understand him either! Is he a man or a mouse?')

Lily got up abruptly. She clattered the cups and saucers together and took them out to the scullery. She didn't want to get drawn into this discussion; even less did she want it to move on to herself and Jim. She didn't want Beryl telling her what she should be doing, when she knew perfectly well. Oh, come on, Sunday! Now she knew what she had to say to Jim, she just wanted to get on with it.

Chapter 24

'When did I last see you? It's got to be over a year.'

'It was the Easter before last. At the egg-rolling.'

The whole village of Bidbury turned out for the annual jamboree on the local 'big hill'. This was followed by an Easter Bonnet Competition for the children, and a plate tea laid on by the Parish Council on the green – or 'In Village Hall if Wet' – though it would have taken a monsoon to keep the village children from the actual egg-rolling – and some of the adults, too.

'Of course. I remember now.'

Jim took a long swig from one of the bottles of lemonade that had been brought out to the field in creaking baskets, along with jugs of tea, piles of sandwiches, and hunks of cake. The weather wasn't

267

sunny, but it was hotter than if it had been, heavy and humid, and it was thirsty work against the clock to get hay carted and back to the yard, the rick built and the tarpaulin over it before the thunder started its drum-roll over the hills.

'I must have missed you when you came for the hens,' Margaret went on. 'Didn't see you Christmas, either.'

'No, we only got a couple of days off from the shop. And with the trains, or lack of them, it wasn't worth the trek.'

'Right.'

Margaret Povey had the slow, extended vowels of the locals in that part of the world. 'Came' sounded more like 'come'; 'right' was 'roight'. Jim's father had the same rounded accent, though his Hinton-born mother had never picked it up, and it had been pretty much ironed out of Jim by the grammar school, and even more so by Marlow's.

'You've left school now, I think my mum said?'

'No choice,' Margaret shrugged. 'When Eric signed up, then got taken prisoner . . .'

The Poveys hadn't had a good war. Margaret's brother Eric, Jim knew, had died in a German camp; her other brother had already been killed at Dunkirk. Ted Povey had been left to run his farm on his own with the help of a Land Girl – and Margaret in the dairy.

'I'm so sorry, Margaret. You've all had a hell of a time,' said Jim. Then he remembered. 'But I thought . . . You used to like drawing, didn't you?'

Margaret's pictures had been regularly pinned up on the wall at the village school. Faced with the inevitable jar of catkins, most pupils, Jim included, had produced ham-fisted representations with so much rubbing-out they'd made holes in the paper. Margaret was a few years below Jim at school, but the jar of catkins was a kind of teacher's pet, brought out every year, and when it was the turn of her class to draw it, she'd produced a delicate and detailed study. The headmistress had entered it for a competition: Margaret's work had earned a Highly Commended certificate that had been presented to her at assembly.

Margaret stirred the cut hay with her foot.

'Yes, I wanted to go to art school. In Birmingham. Or London, even. No chance now.'

She sounded so dejected; Jim felt for her.

'You never know. It might not be too late. You're still doing your drawing, I hope?'

'When, exactly?' Margaret exclaimed. 'You've gone soft, Jim! You've forgotten what farming's like! Seven days a week, up at five for milking and then taking the cows back out, delivering the churns, buttermaking, feeding the calves, taking the bull calves to market . . . Bringing the cows in again for afternoon milking, and in between I have to help Mum in the house and do what I can for Dad.'

Jim dipped his head. Margaret had a point, as his few days back had reminded him. Haymaking, for a start . . . Townies saw it as charming – smocked yokels chewing on straws, dog roses in the hedge, cider and strawberries for tea. Back-breaking toil, more like; rivulets of sweat; hay seeds in your hair, eyes, mouth, down your shirt; blistered hands from the pitchfork – that was the reality. But the reward was the security of well-fed animals all winter, when the fresh air that townies said they craved was driving rain or a howling gale and the cattle up to their hocks in mud. Even so, it was a way of life, and no farming family would ever wish to change it.

Jim looked at the girl standing beside him. She'd been a tubby little thing, with wiry hair in two fat plaits: it had seemed a miracle that a pencil in her chubby fingers could produce such delicate work. She was taller now in her breeches and Aertex shirt, the weight fallen off or redistributed, and her hair cropped short into her neck. It wasn't quite a case of ugly duckling into swan, but a passing mallard would have surely given her a second glance. Margaret had grown up.

'I'm sorry,' Jim said again. 'It's a funny thing, this war, isn't it? For some people it's one big sacrifice – for others, one big opportunity. But you mustn't give up your drawing, Margaret. Really – you mustn't give up hope.'

'I saw Margaret today,' he said conversationally to his mother that evening. She was darning a stocking in the fading light from the window.

It was only half past eight, but his father was

already upstairs getting ready for bed. He'd deteriorated since Jim had last seen him, moving only in a vicious circle of bed and chair, the lack of movement and fresh air weakening his muscles and making his bronchial chest even worse. The small sums he'd been bringing in doing odd jobs around the village had dried up: he couldn't even cope with jobs around the house, hence the list for Jim. Even now Jim was working through it, examining a bit of skirting that had come away from the wall and that his father couldn't get down to fix without a coughing fit.

'Grown up, hasn't she?' observed his mother.

'Yes, she has. A shame she's had to give up on the idea of art school though,' said Jim.

'Oh, I don't know.' His mother bit off a length of thread. 'She's not the first and she won't be the last who's had to give up on her dreams.'

'Maybe she needn't. I was trying to tell her not to.'

'Were you? Well, of course, that's not the only dream she had.'

'No? She didn't say.'

'She wouldn't, would she? Not when the other dream was you.'

'What?'

Startled, Jim knelt back on his haunches. His mother stopped work too and looked at him, her only son, her only child.

'You've only ever seen her as a little girl. But she's always held a torch for you, Jim.'

'No! Rubbish! I never saw it!'

'You wouldn't.' His mother shook her head and resumed her work. 'Short-sighted in every respect.'

Jim considered the idea, but still considered it ridiculous.

'No, I can't believe it. All right, maybe a sort of silly crush, the sort little girls have on older boys.'

'But she's not a little girl, is she, not any more. She's the same age as that Lily! And that torch hasn't gone out, I can tell you.'

Jim tensed. He knew what was behind this. His mother resented the fact he'd moved away, the more so because it was a situation she'd inadvertently created.

She'd had her hopes and dreams too – for him. So when Jim had finished school, she'd written to Cedric Marlow, reviving the long-dead family connection. The hope was that he'd offer to help Jim through agricultural college to get a proper farming qualification, rather than starting out as a farm labourer like his father had. But the letter hadn't been clear enough. Instead, Cedric had offered Jim a position at Marlow's – one that neither Jim, nor, at the time, his mother, had felt he could turn down. But now, every time he visited, she hinted that she'd like him home.

Jim sighed. All these conversations ever did was to make him feel guilty. He knew she had a hard life, and one which was only going to get harder, but he sent her everything he could spare from his wages after what he gave Dora for rent. Why else were his suits the most threadbare of any salesman's, why else did he haunt the library, not the bookshop? Even though he'd explained time and again that his place was in Hinton and at Marlow's now, his mother obviously hadn't given up, and she wasn't going to.

'She misses her brothers, that's all,' he said firmly. 'Perhaps she sees me as a substitute.'

'You can believe that if you like,' said his mother crisply. 'I'm sure she does miss them, and she's not the only one. But she's all Ted Povey's got now, with both his sons dead. So who's going to take over the farm when he's gone? That's all I'm saying.'

It wasn't all she was saying, and they both knew it. She was ramping up her campaign to lure him back, and using Margaret Povey and her father's farm as bait. Well, he wasn't having it.

'I think I'll leave this skirting till the morning,' he said evenly. 'The plaster's damp and the wood's warped. I'll re-plaster the wall tomorrow, leave it to dry, then cut a new bit of wood and slot it in. If that's all right with you.'

He stood up and stretched his back.

'Now I think I'm for bed. It's been a long day.'

'I know it's been a long time, Ivy. But you can't give up hope.'

Dora poured them both a cup of tea from the fat brown teapot. Susan was sitting happily with them at the table, chuntering to herself and slurping a bowl of bread and milk with *Peter Rabbit* open at the page where Flopsy, Mopsy and Cotton-tail were enjoying the same.

Dora stirred Ivy's tea and pushed the cup towards her. Brandy was not on offer.

'I've managed it with Eddie at sea all these years, I know,' mourned Ivy. 'But with Les, it's different. It's like all the stuffing's gone out of me. I've got no get-up-and-go.'

'You've got enough to get you to the pub!' Dora snapped. 'You can't give in like that – especially not like that! You've got to stay strong. Beryl can't be expected to do it all, not look after herself and the baby and you and Susan. Not when she's just as worried about Les as you are.'

Ivy shook her frizzy perm sadly.

'It's all right for you. You've heard from your Reg. But I'm telling you, Dora, when it goes on, it's worse hearing nothing than hearing the worst!'

'You don't mean that.' But Dora sounded contrite. 'Look, I know us hearing makes it hard for you – even harder. But think about it, Ivy. If you heard from Les tomorrow that he was all right, it wouldn't mean that much, trust me. I'm not off the hook with Reg – I'm still worrying about him now, don't think I'm not! They're still out there, and things aren't getting any better – and it doesn't look like they're going to. But what can we do about it from here? Nothing! So we've got to pick ourselves up, news or no news, and keep on going! One foot in front of the other! Battered, not beaten! Down, but not out!'

It was a long speech for Dora, and one that, had it known, the Ministry of Information might have liked on record for one of its bracing exhortations to Britain's 'heroines of the Home Front'. A dollop of Dora's good common sense would have been a fine side order with the plate pie that she'd brought with her.

'What'd Les say if he knew, eh?' she went on. 'Caving in like this? When he's counting on you to be a help to Beryl and the baby?'

Ivy's puddingy face crumpled and her chins wobbled.

'Stop it, Dora,' she begged. 'Please. That's enough. You're making me feel right ashamed.'

'Good!' retorted Dora.

More stick than carrot after all, then.

But sensing an advantage, she pursued more gently.

'I don't want us to fall out, Ivy, but you've got to buck yourself up. Stop this nonsense.'

There was a pause. The clock ticked. Susan licked her spoon. Then Ivy levered herself up, and on heavy legs went to the sideboard. Dora watched her open a drawer and fumble through the jumble of string, pencil stubs, and paper bags – things that thrifty housewives like Dora and Ivy would always have saved, but which were real treasures now. From the back of the drawer, Ivy produced a quarter-bottle of three-star with an inch left in it.

'I'm out of readies to pay for another anyway,' she explained, bringing it over. 'I couldn't afford a half-bottle as it was. This is all that's left, Dora, and that's the truth, I swear on my life.'

She placed the bottle on the table. Susan looked up briefly, then went back to her slurping.

'Take it with you,' said Ivy. 'Then I won't be tempted.'

'Me?'

'Yes, you. Do what you like with it. Put it in your Christmas cake.'

'Bootleg brandy in my house?' Dora was outraged. 'Thanks very much! Get me arrested, why don't you? Not likely! This is going down the sink where it belongs, before the police come sniffing it out.'

With Ivy and Susan gaping after her, Dora carried the bottle at arm's length, as if it were poison, to the scullery, where Beryl was washing her smalls in a basin.

Dora made her stand aside while she poured the liquor away.

'It's a sorry waste,' said Beryl. 'I'd have had that!'

'Too late,' said Dora firmly. 'Now soak this label off for me, there's a good girl, get rid of the evidence. The bottle'll come in useful for something, or it can go in the salvage.'

She wiped the palms of her hands on her skirt, as if simply carrying the bottle might have sullied them. Wide-eyed, Ivy and Susan watched from the doorway. 'Well?' demanded Dora. 'You told me to do what I liked with it!'

Shocked by Dora's decisiveness and shamed into silence, Ivy shepherded Susan to the sink to clean her teeth, then took her up to bed.

Dora helped Beryl peg up her undies on a line strung over the sink, then they went back through. Baby Bobby was asleep in the pram. Beryl kept him downstairs till his late feed, she explained, then they both tucked themselves up.

'My exciting life,' she said wryly.

'You're doing a grand job, Beryl.' Dora touched her arm fleetingly. 'He's a lovely baby. Getting a real look of Les about him, don't you think?'

'Definitely,' agreed Beryl. 'Les's forehead, and his chin. I'm going to send another photograph when I can get out to get one taken. And when I can get my hands on some peroxide. I don't want Les thinking I've let myself go. And I've got my customers to think about, as well. I've got to look the part for them.'

'Lily told me this dress business seems to be taking off. I take my hat off to you, I don't mind saying.'

Beryl shrugged. 'Gives me something to think about, anyway.'

'Exactly,' agreed Dora. 'Head down, chin up, that's the answer. That's why I keep myself busy. It's the only way. Then when my head hits the pillow I'm too dog-tired to lie awake worrying.'

'I'll make sure Ivy gets back to work tomorrow,' Beryl assured her. 'That's three nights she's missed now. I did ring them up, made out she'd done her back in.'

'She doesn't want to lose that little job.'

Ivy cleaned at the Magistrates' Court. Dora had sometimes wondered if that was how she got some of her inside information about black-market acquisitions.

'They don't want to lose her, by the sound of it. Said she wasn't to come back till she was better.'

The sound they heard now was Ivy creaking down the stairs.

'I'll freshen the pot, shall I?' said Dora. 'Then I'd better head home. Lily's on her own, with Jim still away.'

'What is it with those two?' asked Beryl curiously. 'Is anything ever going to happen there or not?'

'I daresay they know what they're doing,' said Dora. 'But I can tell you, Beryl, I've long since given up trying to predict anything to do with my children, Lily least of all!'

Chapter 25

'Lily! Lily! Don't go in yet!'

Lily spun around to see Gladys positively galloping up Brewer Street towards her.

'All right! All right! Calm down!'

She couldn't think what could be so urgent – they'd only parted at six o'clock yesterday after leaving Beryl. What could have happened overnight that was so important it couldn't wait till they got inside?

Gladys arrived flushed and breathless at her side.

'Oh Lily – what am I going to do?'

'Give me a clue and I might have an answer,' said Lily not unreasonably.

Gladys put her hand against the wall and leant her head against it while she recovered.

279

'In my bag. A letter. Help yourself.'

Lily fished in Gladys's bag and brought out a crumpled letter. The writing, she recognised, was Bill's. Scanning it, she learnt that he'd got his posting – '*and about time, too!*' – but now it was all hands on deck, literally.

'*But I've got leave this weekend, be with you Saturday afternoon!*' he wrote, before signing off with all his love and a long string of kisses.

'Oh, Gladys.'

Lily could imagine what her friend would be feeling. She'd been through it with Reg. Excitement for him – it was he'd wanted – but for herself only panic, hope and fear.

Gladys had practical concerns, too.

'I'll have to ask for Saturday off. And at two days' notice! Do you think they'll give it me?'

Lily could at least reassure her on that – look how Miss Frobisher had let her off to meet Sid. Brothers, boyfriends, husbands, sons – the management tended to be indulgent about last-minute leave requests if a serving man – or woman, come to that – was involved.

'Of course Mr Bunting's not going to say no! Though it might help your cause if we don't get ourselves in the late book! Now come on!'

As Lily had predicted, Mr Bunting agreed without hesitation and Gladys half-floated, half-stumbled through the next couple of days. The Summer Sale would be starting the following week, so both she and Lily were busy, or were supposed to be, in readying the stock and the sales floor. But Lily noticed Mr Bunting tactfully swapping a couple of show cards that Gladys had dreamily placed against the wrong items and re-arranging a display that she'd left dangerously skewwhiff. In the state Gladys was in, she might as well not have been there. She was more of a hindrance than a help.

Gladys, though, was blissfully unaware. All she could think about was the weekend. It could be the last time she saw Bill before he went away for . . . who knew how long? Without telling Lily, she'd been giving a lot of thought to Beryl's advice and she knew it was the last chance for her and Bill. Her last chance.

On Friday night, with Lily's fervent good wishes sounding in her ears, she tore off to catch the shops before they closed. Lily had brought her three eggs from their hens and some tomatoes as a gift, and, using her carefully calculated coupons, Gladys bought bacon for Bill's breakfast on Sunday. She also bought coffee as well as tea, because he'd started drinking that now. It kept him awake on long turns of duty, he said, and it had certainly kept Gladys awake when she'd tried it; nasty and bitter it was too.

'Lady Luck smiling on you today,' said the grocer as she packed her spoils away. 'I've got baked beans if you want 'em?'

Did she ever! Gladys took two tins. Was it a good omen?

Unexpectedly, when she arrived home, her gran was downstairs – in the kitchen in her dressing gown. Though there was nothing medically wrong with her, she rarely stirred from her bed given the chance, but Gladys's late return home had meant she'd had to come down 'to look for a bite to eat' as she pathetically explained.

Gladys was as patient with her as only Gladys could be: anyone else would have swung for her, as Dora often remarked. Before unpacking her shopping, Gladys dutifully set about making her a swift sandwich and putting the kettle on: her gran claimed she was too weak to lift it. But when Gladys spotted her eyeing her purchases (there was nothing wrong with her appetite), even she drew a line. She stated firmly that they were for Bill, and reminded her that he was coming for the weekend.

'You said.'

Nothing wrong with her memory, either, except when it suited her to forget things.

'That'll be nice for you,' her gran added. 'Reckon he might bring some NAAFI chocolate again?' She had a very sweet tooth, those that were left. 'As long as it hasn't got nuts in. You know what they do to my insides.'

Gladys unscrewed the lid of a jar of meat paste and started applying it to the bread, trying to look on the bright side. Gran could be a bit of a bind, but at least she allowed Bill to come and stay over in the front parlour. As long as she still had her meals provided and her bed made, the washing done and her chamber pot emptied, she left them to themselves. She didn't want or expect them to provide company or entertainment; they could come and go as they pleased. The main thing was that her comfortable life wasn't disturbed.

'You go back to bed, Gran. I'll bring this up to you.'

The older woman shuffled contentedly off to her nest of bedclothes. Gladys assembled plate, cup and saucer on a tray, and if she screwed the lid of the meat paste jar back on somewhat savagely, the feeling soon passed. She had far too much else to think about.

Next morning, she set to. She'd bought washing soda and a big box of bicarb, as well as a new scrubbing brush. It was late in the year for spring cleaning, but she embarked on it anyway. Tying her hair up in a scarf, she dragged the back and front room rugs and the hall runner into the yard, hung them on the line and gave them a good whacking with the carpet beater. She washed the floors and wiped the skirtings. She dusted all her gran's fusty ornaments, the clock, the wax flowers under glass and the cracked china shepherd with his dog. She washed the windows inside and out, buffing them to a shine with vinegar and newspaper, running from inside to outside and back again to spot any smears. She cleaned the sink and scrubbed the kitchen table. She scrubbed the front step and the kitchen floor. She plumped the cushions and ironed the best tablecloth. The plates and cups and cutlery were clean enough, but she washed them again anyway. She started at six in the morning and it was eleven before she'd finished and put everything back. Bill had said he wouldn't be there till the afternoon, and, desperate as she was to see him, Gladys hoped he hadn't meant five past twelve, because the next job was beautifying herself.

She washed her hair first, making sure all the soap was rinsed out. Gladys had long since given up on curl papers, but had acquired an old pair of curling tongs, and when her hair had dried, used them to give her poker-straight bob something of a wave. She plucked and Vaselined her eyebrows, a trick she'd learnt from Beryl. She applied a coating of face powder, and a tiny dab of the pink lipstick she'd bought before Christmas, and which she only used for Bill, to make it last. That would have to be it. Her eyelashes were stubby and straight, but even under Beryl's tutelage her attempts with mascara so often left her looking as if she'd been in a prize fight that she left it off. She could always have a go putting some on for tonight, when Bill had promised her 'a proper swanky night out'.

As carefully as a beekeeper investigating a suit in which they suspected a rogue queen might be trapped, Gladys negotiated her new summer dress over her head. It was striped – broad horizontal stripes, which were perhaps slightly unfortunate, as she could never have been described as slim, but it was the colours that had sold it to her – yes, sold, because she'd paid out real coupons and real money. The stripes were white and blue: she'd bought it for Bill, because it reminded her of the sea. It even had a boat neck.

By now it was half past twelve and Gladys hurried downstairs to put together something for her gran's dinner. She was far too excited herself to think about eating, though she forced herself to have some bread and jam. It was carrot jam – ugh – but she was saving her cheese ration in case Bill was hungry when he arrived. She carried a sandwich and cup of tea upstairs and edged it on to the littered bedside chest.

'Thanks, love.' Her gran turned her head on the pillow as Gladys stooped for a copy of *The People's Friend* and a screwed-up handkerchief that had fallen to the floor. 'Rub my neck for me, can you? I must have dropped off awkward-like. There's some liniment somewhere . . .'

Gladys poked about in the sticky clutter of bottles. Reluctantly, because she hated the feel of her gran's doughy skin under her hand, she applied some to the old woman's neck and rubbed it in. It stank to high heaven. She'd have to scrub her nails all over again.

'Have you got everything you need?' she asked. 'Bill and I'll probably go out for a walk.'

Easing her neck this way and that, her gran managed a martyred smile.

'You go and enjoy yourselves. I'll be fine.' But she couldn't resist adding, 'You'll be back in time to make my tea, though?'

It was getting on for three when Bill arrived, by which time Gladys had had to make three trips to the privy, had re-curled her hair four times and re-applied her make-up twice, arching forward like the figurehead on the prow of a ship to avoid getting face powder on her dress. She was exhausted from her cleaning, not to mention the pacing about she'd been doing ever since, reluctant to sit down in case she creased her dress. She'd just opened the front door for the umpteenth time to see if he was coming when Bill rounded the corner. He saw her too and waved. Gladys ran to meet him. He slung down his kitbag and they fell into one another's arms, curls and creases irrelevant.

'It's good to see you. I've missed you,' he whispered.

'Not as much as I've missed you!'

It didn't matter who said what first, as long as they said it. It was what they always said.

Twined together, they walked back to the house, and, safely inside, had a proper reunion, out of sight of the neighbours. When they finally disentangled themselves, Bill said out loud what Gladys had been thinking.

'No offence, but can we get out of here? I need some fresh air after that flipping train!'

Hand in hand, they made their way to the park, which was mostly allotments now, but still had the boating lake, and the ducks – or the ones that hadn't been poached. There were no swings or railings or bandstand – long gone for armaments – even some of the benches had been removed. But they'd come prepared. Gladys's purchases had also included a bottle of lemonade and biscuits: Bill carried an old woollen blanket, which he spread out on one of the few remaining patches of grass.

They lay down, Bill on his back, Gladys by his side, her head pillowed on his shoulder, his arm crooked around her. He breathed deeply in and out.

'Your hair smells nice.'

'Thank you. I washed it this morning.'

Bill gave her an extra squeeze. Gladys took the compliment at face value: she couldn't know what depth of feeling lay behind it for him, what a change it made from the stink of engine oil and wet wool and sweat in cramped spaces. How to lie on the earth in the sun next to a soft female body was like a piece of Heaven after endless days of hard surfaces, artificial light and rough, jostling men.

They lay quietly for a bit, Gladys's hand straying daringly across Bill's chest. Then he put his own hand up and grasped hers. Gladys wasn't sure whether she'd gone too far – (how Beryl would have laughed at that!) – but Bill eased himself up, propped himself on his elbow, and stroked her fingers. Gladys eased into a half-sitting position to match him.

'I can't wait any longer,' he said. 'I want to say this now and get it over with.'

Gladys's heart started an insane hammering. Get what over with? Could it be . . .?

'I've got to tell you about my posting,' he began.

The hammering stopped for a second, then resumed with a deadening *thunk*. Was that all? She'd thought for a moment he might have been going to propose!

'Yes? Go on,' she managed.

'The thing is, Glad, you need to understand – it'll be dangerous – any posting would be – and it'll be long.'

The hammering started up again, harder than before. She'd got it wrong. It had never been a proposal. He was going to say they were through because it wasn't fair to keep her hanging on.

'I don't care,' she blurted. 'I mean, I do, of course – I care that you'll be away, and in danger, but Bill, you can't think – you know I'll wait for you!'

'Oh, Gladys.' He touched his forehead to hers. 'Let me tell you what it is first.'

So he told her: he'd been posted as TO(W/T) to HMS *Jamaica*. It – or she – was a Colony-Class cruiser, launched in 1940, but only now fully commissioned after a refit. For the past month, the ship had been on Acceptance Trials and was now in Scapa

Flow ready to start work with the Home Fleet. All these terms tripped off Bill's tongue, though he did at least explain that TO(W/T) stood for Trained Operator (Wireless Training). But it wasn't until he used the words 'escort duty' and 'cover', 'minelaying', 'destroyers' and 'Northern Barrage', that Gladys started to understand what he was really trying to tell her.

'But I thought when you said . . . you're not going to be in Jamaica, then?'

She wasn't quite sure where Jamaica was, but she knew it was very far away. It must be: she'd seen bottles of Jamaica rum with pictures of a black person on them.

Bill gave a huge guffaw.

'No, you ninny! The name doesn't mean anything like . . . Oh Glad, you do make me laugh. How would that work with . . . I dunno, HMS *Eclipse* or something? It'd only leave dock once in a blue moon!'

'Well, how was I to know?' Gladys defended herself. But there was some hope to be had. 'You said a cruiser . . . so not a warship or a battleship?'

Bill smiled kindly. Nearly three years into the war and Gladys was still as ignorant – or maybe as innocent – as Beryl's little Bobby.

'It doesn't make a blind bit of difference, love. The Jerries don't care what they hit. For a U-Boat, the escort ships can be easier to pick off – they've got to get to them first to get to whatever we're escorting.'

Gladys was silent.

'I'm sorry, Glad,' he said, taking her hand again. 'But it's only fair to spell it out. I'll be away for months at a time. And when we're in dock, I'll be right up in the north of Scotland most like. Of course if I can get a few days' leave I'll come down and see you. But I might never get that long. So it's going to be ages – could be a year, even more – before we see each other.'

'I don't care!' cried Gladys again, relief and pleading mixed in her voice. 'I don't! I'll write, and I'll wait, and I'll be here whenever you can come and see me.'

Light dawned over Bill's face.

'Oh Gladys. You didn't think . . . you did! You thought I was going to say we were through! That's the last thing I want! I just wanted you to understand. Oh, Glad. I'm sorry. Come here.'

He pulled her down next to him again and kissed her gently. He wiped away the tears that she couldn't stop from welling up, and which came from over-excitement and exhaustion as much as emotion. A good thing she'd had the sense to leave off the mascara!

'I know it's no use telling you not to worry. You will. But try and hang on to . . . well, times like this, eh? When we were together, and things were lovely. And believe we'll have them again.'

Gladys gazed at him dewily. He might be going away, but he wasn't leaving her, at least not in the sense she'd feared.

'It's not just things that are lovely, Bill. It's you.'

'Aw, listen to us, what a pair of sloppy dates!' Bill blushed, but he kissed her again. 'You're lovely too, in case I haven't mentioned it lately.'

Then he made a suggestion.

'Now I'm going to shut my eyes for five minutes. Why don't you do the same? We've still got our big night out to look forward to, haven't we?'

Gladys nodded, and Bill fell asleep straight away – he could sleep on a line post, he said – that was the first skill you learnt as a sailor. Gladys didn't sleep or even doze: what he'd told her, and what they'd both said in consequence was still whirling in her head. Not to mention wondering exactly how big a night Bill was planning.

Chapter 26

'Bill! You can't mean . . . not here?'

'Why ever not?'

They were standing outside La Concorde, a restaurant at the smart end of town – the last little pocket of Georgian houses, near the Town Hall and the library. It was where the solicitors and accountants and insurance companies had their offices, the smaller ones in the quaint red-brick buildings, the larger ones in modern concrete edifices with a sculpted Greek key frieze and bronze double doors. La Concorde occupied one of the smaller Georgian buildings, with steps up to a black-painted front door, now standing open, and a bow window with bullseye panes. There were geraniums in a window box, and a menu in a glass case fixed to the wall.

'I asked Sid,' Bill said airily. 'He said this was the best place in town. No more than you deserve, Glad.'

'Sid?' Gladys knew what Sid was like – all talk! It didn't mean he'd ever been there: in fact, she was sure he hadn't. 'But it's—'

She'd been going to say 'not for the likes of us' but she stopped herself in time. Bill had planned it so carefully. He only wanted to make their last evening special: he'd gone to all this trouble for her. She couldn't let him down. She'd have to go through with it, but she wished desperately that her pink crêpe dress looked a bit fresher, her white shoes weren't so grey-white, and that she'd had more time to spend on her hair. But by the time they'd left the park – she hadn't wanted to wake him – it had been after half five, and Bill had said they'd better get a wriggle on: the table was booked for half past six. When they got home, Gladys had had her gran's tea to get, and the sofa to make up for Bill in the front room, and hot water to boil for him to shave . . .

'Come on, then.' Bill put a hand under her elbow and steered her up the steps. 'Let's get on in. I'm starved!'

Inside, Gladys had a moment of relief. The interior was dark: the pink-shaded lamps weren't on yet – so it might not matter too much that her hem drooped, and her hair wasn't perfect. She knew better than to air any concern about her appearance to Bill, because he invariably complimented her, whatever she was wearing.

'Can't miss you in that!' he'd said about her blue and white dress, bless him.

A tall man in a frock coat approached, his undertaker's garb enhanced by his dark, slicked-back hair and hollow cheeks. Just like Bela Lugosi in *Dracula*, mused Gladys – a not entirely comforting thought.

He ticked Bill's name off on a list at a little desk and led them with a flourish – all he needed was a silk-lined cape – to a table for two on the side wall.

'Will this suit Monsieur, Mademoiselle?' he enquired.

Gladys nodded mutely, and Bill grinned as the waiter – Gladys assumed he was the waiter, but why the fancy-dress? – pulled out her chair. As she went to sit down, she felt the chair nudge gently against the back of her legs so that her bottom met the seat abruptly and her legs shot under the table. Still startled, she blinked her thanks and took in the mass of cutlery on the starched white cloth. All that silverware – it looked silver – and one, two, three – three! – glasses? What the heck were they all for?

Bill meanwhile was sitting down opposite. The waiter produced two menus and handed them out with another flourish, before asking if they would care for an '*apéritif*'.

A what?

Thankfully, Bill translated.

'What would you like to drink, Glad?'

Gladys stared, glazed. The most she'd ever had was a half of shandy, but she knew from her extensive picture-going that a cocktail was the thing to ask for in a place like this. Though quite which one she wasn't sure. They had such funny names – was it a Sidecar? A Manhattan? And maybe that was just in America?

The waiter, thankfully, came to her rescue. Perhaps he wasn't quite as forbidding as he looked.

'Perhaps a cream sherry for Mademoiselle? And sir?'

Bill wasn't thrown at all.

'A small rum, if you've got it.'

'Indeed. *Un petit moment.*'

He vanished in a swish of tails.

'He's French, then?' Gladys whispered.

The restaurant was empty – it was far too early for most diners – so it wasn't that she'd be overheard, but the atmosphere was so hushed she didn't dare raise her voice. The spectre of the funeral parlour returned. Bill didn't seem bothered: he answered in his normal voice.

'Could be Belgian, there's a lot of them over here, aren't there? Menu's in French, too, have you seen?'

Gladys looked at the stiff card she'd been handed, and her saucer eyes turned into soup tureens. Not only was the menu in French, it didn't have any prices on it!

She hissed at Bill, but he, turning out to be quite the man of the world, told her this was normal.

'You're the lady. You don't need to know what it costs, 'cos it's not like you'll be paying.'

Gladys smiled weakly. On seeing the place, she'd immediately planned to have the cheapest thing there was: how could she now? Let alone know if she'd like it when she got it.

Desperately she scanned the card. *Blanquette de veau* – blanket of what? *Coq au vin*? If it meant the same as the word Gladys had seen chalked on walls, then . . . but the French ate all sorts, didn't they? Frogs' legs, she'd heard, and snails – it'd be just her luck to pick those. Worried, she read on. *Poisson*? Poison?

The waiter returned with two glasses on a silver salver – more glasses! They'd be running out of space soon. He placed a small stemmed glass in front of Gladys and a small tumbler in front of Bill.

'I send the waiter to take your order in due course,' he pronounced, and withdrew.

'He's not the waiter, then?' Gladys whispered again.

Bill shook his head.

'Something they call the maître d',' he informed her. 'He just swanks about basically. It's a French thing again.'

'Bill! How do you know all this?'

'We had a talk soon after we joined up.' Bill lowered his voice momentarily. 'From one of the officers. In

case we ever had to go to some posh dinner with
the top brass. And when it was time for questions,
some bright spark – well, it was Sid, of course – took
the opportunity to ask about posh restaurants as well.
The knives and forks, by the way, don't worry – you
work from the outside in. Cheers!'

Gladys looked at him wonderingly, so proud that her
heart was bursting. How far he'd come from his miserable start in the children's home and his previous life
hauling ropes on river tugs. Bill lifted his glass. Gladys
chinked hers against his and took a cautious sip. The
drink was thick and heavy and sort of singed her
throat as it went down, but it gave her a warm feeling
right down to her tummy. It was actually quite
pleasant, till a funny aftertaste kicked in. She put the
glass down hastily. An older man, bowed, with an
equally bowed moustache, was approaching.

'May I take your order?'

He was French too, but at least he didn't make
such a song and dance about it. Even so, Gladys
looked helplessly at Bill.

'Why don't you choose for me?'

It was unfair, she knew, but maybe this talk he'd had
had explained French menus as well. Sadly, it hadn't.
It had, though, suggested a cunning way around it.

'What would you recommend?' he asked.

The waiter smiled kindly. He knew that ploy.

'Will you be having anything to start?' He doubted
it. 'The *consommé* perhaps – the soup, miss? Or *pâté*?'

Gladys shook her head. Not at these prices – the ones she wasn't allowed to know. Secretly relieved – he wasn't too sure what either of those things might involve – Bill spoke for both of them.

'We'll go straight for mains, thanks.'

'Then I think perhaps the chicken would suit? It's cooked with shallots and bacon and mushrooms.'

Gladys nodded vigorously. That sounded OK. Things she understood.

'Two of those, then,' said Bill firmly.

'And the wine?'

Bill would gladly have ordered some – he'd taken advice on that, too, from a petty officer who'd been in the wine trade before the war – but he could see that Gladys was having enough trouble with her sherry. She was also frantically miming 'no', and to be honest, the prices on the menu and wine list he'd been handed, though he'd affected nonchalance, had made him wince. Thanks very much, Sid! He wished now they'd gone to the White Lion, the other place Sid had spoken of as being 'proper posh'.

'We're all right with these for now, thanks.'

The waiter smiled and turned away, his shoulders sagging a little. Clearly a fortune was not going to be made from this couple tonight. And little hope of a tip, either.

In Bidbury, in his bedroom under the eaves, Jim was packing.

Things had been strained between him and his mother since the conversation about Margaret Povey. On the surface he'd remained the polite and dutiful son, but the intent behind what she'd said, the idea that he might 'get his feet under the table' at Broad Oak Farm by hitching himself to Margaret, both annoyed and appalled him. He hadn't thought she'd stoop so low. And there was more than that, he thought, as he folded his work shirts and put them in his knapsack: there was her bringing Lily into it, and not in a favourable light. Jim had picked up a hint of it when he'd brought Lily to Bidbury to collect the hens, and now he had no doubt. His mother had taken against her. Lily had become the human embodiment of Hinton and of Marlow's and of everything that was keeping him from her.

Standing with a pair of underpants in his hand, Jim suddenly saw it clearly. Worse than that, his mother had somehow known from the start that Lily was a rival – to her. She wasn't prepared to lose him to anyone, but if she had to, she intended to hand-pick who it would be, and it would be a local girl. The fact that Margaret came with a farm attached had sealed her fate.

Jim was a peace-loving sort. He loathed confrontation. He hated arguments. He didn't like a bad atmosphere, and that was what his mother had created. It was one thing for her to want him home, and to make that plain. But to try to manipulate him into it with a long list of jobs she couldn't cope with and then to wind Margaret into her plans . . . that was underhand. More than that, it was blackmail.

At the same time, she was his mother. His father was a burden that would only get worse, and there was no doubt she needed more help. Who else could provide it? He was their only child. It was his duty to come home.

Jim sank onto the bed. That was it then, he'd have to make a choice. His past or his future. Margaret or Lily.

As he sat in a stupor, he heard his mother coming up the stairs. He tried to shove his haversack under the bed, but he wasn't quick enough.

'Packing already? Anyone'd think you couldn't wait to get away.'

Jim counted to ten to hold back the reply he'd like to give, which would have been along the lines of her driving him to it.

'You know it's not that, Mother. I'll have to get going early tomorrow, that's all. I thought I'd get my packing done, then we can have all evening together.' He was dreading it, in truth. His father would head off to bed early as he usually did, leaving Jim exposed. 'There might be a play on the radio.' That would fill the time.

'Not even a full week.'

'What?'

'You didn't arrive till after dinner last Sunday. And you'll be gone at the crack of dawn.'

'I didn't realise I had to clock in and out!' This time Jim couldn't stop the retort, and he instantly regretted it. He moved to soften the blow. 'Look . . . I'm sorry. I know you don't feel you see enough of me—'

'No, I don't, and I've hardly seen much of you this week. Not at all today!'

Jim started counting again, but only got to three.

'Only because I've been racing to finish all the jobs you wanted doing!'

Mending the fence, cutting the hedge, lopping the diseased branches from a tree, netting the currants, mending the henhouse, re-mortaring the outhouse, creosoting the shed, fixing the skirting and the wonky shelf, distempering the ceiling . . .

'Well, if you hadn't gone haymaking—'

This time, he didn't get past zero.

'What? That was your idea! You suggested it! In fact you practically forced me to go! And I know perfectly well why.'

His mother said nothing, but turned away. Jim watched her go in silence, but when she'd closed the door – not a slam, just a firm click, which was worse – he sank onto the bed. What a mess! And one he couldn't see any way of solving that would give both him and his mother what they wanted.

Chapter 27

Gladys wondered if she dared leave all the mushrooms. She'd never been very fond of them, and these were very dark in colour, almost black. You had to be so careful with mushrooms . . . maybe she could make that the excuse. She'd managed to eat the chicken, and the baby onions, and the bits of bacon, mostly by scraping off the funny sort of gravy they were in, which had a very peculiar taste. The potatoes had been fine – *pommes vapeur*, they were called – which had meant plain boiled, to her relief – and there'd been green beans, which weren't her favourite, but she'd managed them. All in all, though, it had been the strangest plate of food Gladys had ever tasted, but she wanted to do it justice because she knew it would have cost a lot and she wanted Bill to think she was enjoying herself. She'd drunk nearly all the sherry, even though it made her head feel a bit swimmy – come to think of it, the chicken gravy had had something of the same taste. Did the French eat this fancy stuff all the time? Not that they were now – they were eating all sorts under the Occupation, she'd heard, not just snails and frogs' legs – rats and dogs, poor things. Gladys shuddered. The mushrooms looked more sinister than ever.

Bill had polished off everything on his plate, which he was now mopping with a piece of bread, but then he was used to eating what was put in front of him without question, having grown up on institutional food. He'd also downed his rum, but he was a far more experienced drinker than Gladys would ever be – or wanted to be.

She'd just steeled herself to fork up a mushroom – just the one, for appearance's sake – when Dracula glided past her to the door. Gladys looked up: a couple were standing there, and Dracula was oiling all over them.

'Monsieur Marlow! How wonderful to see you again! *Quelle honneur!*'

Gladys froze, the mushroom dripping sauce.

'Bill!' she hissed. 'Don't look now, but it's him! The one I told you about! Robert Marlow!'

Bill immediately turned to look – the instinctive reaction when told not to. He turned back with a low whistle.

'Blimey! He's got a bit of swank about him. And who's that he's with?'

'That's Evelyn Brimble!'

Gladys had seen her photograph in the *Chronicle*, standing to the side as her mother graciously opened a bazaar.

'When Robert left Marlow's, he went to work for her dad.'

'The boss's daughter? Not daft, is he?'

Dracula was leading Robert and Evelyn to the window table – the best in the room. He whipped away the little wooden 'Reserved' sign and flicked an invisible speck from Evelyn's chair before pulling it out in the same way that he had for Gladys, though Evelyn was obviously more used to the treatment and sat down rather more elegantly. The folds of her dress – a beautiful eggshell blue, and real silk chiffon, if Gladys was right, which was all but impossible to get – almost dusted the floor. So much for Utility fashions!

The menu and wine list were handed to Robert and the price-less menu, as Gladys now knew, to Evelyn. She also knew she was staring, but she couldn't help herself, and when Dracula had finished fussing over them and had taken their drinks order – champagne cocktails, of course, what else? – she found herself looking straight into Robert Marlow's eyes. He did a double-take worthy of a music-hall comic and almost fell off his chair. Then he gave a minute nod of his head that moved it about an inch, and an infinitesimal gesture of his hand, which moved it about half that. Gladys, as if operated by strings from above, nodded back and tried to move her hand in the same way, quite forgetting she was still holding the fork with the mushroom suspended from it. To her horror, the mushroom catapulted straight on to the bodice of her dress.

'Oh! Oh, no!' she cried as the fork clattered to her plate.

The waiter advanced, fearing a worse disaster, but Bill had jumped up, proffering his napkin, and the waiter retreated to fetch a damp cloth.

As Bill tried to dab the stain away, Gladys shrank in her chair. There were quite a few tables occupied by now and she knew everyone must be looking.

Most of them, in fact, were more interested in their food, but the commotion had caught Evelyn Brimble's eye.

'Good God,' she said to Robert in a low voice as he leant forward to light her cigarette. 'This place has gone down! Since when did people like Jolly Jack Tar and his girl start coming here?'

'Shh!' Robert was no man of the people, but he had some sensibilities. 'I know them.'

'What?' Evelyn looked incredulous. 'Have you been helping out at a soup kitchen on the quiet?'

'No! I don't know him at all, well, I don't really know either of them. She works at Marlow's, that's all.'

'She's a shop girl?'

'Yes. Works on Toys.'

'A shop girl, and she's eating here? Your father must be paying them too much!'

'I doubt it! Anyway, he'll be paying. Some sort of special occasion, I expect.'

Evelyn shook her head and blew out a plume of smoke.

'I'm sorry, Robert, but what next? This place used to have such a good reputation. We've had some wonderful meals here. And there's usually someone we know, but honestly, I'll hardly feel comfortable if she's going to be gawping at us all night. Shall we forget it and go somewhere else?'

'What? No! We're not leaving!'

Evelyn sat back, her blue eyes wide. She wasn't used to being contradicted, and certainly not by Robert. She rested her cigarette on the ashtray.

'You're very forceful all of a sudden.'

'Not really, but . . . Evelyn, please. We're here now. Let's just forget about them.'

'I wish I could! I shan't forget that knicker pink dress of hers in a hurry. What a sight for sore eyes!'

But she smiled. Their drinks were approaching and the chance to be catty always improved her mood. The hubbub at Gladys's table had died down: Bill was back in his seat. The other diners were continuing with their meals, and the low hum of refined conversation buzzed reassuringly around them. Evelyn shrugged and picked up the glass that had been placed before her.

'Chin, chin,' she said.

Robert smiled with relief as they chinked glasses and drank. The evening was recovered – until Evelyn spluttered and put down her glass.

'There's something in there!' she said. 'Something clinked!'

'Really? That's odd. You'd better fish it out.'

'I'm going to! I've had about enough tonight!' Crossly, Evelyn picked up her dessert fork and dinked it about in the glass. When she extracted it, dangling from it was a ring.

'Robert! Did you . . .? You did! You planned this! No wonder you didn't want us to go anywhere else!'

But Robert had leapt up and was down on one knee at her side. Gently he took the ring from her and held it out. The diamond blazed in an obliging final ray of sun.

'Evelyn,' he said, 'I love you. I want to spend the rest of my life with you. Will you marry me?'

'What? Really?' Evelyn smiled her dazzling smile. 'Well, yes – yes, of course – oh, Robert!'

She bent and took his face in her hands as the other diners smiled and clapped.

Gladys watched them kiss in open-mouthed amazement. Right there in the restaurant, in front of everybody, no shame at all! Just like in the films, but right in front of her, in full colour, as large as

307

life! The bowed waiter scurried forwards to shake the happy couple by the hand; two chefs, in their white jackets and puffy tall hats came out of the kitchen and did the same. Even Dracula slimed over to offer his congratulations, or Gladys assumed that was what they were – it was just a load of fancy French to her.

When the second fuss of the evening had died down, the staff had gone back to their posts, Robert had resumed his seat, and Evelyn was holding out her left hand and moving it this way and that, admiring her new accessory, Gladys finally found her voice.

'How about that!' she hissed, leaning across the table. 'I'll have something to tell Lily on Monday!'

As if she didn't have enough already.

Bill, though, didn't seem impressed.

'Flash beggar,' was all he said.

Dracula – the maître d' himself – approached to take their plates.

'You enjoyed your meal, I hope.' It wasn't a question: he had every confidence in the kitchen, even with the constraints they were under. 'And the little piece of theatre?' He indicated Robert and Evelyn. 'Monsieur Marlow, he planned it all very carefully.'

Gladys dared a smile. He didn't seem quite so scary now they'd all shared in the excitement.

'Lovely,' she said, though in truth she only meant the Robert and Evelyn bit.

Bill gave a grunt of assent.

'Excellent! And now perhaps a little dessert?'

Gladys opened her mouth. A trolley had been wheeled in while they'd been eating and, sweet-toothed like her gran, she'd thought she could fancy something. You could hardly go wrong with a cake or pastry, could you, even if it had a funny foreign name? She'd spied a creamy-looking cake – what a treat that would be – she could also see a bowl of trifle, which she knew was Bill's favourite. It'd be mock cream on the cake, of course, and the chocolatey-looking decoration would be cocoa and chicory, but if it took away the taste of the main course . . . And as they'd economised on the starters and the wine . . .

'No thanks,' said Bill, without even asking her. 'I think we're done here. Just the bill, please.'

He was quiet on the walk home, too, but Gladys hardly noticed: she had plenty to think about. It was a pity about the stain on her dress. All the dabbing hadn't made much impression on it, but she could have a better go tomorrow with some Borax, and if that didn't work, she could always try covering it up with a brooch. As for the rest – the restaurant, the food, Robert turning up, and the proposal – and she'd been right there, an eye-witness – wait till Lily heard about it! And Beryl! For once she'd be the one with something to report! She imagined the others' excited questions and strove to imprint every detail on her mind. She didn't want to let them down.

It wasn't late when they got back, but they could hear her gran's snoring from the hall. It always amazed Gladys that she could sleep as much as she did, given that she did nothing all day, but at least it meant she wouldn't be thumping the floor with her stick or ringing the little bell in the shape of a crino-lined lady that she employed to get Gladys running up and down the stairs.

'Cocoa?' she suggested as they went through to the back. 'Or a cup of tea? Or I got some beer in, Bill, if you'd like it?'

'A cup of tea'll do fine, thanks.'

'Righto,' said Gladys brightly and led the way to the kitchen. She filled the kettle and put it on the gas. Bill sat at the table, his face propped on his hand.

'Did you enjoy it?' he asked. 'Tonight, I mean? You weren't very talkative. For you.'

'Yes! Of course I enjoyed it! I said thank you, didn't I?'

'Yeah, yeah, you did. But I don't think you really liked the food, did you, or what you had to drink?'

'I – well, it was the first time I'd had anything like it, that's all. It was new to me.'

'We should never have gone,' said Bill bitterly. 'It was all wrong. Wrong from start to finish.'

'Oh Bill, don't say that! Not when you've spent all that money!'

She'd been staggered by the number of notes and coins he'd had to place inside the little leather folder in which the bill had been presented – to hide the total from her, she supposed.

'It's true though, isn't it? And to cap it all, that palaver with that stuck-up pair.'

If Gladys had truly enjoyed anything it was 'that palaver', but she could hardly say so.

'Some last night this has turned out to be.'

Gladys looked at him, agonised. She could try to convince him that she'd loved every minute, but he'd never believe her; she wouldn't believe herself. She felt stupid now, and worse, guilty, for not realising that his silence on the way home was something more than their usual cosy amiability. She'd have to do something: she couldn't bear to see him so crushed. There was only one thing she could think of, the thing she'd been thinking of and dismissing, thinking of and dismissing for the past twenty-four hours.

She moved to Bill's side of the table and gestured that she wanted to sit on his lap. She put one arm round his shoulders and picked up his hand in her free one.

'Bill,' she said, 'don't be fed up. We've still got all of tomorrow together. And' – her heart was doing that hammering thing again – 'we've still got the rest of tonight.'

He shrugged.

'Sure we have. A nice cup of tea and the wireless.'

'No,' said Gladys. It was now or never. 'Not that. We can do something other than that. We can . . . we can . . . we can do it, Bill, if you want.'

Bill's face filled with colour and he leant away to look at her.

'Really? You'd really . . . Oh, Gladys. Do you mean it?'

Chapter 28

Lily, by contrast, was having a far less dramatic evening. As she and Miss Temple had put the final touches to their Summer Sale displays, she'd thought fondly about Gladys and Bill. She knew all about the planned walk in the park and the smart night out, and hoped against hope that Gladys was enjoying herself – that they both were. Gladys had described all the work she'd be putting in on the house and on herself, and Lily had raised a mental eyebrow. She knew Gladys and Bill were a proper couple, in love and all that business, but Bill was being treated like a king, or at least the conquering hero, when he hadn't even seen active service yet! Jim was back tomorrow, and she got a funny feeling thinking about it, and him, but she wouldn't have dreamt of going to that much effort – for any boy, come to that.

To be fair, no extra housework was required for Jim's return: Dora cleaned and dusted, swept and polished, every day, and Lily could well imagine her mother's outrage if Lily had flicked around with a duster, implying that Dora's high standards weren't good enough. Lily had quite enough of cleaning and polishing at work: though she helped her mother without complaint, it was the last thing she wanted to do when she got home. She did wonder sometimes how she'd cut it as a wife, but the thought never bothered her for long. Jim had said, hadn't he, that there were going to be big changes after the war and that people wouldn't just slip back into their old ways. Jolly good, thought Lily: she was counting on the fact that one of the changes would mean women not being stuck at home doing all the chores, day in, day out.

All the same, she was pleased that Friday night had been bath night and that she, and her hair, looked and smelt clean, even with the miserable amount of water that the Ministry of Fuel and Power allowed. The minute Dora had seen the Ministry's 'Five-Inch Bather' film on a rare trip to the cinema, she'd forced Jim to paint a line on the inside of their galvanised tin tub. Lily had objected, on the basis that the rule was intended for a full-size bath: as their hip bath was only half the size, they were surely entitled to twice that height. Dora's look would have made a Nazi Stormtrooper quail in his jackboots and gave Lily her answer. The line was painted.

Unlike Gladys, Lily didn't have a new dress for the weekend, either, just the one she'd been wearing since the start of the summer. It was another, very welcome, cast-off from Renée over the road, who'd given up on it after putting a big rip in the skirt when it had caught on a loose spring in a boyfriend's car. A boyfriend! And with a car! Lily's eyes had widened. Renée was certainly going up in the world – if not quite in the air – as a typist in the WAAF. Dora had mended the tear with tiny stitches – at least it was at the back – and the dress was certainly pretty, lemon and white chequerboard squares with a daisy – white on yellow, yellow on white – in every other one. Lily loved it: it was her happy dress. It made her feel cheerful just looking at it.

When she got in from work on the Saturday night, she put the dress on again because she had a date. Well, not a date as such, but when Sid had told her about his system for speaking to Anthony, she'd realised that the two of them could set up something similar. She didn't know why she hadn't thought of it before. There was always a queue of women – it was mostly women – outside the call box by the fish and chip shop, waiting for calls: now Lily would be joining them. Before Sid had left, she'd checked out the number of the box, and Sid had given her the number of the telephone in the mess at his base. So after tea, and with Dora looking forward to *Old Mother Riley and her daughter Kitty* on the wireless, Lily trotted off.

As usual, the box was occupied and there was the inevitable queue. It might very well be the same at Sid's end, so she parked herself on a handily-placed pile of sandbags to wait. She and Sid had set a limit of half an hour – any longer than that outside their appointed time and he'd decreed they should give up. He didn't want Lily 'hanging about' on her own, he informed her, especially outside the chippy, where she might attract 'undesirables'. And people said *she* sounded like her mother sometimes!

As she waited, Lily wondered if Sid had set a time limit on waiting for his calls with Anthony, but guessed that he hadn't. She suspected they'd have waited all night to speak to one another.

Tonight she was in luck. The queue moved fast – one woman evidently couldn't get through, and came out cursing, another emerged in tears after two minutes muttering 'And with that Thelma! The cheek of it!' Then it was Lily's turn, and only twelve minutes after the appointed time. All she needed now was for the line to be free at Sid's end: the other rule was that whoever got to the phone first would make the call. Lily had come supplied with a pocketful of coins – that was another good thing about the daisy-print dress: Lily loved a pocket. She dialled and held her breath.

The phone was picked up straight away at the other end, but Lily made sure she'd heard Sid say 'Sis?' before the pips went. She posted the first coin from the pile she'd stacked on the shelf. They were off!

They did their usual run-through of the expected topics. 'How's Mum? –' (Fine, sends her love); 'Heard any more from Reg?' (Yes, another letter, but dated end of May, well before Tobruk . . .) 'Where's it been till now? On the back of a camel?'. Then – 'How's the shop?' (Fine, sale preview for account customers on Monday and Tuesday, sale proper starting Wednesday.)

Then Sid asked, as she'd known he would, about Les.

'There's still no news, I'm afraid.'

'Still nothing?'

'Nothing.'

'Well, I know we keep saying it, but they'd have heard from the War Office by now if anything bad had happened.'

'We do keep saying it,' agreed Lily down the line. 'But it's not cutting much ice with Ivy. Or at least, it wasn't.'

She told him how she and Gladys had found Beryl in despair, and how Dora had had to go around and give Ivy a good talking to and pour her brandy down the sink.

'But in good news,' she added, 'proper good news – Bill's got his posting. He's here this weekend seeing Gladys.'

'I know. He asked me for tips on where to show a girl a good time.'

'You? Hang on, he's told Gladys to expect a smart night out. I hope you didn't say something crude about the back row of the Roxy!'

'Thanks, Sis! I spend years cultivating the image of a debonair man about town, and then—'

'Seriously Sid, where did you tell him to take her?'

'I gave him a couple of options,' Sid answered breezily. 'You'll have to wait and see. You'll get chapter and verse from Glad on Monday, I daresay.'

'I daresay I will! So did Bill tell you what his posting was?'

'Not in as many words, but it's not that bad a one, Lil. I mean, hopefully we're talking about him being away for months at a time, not years.'

'Years?' Lily was aghast. 'Is the war going to last that long?'

'I just mean,' said Sid quickly, 'if he'd got sent out East – Japan, Burma, Pacific Fleet . . .'

'Sid, answer my question! Years?'

The thought of everyone fighting for all that time was horrifying, but Sid didn't answer. Instead he asked about Jim.

'Isn't he back tomorrow? Sure you've got time to talk to me? Shouldn't you be beautifying yourself?'

'What for? There's no need—' Lily started, but was brutally obliterated by the pips. She fumbled for more coins, but she'd used her last sixpence, and in her haste, her pennies cascaded to the floor.

'The Lily doesn't need gilding, I know!' was all she heard Sid say before they were cut off.

That wasn't at all what she'd meant; she'd been going to say that she wouldn't have dreamt of it – if Jim didn't like her as she was, then too bad – but Sid was gone. Lily huffed in frustration. They hadn't had the chance to arrange another call, and she hadn't asked Sid anything about himself, most importantly how he was feeling about Anthony, let alone when he'd be going to Leeds, which would mean a different number. Now she'd have to write! She crouched to scrabble up her scattered coppers, hoping that Sid might phone her back. But the booth remained frustratingly silent apart from some testy rapping on the glass from a woman with a headscarf and a jutting jaw doing a fine impersonation of Goebbels with a gastric attack.

The headscarf made her think of *Old Mother Riley*, and Lily realised that she didn't want to go home straight away. Giving way to Goebbels with her sweetest smile, she wandered slowly off. If she detoured through the park, she could rehearse one more time what she planned to say to Jim. She'd decided she was going to start with Sid and Anthony, finishing up with what Sid had said about telling people truthfully how you felt. If Jim didn't take the hint, she could back off – it was one thing to take a risk, another to make yourself look a fool. That seemed to her a sensible way to proceed, and she was secretly proud of herself for working it out.

Of course, Jim would have his turn too, before they got to the big stuff: she wanted to hear how his week had gone. She knew his mum would have made a fuss of him and wondered if she'd made him a special farewell tea, like her mum did whenever Reg or Sid came home. She hoped so. Jim deserved it.

Jim's mother, of course, had been making a fuss of him all week, but not in the sense that Lily was imagining. His last night didn't look as if it was going to be much different.

Jim couldn't believe it – just when he needed it, the BBC had failed him. After a frankly tedious edition of *Experts in Khaki*, neither Jim nor his mother had been exactly entranced when *Old Mother Riley* came on.

'Load of nonsense,' she snapped. 'You don't want this on, do you?'

Jim shook his head, though he was dreading the conversation he knew was coming. He'd planned it all out in his head while finishing the last of his packing, and thought he might have come up with a solution that could suit. But as he opened his mouth to speak, his mother gave him a reprieve. Like she had the last time he'd visited, she dragged him into the scullery and started bringing things out of the larder. Soon the table was covered with jars and bottles.

'I'm not sending any of my strawberry jam,' she said. 'I couldn't get it to set this year, and I won't have anyone thinking I don't know how to make a preserve. But I've got a jar of damson left, and how about some quince cheese?'

'I'm sure anything would go down very well,' said Jim awkwardly. 'But, really, Mother—'

It wasn't as if Dora was a bad housekeeper or a poor cook – far from it – but he could hardly point that out. Anything that implied that Hinton was less than a hellhole, and food at the Collinses' any more than a starvation diet would only cause further red rags and bulls to appear in his mother's line of vision.

'Don't you go saying there's no need. I hear *Kitchen Front* too, you know, and read the paper. All about the queues in towns for food and using up leftovers I wouldn't feed to the pigs. We're very blessed out here.'

'I know. And thank you.'

She was only trying to be helpful – as well, of course, as displaying her jam and preserve-making skills. And delivering another strong hint about the advantages of the countryside.

'There's a brace of pigeon in the outhouse. And some cream in a pot on the cold slab, don't forget to take it.'

'I won't.'

That was it. Neither of them could wring any more out of the topic of provisions, and a silence fell. Jim took a deep breath. Now was the time.

'Mother,' he began, 'I've been thinking. I know life's tough for you, with Dad less and less able, and I admire how well you manage. But I can see it's exhausting. I think you need more help.'

His mother, who'd been straightening her saucepans so the handles all stood at the same forty-five-degree angle on the shelf, spun around so fast she knocked one of them out of true. Jim realised from the look of hope on her face that he had better make things a bit clearer, and fast.

'So what I suggest,' he said emphatically, as if speaking to someone hard of hearing, 'is getting someone in to help. A girl from the village to help in the house, a boy to help in the garden, whatever you need, whatever you prefer. And I'll find the money to pay.'

His mother stared at him. The silence before had been heavy but not hostile. This one felt flinty.

'That's it, is it? That's your best offer? Fob off your responsibility on somebody else?'

'It's not like that—'

'Yes, it is! That's exactly what it's like. You're casting us off, your own flesh and blood, your own parents, your own home, and I'll tell you for why! You'd rather have your town life and your posh shop and your precious Lily and her family! That's how important we are to you! Thank you very much!'

She pushed past him, and he heard her go upstairs. Jim dropped onto a chair and put his head in his hands. He'd thought it was a reasonable solution, but he could see now that his mother wasn't going to settle for anything less than blood – she wanted him and no one else.

Chapter 29

It had all turned out perfectly, thought Gladys as she lay contentedly in Bill's arms. Just perfectly.

'Do you mean it? Really mean it, I mean?' he'd asked her back in the kitchen what seemed like hours ago, another lifetime ago.

His eyes had scanned her face. Gladys could feel his heart hammering against hers, hammering as hard as her own: if they hadn't been encased in pink crêpe and blue serge, they'd have been striking sparks off each other. She opened her mouth to reply, but nothing came out. All she could hear was the hissing gas and the wheezing kettle, as loud as a rushing train. Shaking her head slightly to clear it, she tried to speak, to tell him 'Yes, yes, of course!' – but her hesitation was fatal. Bill pushed her away.

'You don't, do you? You don't really want to! You're just saying it because you think it's what I want!'

'Don't you?'

Bill jumped up, tipping her off his lap.

'No,' he raged. 'No! Not like this! Not like some sort of consolation prize! Because you feel sorry for me! Or because you think it'll make things better! This isn't how it's meant to be!'

'Then how do you want it to be?' pleaded Gladys desperately. 'I thought you loved me – you say you do – and if you love me, surely you want to—'

'Oh, Gladys. Gladys.'

He wasn't shouting now: he was her calm, gentle, lovely Bill again. He sat down and pulled her back on to his knee.

'I do love you and that's why, even though it's killing me, I want to do things how you want. How I know you want to. That's why – oh, look—'

He fumbled in his pocket and brought out a small leather box.

'This isn't how this was meant to be either. I was going to do it in the restaurant. But I could tell you didn't feel right there, not really, and neither did I. It was too stuck-up for us, and there was all that business with your dress, and then that flash Harry jumped in on the act!'

Gladys was hardly listening: her eyes were fixed on the box. Her heart was going insane. It wasn't a hammer any more, it was a piston; it was a pickaxe. It was a whole iron foundry.

'So. Here we go.' Bill flicked open the lid. Inside, sitting in a little slit in a cushion of black velvet, was a ring. A diamond. 'I love you, Gladys. Will you marry me?'

Again Gladys's voice failed her. All she could do was fling her arms around Bill's neck and sob into his sailor collar.

They'd moved after that, first to the big saggy armchair in the other room for a proper cuddle and for Gladys to dry her tears, and then to the rug, the one that they'd taken to the park, and which Bill had laid down on the floor. They didn't put up the blackout, but it was properly dark now and the only light came from a moon in its last quarter.

There they lay and talked.

'Let's get one other thing straight from the off,' said Bill as he stroked her hair, and Gladys, just like Evelyn, turned her hand this way and that. Her diamond, being considerably smaller, could hardly be said to blaze, but it still gave the occasional twinkle in the moonlight. As far as Gladys was concerned, anyway, it was the Koh-i-noor. She dragged her attention back to Bill. Her lovely Bill. Her fiancé Bill!

'This isn't some kind of bribe. I'm not the kind of bloke that asks a girl to marry him just so's he can have the honeymoon before the wedding. That's not what you want, I know that, knowing you like I do. So' – he couldn't help sounding a bit regretful – 'I can wait.'

'Are you sure?'

'Gladys. Of course I'm sure. Think about it. Are you saying you want to be caught out like Beryl? But caught out worse than Beryl?'

'How, worse?'

'Let's say we did do it. I know we'd be careful, but . . . well, these things happen. What if you fell pregnant? I'm off tomorrow. You'd be stuck here on your own, getting bigger and bigger, and no chance of me getting back to wed you to save face!'

Gladys took his face in her hands, his dear, freckly face with the snaggle-toothed grin and the slightly, just slightly, jug ears.

'That's the loveliest thing anyone's ever said to me,' she said. 'Well, apart from you asking me to marry you, of course! To think you'd put me and what I want before what you want. I do love you, Bill.'

'And I love you, you silly sausage!'

Then they kissed and cuddled some more, and before too long, with reluctant little murmurs and much going back for more, they kissed each other one final goodnight and fell asleep.

Jim left almost before the dawn. In the cool early morning quiet of the kitchen, with the wood pigeons fluting outside, he sat at the table and wrote a note. After a while, he scribbled his name, and added something that might have been a smudge. Or possibly a kiss.

He shouldered his knapsack, bracing himself for the added weight of the provisions his mother had given him. Patting the dog goodbye, collecting the pigeons and not forgetting the cream, he crept out and down the mossy path, its border of blue geranium and lady's mantle soaking his ankles with dew. Pulling those up and replacing them with vegetables would be one of the first jobs to be tackled, he reflected. He dealt carefully with the rickety gate and turned for one last look, in case his mother should be at the window, but the blackout was still up in the front bedroom. Jim adjusted the straps of his rucksack on his shoulders and set off smartly down the lane.

He struck lucky. Just outside the village he thumbed a lift on a hay cart as far as Evesham, then a potato lorry took him to Worcester. He had to wait over an hour for a train – the one he'd been aiming for had been commandeered for troop movements – but at least it gave him time to think, not least about what he was going to say to Lily.

The train, once it got going, didn't have too many delays, and by noon he was back in Hinton and swinging down Brook Street towards the Collinses'. His rucksack was heavy, and the pigeons, tied at their feet, bumped against his thigh, but his resolve was firm as he saw the whitened step of number 31. He turned into the cool of the entry.

Since the start of the war, there'd been little point in hazarding anything like an arrival time when you had a journey to make, but they certainly wouldn't be expecting him yet. From the back alley Jim could hear Dora clattering about in the kitchen over some music on the wireless. Good – it would mask the sound of the latch. He eased the back gate slowly open, peeped past it, and struck lucky for a second time, seeing Lily before she saw him: she'd just come out of the house. She was in her yellow dress with her hair all tousled, and she was holding a colander and a knife. About to cut some beans, no doubt.

Jim's heart gave a jump–skip. He must try, at least to start with, to keep things as normal as possible.

'Hello, you.'

Lily stopped dead.

'Jim!'

'Hello,' he said again, as he walked towards her. 'Have you missed me?'

'Missed you? Why, have you been away?'

Lily had been practising sounding normal too – and she was quite pleased with the result. She sounded natural enough, she thought, even if her voice was perhaps a little higher than usual. Determined to keep things that way, for now at least, she nodded towards the pigeons.

'You shouldn't have.'

Jim grinned.

'Sorry. The village shop was fresh out of stripy rock and trinket boxes covered in shells. I think your mum'd prefer these anyway, don't you? I'd better get them in the cool, though. Shall we go in?'

Dora clucked over him, and the various jars, and as for the pigeons – she had plans for those.

'One for us, and one I'll give to Ivy,' she said. 'It's very kind of your mother, Jim. How are they, your parents? And how was your holiday?'

Lily wasn't the only one who'd been rehearsing, and Jim gave them the potted version he'd prepared on the journey: ('They're fine, but some holiday! I ache all over!') and, over dinner he heard all the Hinton news. There was plenty of it – Sid's posting to HMS COPRA and how it had come about, and Bill being back on leave ahead of his posting. They also had to tell him that in the week he'd been away, there'd still been no news of Les, and no recent news from Reg, come to that.

Lily chipped in from time to time, but she let her mother do most of the talking. She couldn't quite believe that Jim was back, looking lithe and tanned, his hands pocked with nicks and scratches – from the work he'd been doing presumably – and his hair in need of a cut. Dora would have to see to it later – he couldn't go back to Marlow's like that.

Finally the table was cleared, the washing up done, and Lily and Jim were free. Dora settled down with a basket of mending and the wireless, so Lily knew they wouldn't be disturbed.

'Shall we sit in the yard?' she suggested. If she didn't tell him all she had to tell him about Sid, as well as say what she'd been working herself up to say soon, she'd burst.

Jim agreed; he had plenty to say to her too. In unspoken agreement they went outside to perch in their favoured spot, the edge of the veg bed with the sun on their backs.

'Come on then, spill,' said Jim. 'You were very quiet at dinner. What is it? Gladys? Beryl?'

Lily shook her head.

'You know as much as I know there.'

'You, then. Is it work? You can't have fallen out with Miss Frobisher? Are you moving department? Been promoted over my head?'

Lily shook her head impatiently.

'It's nothing like that. It's Sid.'

Quietly, and haltingly in the beginning, Lily told him the full story, the real story about Sid, and about Anthony. She told him how difficult it had been to draw it out of Sid, and how she'd only heard it bit by bit. She told him plainly and simply, not dressing it up, not dressing it down, including how she'd hated evading his questions about her meeting with Sid at Snow Hill, and the sad, sudden way Sid's love affair had ended.

'Oh, Lily,' was all Jim said when she'd finished.

331

He didn't sound shocked; he sounded sorrowful. 'But that's dreadful. I don't mean Sid being how he is,' he added hurriedly. 'That's the way he's been made and that's an end to it. I never would have thought it, but I suppose that's just because I fell into line with everyone else and assumed it would be a girl.' He sighed and shook his head. 'Anthony sounds a terrific bloke. But what a way for it to end. And what a way for him to find out.'

'I know. He was in an awful state when he first got home.'

'Of course he was. But the other thing is – how awful for you.'

'Me?'

'Yes. I can't believe you kept all this to yourself – not just for the last few days, but for months.' Now he sounded almost admiring. 'I didn't think you had it in you.'

'Thanks!'

'You know what I mean.'

Did she?

'It's a compliment, silly.'

'It's not me who matters. I couldn't tell you till Sid said I could. And then you weren't here. But you're not . . . you don't . . . well, you really don't think badly of Sid for it?'

'Of course not! I know some people – most people, probably – do, and think it's a cardinal sin and every-thing, but you can't fight your nature, can you? It's just the way some men are made – and women too – and the sooner everyone accepts that . . . I think Sid's damn brave to come clean. It can't have been easy.'

'It's funny,' said Lily thoughtfully. 'When he had to take this posting to HMS COPRA, his line to Mum was that she wouldn't have to worry about him like she does about Reg. But knowing what I know, I worry about him more. It's just as dangerous. If he got caught.'

'I'm sure he'll be careful. And in time, well, maybe things'll change. The law, I mean. And people's attitudes.'

'You think so?'

'I hope so.' Jim brushed a bit of moss off the veg bed wall. 'And your mum really has no idea?'

'I don't think so. How could she? And I don't know how Sid could ever tell her. I don't think she'd take against him – but she'd be shocked, I'm sure.'

'Quite possibly. But in the end . . .' Jim sighed. 'You've got to be who you are. Do what you have to do. You can't duck these things.'

'No. You can't.'

Lily swallowed hard. That was the first part over. Now for the really difficult bit. Herself and Jim. Another thing not to be ducked.

Chapter 30

She didn't dare look at him, so she looked at where their knees almost touched, his in his old drill trousers, hers under the yellow and white squares of her dress. What had Sid said? What had her mum impressed upon her since she was a little girl? Just tell the truth . . .

But as she opened her mouth, Jim leant forward and clasped his hands between his knees. Get on with it, he thought. Just follow Sid's example. Better the difficult truth than the easy lie.

Inevitably, they both spoke at once.

'You first,' said Jim. Coward! he thought.

'No, you.' Chicken! she reproached herself.

Jim gave in. He sat back again.

'All right,' he said. 'I need to tell you about something that happened when I was home.'

'OK . . .' said Lily, puzzled. 'What?'

'It's my mother,' Jim began. 'You know she's hinted before, like when we went to get the hens, that she wanted me to go home. That she needed more help. Well, this time she rather upped the ante.'

What? No – no, it couldn't be! Not now! Not when she was about to . . .

'What? How?'

Somehow Lily forced the words out past the concrete that someone seemed to have poured down her throat. Jim sighed.

'I heard a lot about how difficult it was getting for her to manage my dad on top of the house and the garden and the laundry she takes in and everything. He's quite a bit worse, to be fair. So I made all sorts of suggestions, like getting in someone from the village to help, but the truth of it is, it's me she wants.' He gave something between a snort and a laugh. 'She dangled all sorts of inducements.'

The concrete was setting fast, but if her throat felt paralysed, Lily's knees threatened to make up for it in activity. She could feel them starting to shake, and pressed them together. Inducements? That was what Beryl had said Gladys should offer Bill. Lily hadn't liked the sound of it then; she liked it even less now.

'Inducements? Such as?'

'Oh, well . . . perhaps that's a putting it a bit strong.'

Jim hadn't meant to get that far: knowing what Lily was like, he'd expected her to have interrupted sooner. He'd have to flannel now, and he didn't want to, but what could he say? That his mother had as good as proposed an arranged marriage, pairing him off with Margaret Povey to get his – or her – hands on Broad Oak Farm? He couldn't present her in that bad a light. It would be disloyal.

'Oh, you know,' he shrugged. 'The healthy life in the countryside, fresh air, exercise . . .'

It was an inducement of sorts, thought Lily: Jim did love and miss the countryside, she knew. But there were other thoughts jostling in her mind, and drilling through the concrete throat.

'But Jim, you send them money. Your mother couldn't pay you. If you're not earning, surely, every-one's worse off?'

Jim had raised the same point with his mother, but she'd had the answer ready.

'With me there, she reckons I could make the garden more productive. We could sell some of the stuff, veg and fruit. And I could get always get work on local farms.'

All Lily's fears from earlier in the year came rushing back.

'But they've got Land Girls, haven't they?'

'Some have. And they're doing a great job, don't

get me wrong. But at busy times – harvest, haymaking – farmers can always use an extra pair of hands.'

Lily couldn't argue with that. But she could still argue. She would argue this for all she was worth.

'But what about Marlow's?' she objected. 'After Mr Marlow's trusted you, given you more responsibility? And you're getting on so well with Mr Simmonds, and there's the *Messenger*, and all the ideas you still want to develop . . . you've got a future there, Jim, you know you have – it's only just started!'

Never mind his future at Marlow's. What Lily really wanted to say was 'What about <u>me</u>? And us? Haven't we got a future?'

'So what did you say to her?'

'It was very difficult.'

Jim spoke slowly and deliberately. If he was going to say he was leaving, Lily just wished he'd get on with it. She was pressing her knees so hard together now she could feel bone grinding against bone.

'She's my mother. Of course I feel for her. So, in the end, I had to say—'

They'd been so engrossed that they hadn't noticed the footsteps down the alley. Now the back gate burst open, and with it, a volley of sound and the flapping of an envelope.

'It's Les! He's all right! He's safe, he's all right – oh, Lily, he's safe, and he's coming home!'

Barely a day passed without a visit from Beryl and, Lord knew, she'd made some badly-timed entrances.

But this time . . . but what could they do when Beryl had waited so long for a letter and had been so brave, and now had such wonderful news? Hoping she could trust her shaky knees, Lily jumped up.

'That's wonderful!' To her amazement, her voice sounded almost normal.

Beside her, Jim had stood up too, and had even managed a smile. When he spoke, though, he sounded puzzled.

'But how did you hear, on a Sunday? There's no post.'

Beryl waved the envelope.

'Look at this! Trust him!'

Lily glanced at it. Then looked again, and then at Beryl.

'Yes!' said Beryl in triumph. 'I know! If I've told him once I've told him a hundred times about his bloomin' awful writing! We're number 26, but because he didn't form the six properly, the letter had only gone and went to number 20!' In her excitement and indignation, Beryl's grammar had gone AWOL. 'They've been away visiting their daughter in Whitstable, they only got back today and brought it straight round.'

'So it's been sitting there since . . .'

'A whole week!' said Beryl. 'While we've been going round the bend!'

'But why's he coming home?' asked Jim. 'I thought he'd be there for the duration.'

'Didn't we all. Read it!'

Hands shaking slightly, still trying to collect herself, Lily extracted the letter and angled it so that Jim could read it at the same time.

Dear Beryl – and Mum and Susan,

Sorry I haven't been in touch, but I haven't been too good. Long story short, I hadn't felt right off and on almost since I got here, gippy tummy, hot and cold, headaches and that, put it down to the heat, then I passed out at the wheel, luckily only me in the truck. Don't worry, I wasn't badly bashed up, but they carted me off to hospital. Then, well, it's been a while now, and this is the first time I've been well enough to write.

With a look to check that Jim had got to the end of the page too, and had understood the slightly garbled account, Lily turned over.

They say it's a kind of fever they have over here. Not malaria, don't worry, but from mosquitos, though. Must have got bitten the minute I got off the boat! But good news – great news! They're sending me home. I don't know when or how, but I'll be back with you and Bobby. Give him a big kiss from his dad, and one for you too. Can't wait to see

you. Love to Mum and Susan. Hope you are
all well and real sorry if you've been worried.
I love you, doll, Les xxx

Lily folded the letter and handed it back.

'Beryl, I don't know what to say. Poor Les!'

'Poor Les! Weeks, he's been in hospital, it sounds like! So he was never anywhere near Tobruk! Or that Mersah Matruh place, or where the fighting is now. After all that worrying, and driving poor Ivy to drink! She'll have his insides for elastic when he gets back, she says!'

Poor Les! thought Lily again. But at least thinking about other things was slowly reconnecting her with reality. Jim had recovered himself too.

'You know she won't,' he grinned. 'He'll get a hero's welcome, flags, bunting, fatted calf, the lot.'

'Quite right,' agreed Lily. 'He may not have been in the fighting, but weeks in hospital, Beryl? What he's had sounds horrible. It must be if they're sending him home to recuperate.'

Beryl softened.

'I know. I hope he really is all right and not just putting on a brave face. Still, we'll know soon enough.' She stroked the letter and held it to her chest. 'I can't believe it. Is your mum in? I must tell her!'

'She's inside,' said Lily.

'I hope she's sitting down!' called Beryl over her shoulder, moving off at a lick. 'Ivy would have come round, but she said her legs wouldn't carry her, they were shaking that much!'

Lily knew the feeling: remembering where she and Jim had got to in their conversation, her own knees were starting to feel percussive again. She sank down on the side of the veg bed. Les was coming home to Hinton, which was wonderful. But did the scales have to be balanced out by Jim having to leave?

Shaking his head at Beryl's excitement, Jim sat down too.

'After all that!'

'I know. But I'm so happy for her. They can be a proper family now.'

'Yes, he's had a rough time. Sounds like that mosquito did him a favour though. Anyway . . .' Jim pushed his hands through his hair, making it more tousled than ever. 'Where were we?'

Lily's throat began to close up again.

'You were about to tell me you're moving back to Bidbury.'

'What? Whatever gave you that . . . No, I wasn't!'

No? Lily's throat was not cooperating, and Jim carried on.

'Oh, Lily, I'm sorry – I'm so sorry! I didn't mean you to think – oh, but it was awful, I felt such a heel. She countered every objection I made; she got upset and cried – I didn't know what to do. In the end, I came up with a compromise. It's not what my mother wants, but she could see it's the best she's going to get.'

'A compromise? What sort of compromise?'

'I'm going to go more often.'

Lily couldn't believe it. He wasn't leaving! Les was coming back, and Jim was staying too!

'Oh!'

It was wonderful news, but she was so stunned, so disbelieving, it was all she could manage.

'I'm not sure how often,' Jim went on. 'Or quite how I'm going to do it. But as many weekends as possible.'

Hang on. Hardly any workers got whole weekends off: shop workers didn't even get a half-day on a Saturday. Jim surely couldn't get all the way to Bidbury and back on a Sunday and do anything worthwhile while he was there? He could see her doubt.

'Like I said, it's not perfect. I'll have to leave straight from work on a Saturday and come back very late Sunday night. I may even have to go cap in hand to . . . to Uncle Cedric, and ask for unpaid leave or something, so I can stay over on Sunday nights too.'

Uncle Cedric! Jim hardly ever used that term – and he'd never, never, ask a favour of him unless it was vital. If he was prepared to do that, he must really want to stay in Hinton. He didn't want to leave Marlow's – that much was clear. But could there be a bit more behind it? Could perhaps it be also that he didn't want to leave her?

She turned to look at him at the same time as he turned to look at her.

'I'm not going back, Lily. I belong here now. For good.'

Lily felt faint with relief. She swayed slightly, and as she did, Jim moved his arm to steady her. Their faces were inches apart, and suddenly she couldn't see him so clearly. She wasn't sure if it was because her head felt strangely light, or because her eyes had gone a bit blurry, or just that his face was so very close.

'You're here! Oh, good! We had to come and tell you!'

It was Gladys and Bill, looking as pleased as two cats fresh from waxing their whiskers and choosing matching pyjamas.

Yet again, Lily and Jim had been so absorbed that they hadn't registered the footsteps, the latch, the gate . . . none of it.

It was a dream; it was a nightmare. Lily got unsteadily to her feet, even more unsteadily than when Beryl had burst in, and before she knew it Gladys was upon her, waving her left hand in front of her and dragging Bill behind her with her right.

'Look, Lily, look! Lily! Lily! Look! Look!'

Lily blinked and saw the tiny diamond as it was rotated inches from her eyes.

'Last night!' cried Gladys. 'Bill asked me to marry him! We're engaged!'

There was nothing else for it. They had to go indoors, where Dora had laid aside her mending and was listening to Beryl's plans to give Les a hero's welcome.

'Of course I'll make a cake,' she was saying, 'but I can't till he's actually here. How can I if we don't know when he'll be back?'

'Yes, all right,' conceded Beryl. 'But when you do, make it a big one – and you will ice it, won't you, Dora, somehow? And spell out "Welcome Home"? I bet Ivy could get her hands on some of those little silver balls, and—'

'Mum? Beryl?' Lily plunged headlong into Beryl's non-stop torrent. 'Look who's here! And they've got some good news too!'

As she spoke, she pushed forward a flushed Gladys and a blushing Bill. Once again, Gladys flourished her ring, and there was another flurry of 'Look, look!' and 'Guess what?' Beryl shrieked and jumped up, and Dora said, 'Well, I never!' Then they both hugged Gladys while Bill stood back looking both pleased and sheepish. Then Lily hugged Gladys all over again, and then, for good measure, everyone hugged Bill, even though no one knew him very well, while Jim stood on the sidelines looking rather pink of cheek himself.

On top of Beryl's news, which she relayed all over again, even more excitedly this time, this called for a major celebration. A pot of tea was made, and scones produced, along with Dora's gooseberry jam and Alice's recently-unpacked damson.

While Bill concentrated on the scones, Gladys breathlessly relayed a minute by minute account of the previous day's events.

'So we end up in this Frenchie place.' Bill finally got a word in. 'Recommended by Sid if you please – I don't know what he was thinking! Must have got me mixed up with Maurice Chevalier!'

Gladys's besotted gaze said that in her eyes her fiancé was Maurice Chevalier, with a touch of Spencer Tracy and a dash of Errol Flynn.

'Dead posh,' she cut in. 'You can't imagine. Menu all in French. And the waiters as well. Tablecloths, starched, and silver knives and forks. Silver!' Everyone marvelled, but Gladys wasn't done yet. 'So posh,' she added weightily, 'that who should come in but Robert Marlow.' She paused to let the full import of this sink in before concluding exultantly, 'With that Evelyn Brimble!'

'No!' exclaimed Beryl. 'His girlfriend,' she added, in case Dora wasn't fully aware of who was who.

'No, not his girlfriend,' said Gladys smugly. 'Not any more. His fiancée. He proposed to her right then and there in the middle of the restaurant!'

'No!' exclaimed Beryl again, robbed of the power of further speech.

'A right flash Harry,' Bill muttered to Jim, who raised his eyebrows to signal agreement. He might have revised his opinion of Robert slightly, but it was still a fair assessment.

345

'So they're engaged!' Recovered, Beryl turned to Lily. 'What did I tell you? You still think he's Bobby's dad, do you?'

Lily had come clean about her blunder in the hospital to Gladys and to Jim, but Dora was looking mystified. Lily glared at Beryl and had to explain her misguided suspicion on hearing what the baby was to be called.

'Never mind that.' Jim stepped in to rescue her from further embarrassment. 'You see what this means, don't you?'

Everyone looked at him expectantly.

'Come on, newshounds!' he exclaimed. 'It's a double scoop for *The Marlow's Messenger*, isn't it?'

Chapter 31

Once everyone had helped clear the table, Bill and Gladys said they had to go. They were seeing the vicar.

'The vicar!' exclaimed Beryl. 'I thought you said you weren't getting married for ages?'

'We went to the service at St Mary's this morning, didn't we, Bill?' beamed Gladys. 'And the vicar was lovely. We want to find out how it's done, for when it does happen. And, Lily – I haven't said, I'm just assuming, but if he asks what we've got in mind – you will be my bridesmaid, won't you? Please?'

Over the tea and scones – though she'd eaten suspiciously little – Lily's heart rate had slowly gone back to normal. Although she was still trying to absorb what Jim had said, bit by bit she'd been able to take part in the conversation, even though she was never entirely sure if what she was saying made sense or was a reasonable response to what she'd only half-heard. Luckily, as so often with Gladys's tales, a 'Really?' or a 'No!' was the only rejoinder needed. By now, thankfully, she was more or less functioning as normal, and was able to give Gladys the reply she deserved.

'I thought you'd never ask!' The two girls hugged again. 'I'd be most put out if you hadn't! Of course I will. I'd be honoured!'

'Watch it, Lily,' Beryl was putting her jacket on. 'That's twice already. Three times a bridesmaid . . . You know what they say . . .'

'I'm quite safe, thank you,' said Lily, cringing at the mention of anything bridal relating to herself with Jim standing right there. 'I can't imagine Evelyn Brimble asking me!'

'There's Sid and Reg, don't forget,' Gladys reminded her. 'They're bound to want you for a bridesmaid.'

'I can't see anyone catching Sid for a bit,' grinned Bill. 'It'll take some girl to pin him down!'

For a bit? Never, in fact. Lily gave Jim a sidelong look, but he was staring out of the window.

'Oh, that's all right, then,' concluded Beryl. 'That'd make four, wouldn't it, so the curse is lifted.'

Lily gave a half-hearted smile. All this nonsense about her being – or never being – a bride, when she and Jim couldn't even get beyond being friends. She still hadn't said her piece, and if there were any more interruptions this afternoon, she never would!

'And there's one thing you needn't worry about, either of you,' Beryl added. 'The dresses. I can sort that out. It'll be my wedding present to you, Gladys.'

'Really?'

'With everything else going on, I haven't said, have I?' Beryl resumed the limelight, a spot she'd graciously ceded to Gladys and Bill. 'I've got my first booking – the girl marrying the bloke in the Black Watch. She came round yesterday, paid a deposit and everything!'

'That's marvellous!'

'Well done, Beryl!' Even Dora sounded impressed.

'And that's after only a couple of weeks and a couple of inquiries! By the time you two tie the knot, I'll have plenty more frocks. In fact, if I hear of anything going, you can come with me and try it on then and there. Same with a dress for you, Lily. Unless you fancy making something, Dora?'

'Oh, no, you're not catching me like that again!'

Dora wasn't falling for Beryl's tricks this time.

'Fair enough. But that reminds me!' Beryl rounded on Jim. 'I wanted to ask you, Jim. About keeping accounts. What the heck is double-entry book keeping?'

Everyone laughed. Jim said he wasn't the man to ask, but Beryl wasn't having any of it, and inevitably he found himself agreeing to a tutoring session.

'Let me know when it suits,' Beryl cried gaily,

though her smile faded when Dora produced the much-travelled pigeon for her to take away.

'Not exactly the accessory of the moment, is it?' she grumbled.

'You won't be saying that once it's in a pie. And tell Ivy to get it cooked as soon as, before it gets high. It's been dragged halfway across the Midlands as it is.'

'As long as she doesn't expect me to have anything to do with it, except eat it.' Beryl kissed Gladys and Bill all over again. 'Congratulations, you two. I hope – no, I know – you'll be very happy.'

'I'm sorry we can't stay,' Gladys said quietly to Lily as she saw them all to the door – the front door, in honour of the occasion. 'We could have sent Bill and Jim to the pub, and I could have told you everything. What really happened once we got home. But Lily, so you know . . . I didn't have to use Beryl's . . . inducement.'

Lily had been wondering. She'd been examining Gladys's face to see if there was some sort of transformation, the one she imagined that might happen when you took that final step with a boy. Gladys certainly did look different – glowing – but that could simply have been thanks to the ring on her finger. Lily was relieved to hear that to get what she so badly wanted, Gladys hadn't had to lose what she had.

The other three had gone ahead into the street, and Gladys put a hand on Lily's arm.

'One more thing. We won't let Beryl bully us about the dresses. This is my wedding. We'll have what we want, not what she picks for us.'

'Fine by me,' said Lily, amazed at the air of authority Gladys's new status had bestowed on her. Next she'd be bossing Lily around and calling Dora by her first name too!

Gladys hadn't finished yet.

'And I'm sure you've noticed, but Jim can't go back to Marlow's like that. Someone'll have to cut his hair before tomorrow!'

'I know. Mum can do it.'

Lily sounded cheerful enough, but her heart took a dive. After all the interruptions, standing around watching Jim have his hair cut was only going to hold things up still further. Was she ever going to be able to say what she needed to him?

Dora hadn't missed Jim's raffish appearance either. By the time the two of them came back through she'd set a dining chair over a square of newspaper and was sharpening her scissors.

'Can't have you going back to work looking like a hooligan,' she declared. 'Sit yourself down.'

With years of practice on her sons, she draped a towel around Jim's shoulders and confidently attacked. Lily watched with a strange feeling welling inside her as her mother tipped his head this way and that. Just a couple of hours ago that head had been very close to hers. Had she imagined it, or had something been about to happen between them?

She fidgeted edgily. Dora cut and trimmed, until, having inspected Jim from every angle, she finally announced herself satisfied. Jim folded the towel and carefully collected the newspapers so as not to scatter any snippings. He went to get rid of them as Lily put back the chair.

When he reappeared, he looked at himself in the mirror over the fireplace.

'Crikey, But I suppose I'll get away with it as long as they haven't had an escapee from Dartmoor.'

'Get away with . . . Oh, get away with you! I've only given it a trim!' Dora was wiping her scissors before putting them away.

Jim grinned.

'Only teasing. Thank you. You save me a fortune at the barber's. Doesn't she, Lily?'

Lily nodded. She'd rather liked the tousled look, but now she found the boyish nape of his neck, a thin stripe revealed where his hairline no longer met his tan, positively piercing.

But Dora was already on to her next task.

'Right then. Tea. Anyone ready for it?'

Lily looked at Jim. Not something else to get in the way.

'We've had it, haven't we?' he asked. 'I'm still pretty full of scone.' He looked to Lily for confirmation. 'You?'

'Stuffed,' she said unromantically. 'Nothing else for now, Mum. If that's all right.'

'All right? I'd be glad of the chance of a sit down.'

They'd been sitting down all afternoon, but both Lily and Jim knew it was Dora's way of saying she'd be glad of a bit of peace and quiet. It made it easier, and quite natural, then, for Jim to suggest that he and Lily went for a walk.

Outside the back gate, they stopped.

'Where to?' asked Lily as usual. 'Canal, park? Park, canal?'

'I thought we could go somewhere different.'

Lily drew her head back, amazed.

'Is there anywhere different?'

'Yes. Juniper Hill.'

'To Violet's? I mean – Mrs Tunnicliffe's?'

'Not to the house,' Jim said patiently. 'But when we went before and you were in with her, I did a bit of exploring. At the top of the hill, there's a footpath and it leads to . . . well, you'll see.'

'A mystery tour! All right.'

It was a beautiful evening to be out. Balmy, they'd have called it in books, Lily thought, the heat of the day dissolving to gossamer in a sky of palest blue, with hints of pink and gold on the horizon.

They couldn't pick up where they'd left off, not yet, thought Lily. She didn't want to say what she had to, not like this, not walking along. She'd waited this long, she could wait till they got there – and it wasn't as if they didn't have plenty of other things to talk about – admittedly brides and weddings. But at least they were other people's.

'Quite an afternoon,' she began.

For once, Jim had matched his pace to hers rather than the other way around.

'You didn't see it coming? Gladys and Bill, I mean? No great surprise, surely.'

There was no need, now, to mention Gladys's despair that her engagement would never happen.

'No, not really. It's what Gladys wanted from the start, and Bill's such a good sort. It's a proper happy ending. But what about Robert and Evelyn? Is that a happy ending too?'

'Hah!' exclaimed Jim. 'Now you're inviting me to be cynical.'

'Am I? You're the one who said he seemed besotted when you saw them at the White Lion.'

'True. But I do ask myself whether they'd be getting married if Evelyn was a penniless orphan.'

'You think it's only because she's the boss's daughter?'

'No, not quite. He fell for her before he worked for Sir Douglas, I'm sure. But the fact she's now also the boss's daughter doesn't do any harm either.'

'That's awful! You make it sound like a marriage of convenience.'

Jim shrugged, but not in response to Lily – more to shrug off the unwelcome memory of his mother's shameless parading of Margaret Povey with the same aim in mind. He steered the conversation onto less bumpy ground.

'Well . . . perhaps I'm being mean. Robert may have nearly cost me my job once but he has come out to bat for me lately, hasn't he, about my ideas for Marlow's. And I don't see him having an easy time as Evelyn's husband, keeping her in the style to which she's accustomed. So perhaps we're quits.'

'Quits enough for you to get an invitation to the wedding?'

'Oh yes, because you'd love to see me looking a right Charlie in a morning suit, wouldn't you? I wouldn't hold your breath!'

'Pity,' smiled Lily. 'I bet Beryl'd love the challenge of finding you a top hat and tails! Beryl the business-woman,' she marvelled. 'Who'd have thought it?'

'She's amazing, isn't she? Such energy.'

'Yes, poor Les won't get much rest and recuper-ation with her around! Still, she's a good sort too. And a force for good. The world needs people like her.'

And people like you, Lily, Jim thought warmly, but he didn't say it. He'd waited this long. He could wait till they got there.

Chapter 32

They were at the foot of Juniper Hill now, and started up the slope. On their previous visit, Lily hadn't noticed much beyond Violet's house: now she saw that at the top of the hill, the road met a thicket of trees before curving around to the right. Maybe the little copse was where Jim had done his exploring.

Violet's house was about halfway up. A vast grey cat was sitting Sphinx-like on one of the stone pillars at the gate. It opened its eyes a slit as they approached, then closed them again.

'What an enormous creature!' exclaimed Lily. 'I'm surprised it can get up there.'

Jim pointed out a log carefully angled at the side of the pillar.

'It's got a helping hand.'

'Hello, you!' Inanely, Lily addressed the cat. 'And what's your name?'

The cat declined to answer but graciously inclined its head so that Lily could stroke it, then raised it to indicate that it would be preferable if she transferred her attention to the thick fur under its chin and especially the unreachable bit under its collar. From the collar dangled a shiny disc announcing that his name was Theo.

'Artful,' said Jim, looking on at the purring and preening.

He didn't approve of cats because of the destruction they wreaked on his beloved birds, though this one was too portly to do any harm, as Lily pointed out.

'He couldn't catch a bird unless it dropped into his paws, could you, hey? Even then it'd probably be too much effort to bite its head off.'

Theo shook his head, rattling his disc, then dropped it in a gesture of thanks, or, more likely, dismissal. Lily took the hint and took a proper look up the drive of the house. When they'd been there in the spring, the daffodils had been out and there'd been primroses in pots on the steps. Now they were finished and two stone urns were filled with pink geraniums. A low, sporty car was parked on the gravel.

'One of the sons, I bet,' she deduced. 'I'm glad they haven't just left her to it. They're keeping an eye on their mother.'

It was another unwelcome reminder for Jim.

'Shall we get on?' he said brusquely. 'Though *you* may want a helping hand up the last bit. It's quite steep.'

Without waiting for an answer, he held out his hand. Before, Lily would hardly have registered it. Jim had pulled her up so many times from benches, from the veg bed wall, from the grass in the park, or in the winter helped her over puddles or patches of ice and she'd thought nothing of her hand in his. Now, of course, it meant – or might mean – something quite different. But she took it, trying not to think about it, and he hauled her up to the top of the slope, huffing and puffing and pretending she was a dead weight.

At the top, he let go of her hand and pointed. It wasn't the trees they'd been aiming for after all – they were fenced off and obviously private. But alongside the fence was an overgrown path.

'A footpath?' she queried.

After all her worries about Sid being slung into prison, it'd be a fine thing if they were the ones to get arrested for trespassing.

'No sign any more, but yes, I checked on the map. Well, come on, or do you want a blindfold to keep the mystery going?'

Lily declined the blindfold: the path was stony and only wide enough for them to walk in single file. It was overgrown with cow parsley gone rank and nettles, which Lily had learned to love because back in the spring, along the cut, Jim had pointed out the butterflies' eggs on the undersides of the leaves. The small tortoiseshell was one of the ones that favoured nettles above anything else, he'd told her, and there were a few of them fluttering about now in the late sunshine. The path wreathed this way and that before it ended suddenly in a narrow expanse of grass.

Jim led the way to the edge. The slope they'd climbed fell away on the other side, but instead of houses, a path scissored down into a cloak of trees. Stitched into the valley were a few cottages and a low white building that looked like a pub. Beyond that, fields stretched away, a ribbon of road unravelling through them.

Lily stood amazed.

'I never knew this was here!' she exclaimed. 'Just the other side of town and it's the countryside!'

'That's right. It took me by surprise too. It's another world, isn't it?'

'All these years,' Lily marvelled. 'I've only ever known about the park and the canal. And this was here all the time! But this land, where we're standing, it doesn't belong to anyone?'

'It's common land,' said Jim. 'I looked it up. Someone owns it, but common people – that's us – have rights. To walk on it, of course, and other things – collect firewood for instance—'

'That's handy!'

'And graze our sheep, or in the autumn, bring our pig to root out acorns if any drop over from the trees.'

'Let's get one, quick! But Jim, you might have said. You've known about this place for months and you've never let on!'

'You're not the only one who can keep a secret,' he said, meaning Sid, she supposed. 'Anyway, I was saving it. For the right moment.'

There was no breeze, nothing at all, but Lily suddenly felt shivery.

'Shall we sit down?' he asked.

They sat side by side on the grass, their arms around their knees, looking out at the view as the sun inched lower in the west.

'I still wasn't sure, even today,' he began. 'There's been so much . . .' He gave her his twisty smile. 'So much emotion already this afternoon. I was a bit worried that coming over to Violet's again would upset you. Bring it all back. In a bad way.'

She looked at him, her heart swelling. How very thoughtful he was. But when she thought about Violet's death now, all she could remember was Jim holding her while she'd cried.

'How could it?' she said quietly. 'When it's so beautiful here? And so peaceful. Even if it had . . . it would have been worth it.'

'That's all right then.' Jim took a deep breath. 'So, for the second time of asking, where were we?'

'I think,' said Lily, summoning all her courage, 'I think you might have been about to say something about—'

'You and me?'

'Yes.' It came out not much above a whisper. 'If there is a you and me.'

'Oh, I think there is,' said Jim. 'Don't you?'

'Oh, yes,' said Lily fervently. 'Yes, I do!'

At last, she thought, at last!

'Well, that's good.' Jim let out a breath, which was half relief, half a laugh. 'We got there – at last!'

Lily burst out laughing, and so did he, properly now. And suddenly everything was just as it always had been between them, but even better.

'Oh, I know!' she cried. 'I know! When everyone kept turning up one after the other . . . there were times this afternoon when I wondered if we'd ever get round to it at all!'

'Some things are worth waiting for.' Jim took her hand and laced their fingers together. 'I still wasn't sure . . .'

Surely he couldn't have doubted her? But then she realised that if he'd given her no clear signals, she hadn't really given him any either. All the fuss she'd made about him joining up, and then about him leaving for war work, might just have been petulance at being left behind, years off making any proper contribution to the war effort herself. And though he'd never shown it, Jim could have taken her refusal to talk about Sid when he suspected, quite correctly, that she was keeping something back, as evidence that she didn't trust him.

She looked at his face, all angles, his glasses as ever slightly out of true, at his newly-trimmed head, such a lovely shape, and at his long fingers twined with hers. His hesitancy moved her more than any flowery declaration could have done.

'Weren't you?'

He turned turned to face her, serious.

'Well, we're taking a bit of a risk, aren't we?'

'Meaning?'

'Whatever happens, Lily, I don't want us to stop being friends. I would never want that.'

Wasn't that exactly what she'd said to Sid?

'I've thought about that too. If things went . . . wrong.'

They'd only so recently started to go right, she could hardly bring herself to say it.

'We'll have to make sure that doesn't happen, then, won't we?'

Lily nodded. She'd never been happier, and she wanted to go on being happy, but there was something else.

'Can I say something?

'You've never needed my permission before!'

'This is different.'

Jim pulled back and looked at her, half suspicious, half smiling.

'You're not going to go all submissive and little woman on me, are you? I'm not sure I could cope!'

'No! That's exactly what I don't want to happen!'

'Oh, terms and conditions, I see,' he grinned. 'Go on, then.'

'All right. Look, Jim, now we're being honest, I really . . .'

This was going to be difficult. She half wished she hadn't started, but she had, and he was watching her, waiting, so she had no option.

'I really like you, Jim . . . a lot . . . but . . .' She'd thought such a lot about what she wanted to say, and how she was going to say it, but now the words all came out in a rush, pushing into each other like people scared they'd never get to the head of a queue. 'I don't want us to turn into the sort of sloppy couple that Les and Beryl were when they got together, or like Gladys and Bill today, all wedding bells and seeing the vicar. I mean, it's right for them, it suits them perfectly, but I don't think I could . . . I don't think we could . . . I'm not ready for all that yet!' She huffed in frustration. 'Oh, I'm not putting this very well. Basically, I don't want anything to change!'

Jim threw back his head and laughed. He took her other hand in his.

'You are so funny! You're so unlike other girls! Thankfully,' he added, in case she took it the wrong way. 'Look, Lily. I understand. We'll do this our own way. For a start, I wouldn't dream of embarrassing your mother by sitting smooching in front of her—'

'Oh no, that'd be awful!'

'The important thing for me was to say what I've said – what we've said – and for us to know that we mean something to each other. To get it out into the open between us. We don't have to rush into anything else, do we? We know how we feel, that's all that matters.'

Lily squeezed his hand. She could have drowned in the wave of relief.

Jim grinned again.

'So no bottom drawer? No planning your trousseau? No resentful, brooding looks when Gladys and Bill get married?'

'None of that! Never! I promise! And at work . . .' She tailed off.

'Ah yes, work,' said Jim. 'The other reason I want to stay in Hinton.'

So she was the first reason? A pale moon had just started to show itself, and Lily could have leapt right over it. Jim turned their joined hands this way and that.

'Look, we'll tell our friends, your mum, Sid and Reg . . . But we don't have to make a big thing of it in front of everyone else – our bosses, for instance – if you don't want to.'

The waves of relief were becoming tidal.

'Well, I was hardly going to go confiding in Miss

Frobisher,' she said. 'I know you've got the chance to go far at Marlow's. And you will. But she seems to think I've got – what do they call it . . .'

'Potential?'

'That's it, potential as well.'

'Well, I could have told her that,' said Jim. 'The way you were telling me how to arrange my Tudor dining set the day my department moved in next to yours!'

'I did not!'

'Yes, you did! But I know what you're saying, and you're right. The minute a girl announces she's got a boyfriend, people make assumptions about what'll come next and don't think she's serious about her job, or at least not about progressing very far. And I'd never want to hold you back.'

'Nor me, you. You've got a real future at Marlow's – if we can get through this war!'

Jim nodded.

'War permitting, I think we both have. We've both got things we want to achieve, things to prove, even, to ourselves and to the people who've put faith in us. And since it's taken us a year to get to this point, well, here's a radical thought. For now, let's just enjoy it for what it is.'

It seemed the perfect summary of their situation, and Lily had never felt so content. Jim too felt the tension and anxiety that had built up during his time in Bidbury finally ebb away. There was still the problem of keeping his mother at least reasonably happy with the compromise she'd reluctantly agreed. But that was for another day. He wasn't going to think about it now. He'd make it work.

'So you can rest easy,' he smiled. 'I certainly don't plan on going public in *The Messenger*. I've got my double scoop. I don't need to make it a treble. OK?'

Lily nodded. She was beyond words – a rare enough event, and Jim wasn't going to let it go to waste. He leant forward and touched her lips with his own, then again, for longer this time. Then he leant back and looked at her.

'Still OK?'

More than OK; Lily could only nod her head.

'Good.' He kissed her once more, for even longer, then let go of her hands and pulled her in against his side. 'That's how we'll do things, Lily. One step at a time.'

Lily laid her head on his shoulder and looked out at the view.

'Can we stay here for a bit?' she said. 'I'd like to do what you said. Enjoy it for what it is.'

And it truly couldn't have been better.

Author's Note and Thanks

If you've read the first book in the series, *A Store at War*, you'll know that my fictional Marlow's was inspired by a real department store – Beatties of Wolverhampton. It started out as a small draper's in 1877 and grew over the years to encompass twelve stores across the Midlands before being taken over by House of Fraser. Affection for the store was so great in Wolverhampton itself, though, that after a local campaign, the Beatties name was retained, and the store still sits proudly facing Queen Square.

James Beattie's great-granddaughter, Vicky Redshaw, has been incredibly generous about the books, and the current Beatties manager, Debbie Eggerton, and former staff members Anne Sharples and Mike Baker kindly shared their memories and memorabilia. Exploring behind the scenes, I even uncovered the famous Beatties rocking horse which entertained generations of children – the Marlow's equivalent will feature in plotlines to come.

Huge thanks are also due to my lovely agent, Broo Doherty of DHH, who loved Lily's world from the start, and my editor Lynne Drew, who shared that belief. Also at HarperCollins, Emilie Chambeyron, Ellie Wood and Sophie Burks all worked hard on my behalf, while Claire Ward and her team came up with the stunning cover designs. My thanks to them all.

Friends and colleagues have always been a huge support and inspiration. I want to thank everyone I've worked with on *The Archers* and other shows, with and from whom I've shared and learnt so much. Very special thanks go to Mary Cutler for thirty years of friendship and to Keri Davies for his help with the initially scary world of Twitter. A host of other friends have shown more interest and patience than I deserve and been understanding when meeting up had to be sacrificed to deadlines: I now owe several lunches, drinks and cups of tea.

My family is tiny – husband here, daughter and her family in Kenya – but I hope they know they mean everything to me. As they say in Africa: 'We may be far apart, but we all share the same sky' – actually, Skype and Whatsapp.

Finally, a huge thank you to all the readers who've also loved Lily and Marlow's – and have told me so. If you'd go one step further and post a review on Amazon or GoodReads, I'd be so grateful – nothing makes an author happier than a happy reader's review!

If you enjoyed

Wartime for the Shop Girls

read on for the first chapter
of the next book in the series,

Heartache for the Shop Girls

The writing above the clock on the first floor of Marlow's read *'Tempus fugit'*. That, Lily had learnt meant 'Time flies.' Well, if time was flying this morning, it was a bird with a broken wing, a Spitfire spluttering home with half its fuselage shot away, a bee drowsily drunk on pollen. It might be half-day closing, but with the sale over and many customers away, Wednesday mornings in August could seem longer than full days.

August was the strangest month, thought Lily, as she spaced the hangers on the girls' pinafores the regulation half-inch apart. It had a sleepy, droopy-eyelids feel, and it was still summer, but it often felt as if summer was over, with a blank white sky, shorter days, the leaves crisping and the shadows lengthening on the grass. And things happened in August – not always good things. The Great War had started in August, and so had this one, pretty much, with the wait for Hitler's 'undertaking' that never came.

She looked across to Furniture and Household, hoping to catch Jim's eye, but he was with a customer. He was tipping a kitchen chair this way and that, demonstrating its sturdiness. Jim took lots of things seriously – and plenty not so seriously. It was a combination that had first attracted her to him – but whether he was testing or teasing her, Lily had accepted the challenge.

'Miss Collins! Customer!'

Lily snapped to attention, and smoothed down her dress as Mrs Mortimer approached. She was one of the first customers Lily had served after her promotion from junior to sales, and a kind, tweedy soul so it had been a gentle dunking, not a baptism of fire.

Mrs Mortimer would only be looking – or 'doing a recce' as she put it – on behalf of one of her busy daughters or daughters-in-law before she, or they, returned with the essential coupons to make the purchase. But it was all good practice.

She began as she'd been taught.

'Good morning, Mrs Mortimer, how are you? How may I help you?'

***

On Toys next door, Lily's friend Gladys was dusting Dobbin, the much-loved Play Corner rocking horse, and thinking much the same about the time. When you had nothing to do on your afternoon off, a long morning didn't matter, but when there was something you were looking forward to – my, did it drag!

This afternoon there was a little party planned at Lily's, a welcome home for their friend Beryl's husband. Les Bulpitt had been invalided home from North Africa, to everyone's relief and delight, especially Beryl's, now a proud mother to baby Bobby. Les had been away for Bobby's birth, so hadn't seen his son as a new-born. Now he was home they could be a proper family.

Gladys sighed happily. Thoughts of contented married couples always led to thoughts of her fiancé, Bill, and how contented she'd be when they were married, and especially when they started their family. A husband and children were all Gladys had ever wanted, and Bill was the answer to years of fervent prayers. Had it been wrong to pray for something like that, Gladys wondered now, when there were bigger things to pray for, like an end to starvation and cruelty and persecution? She probably ought to pray for forgiveness for having been so shallow and selfish, but she was too busy praying for a speedy end to the war and for Bill to be kept safe in the meantime.

***

On Furniture and Household, Jim had made his sale.

'If you'll sign here, please, Mrs Jenkins, I'll send this up to Cash Office to get your receipt.'

He stuffed the sheets into the little drum, rolled it shut and inserted it into the pneumatic tube. Off it whizzed upstairs. Jim smiled at Mrs Jenkins, another of the store's regular customers.

'I'm not sure when we can deliver, I'm afraid,' he began. 'With the new petrol regulations...'

Mrs Jenkins held up her hand.

'Don't worry, a few days won't matter. We've been without a kitchen chair for months – I had to give cook one of the dining chairs when the old one got past repairing. I'm grateful you had anything, even second-hand!'

'The Utility scheme should help,' said Jim. 'We should get more regular supplies.'

Mrs Jenkins looked sceptical.

'Newly-weds get first dibs, though?'

'Oh, yes. And anyone who's been bombed out.'

The tube throbbed as the cylinder plopped back into the little cup at its base. Jim retrieved it and handed Mrs Jenkins her copy.

'I'll telephone,' he promised, 'with a date for delivery. I hope within the next week.'

'Marvellous – well, as good as it gets these days! Thank you. Goodbye!'

'Goodbye.'

Jim closed his sales book and looked across to Childrenswear, hoping Lily was looking his way. But she was with a customer, Lily's blonde curls bent close to Mrs Mortimer's grey head as they examined the smocking on a summer dress.

The clock showed half past twelve. Only half an hour to go before all four lights below it would be illuminated, the sign that the last customer had left the store and commissionaire had bolted the doors and drawn down the blackout blinds.

Thirty minutes to go, then freedom...or was it? Jim had a funny feeling that there'd be a list of jobs for him ahead of the afternoon's little party. No change there, then! In a year as their lodger he'd realised that it was Lily's mother Dora who made work for idle hands. The devil never got a look-in.

***

'Really, Jim, is that the best you can do?'

'What? I'm at full stretch here, I'll have you know!'

'Come off it!' Lily scrutinised his efforts. 'What's the point of a banner if it looks like a drooping petticoat?'

Jim lowered his arms and the 'Welcome Home' banner he'd been holding up slumped dispiritedly to the floor.

'That's better.' He eased his neck and shoulders. 'My arms were nearly dropping off.'

He might have known he wouldn't get away with that.

'How can they drop off when they're above your head?' Lily retorted. 'Drop implies down, doesn't it? Tch! And to think you're the one with the School Certificate!'

Jim looked at her, head on one side, mouth twisted. Only a few weeks ago the two of them had finally admitted that their friendship had grown into more than just that. But their fledgling romance didn't mean they weren't still friends first and foremost – friends who teased each other relentlessly.

To show she was on his side really, Lily dragged over a dining chair. Jim was over six feet tall but her mum had been adamant that the banner had got to be thumb-tacked to the top of the picture rail, not the front – she wasn't having it look as if it had woodworm. To say Dora Collins was house-proud was a bit like saying Hitler had simply got out of bed on the wrong side on the day he'd invaded Poland.

'Haven't you two finished yet?' Dora, pinny wrapped across her slender frame, hair bound up in a turban, appeared from the scullery, sounding stern but only concerned, as always, that everything should be just so. 'There's still lettuce to wash and tomatoes to slice, sandwiches to make…'

She was carrying a sponge cake on the best cut-glass stand. The icing and the little silver balls which Beryl had requested had of course been impossible, but it still looked delicious. Dora Collins wasn't to be beaten in the cake-making stakes, and thanks to the hens they kept in the yard, cakes in this house didn't have to be made with foul-smelling dried egg, either, even if it meant sacrificing sugar in tea.

Jim and Lily exchanged a 'that's told us' look and Jim scrambled up onto the chair, having first, of course, removed his shoes. Dora might have been turned away, setting the cake in the middle of the table, but she had more eyes in the back of her head than a whole platoon of snipers. Lily passed up the tacks, and soon the banner was in place to everyone's satisfaction.

Ivy and Susan, Beryl and Les, Gladys – Dora checked she'd set out enough plates. That was five, plus the three of them – yes, eight in total.

Banner fixed, chair replaced, Dora marshalled Lily and Jim into the kitchen.

'Now,' she instructed. 'Let's get a bit of a production line going. If I slice the bread –'

'Jim can spread the marg, and I can fill.' Lily finished the sentence for her.

Jim smiled to himself.

'The apple doesn't fall far from the tree,' was one of Dora's many favourite maxims and it certainly explained where Lily's organisational skills – he wouldn't have dared call it bossiness, not to her face, anyway – came from.

***

'Aw, you shouldn't have!'

'But we did! And it's all for you, Les!'

Beryl hung on her husband's arm as they stood in the doorway, Les grinning at the spread. But he wasn't the Les that Lily remembered. He looked very different – thinner, and paler than you'd expect after months in the desert. But she'd been silly to expect him to look brown, Lily realised – most of his tan would have disappeared in the weeks he'd spent in hospital and a further few getting home on a troop ship. He looked older somehow.

'Me and Susan made the banner, Ivy and Dora's done the tea . . .'

Beryl steered Les into the room as Les's sister Susan, carefully carrying baby Bobby, came in behind them.

Beryl had scribed the 'Welcome Home' in big fat letters, but she'd let Susan do the colouring, which was why it was all wonky and went over the lines. Les's sister was thirteen, but she'd been born with all sorts of difficulties. With a weak heart and poor eyesight, co-ordination wasn't one of her strong points, not that she had any, really. 'Backward' was the kindest description.

'How are you?' Jim pumped Les's hand but Lily could tell he was just as shocked as she was by Les's appearance.

'He needs feeding up, that's what!' clucked Ivy, Les's mum. Still in her shapeless duster coat and even more shapeless hat, she was adding her contributions to the table – a plate of sausage rolls and a dish of junket.

'That's right,' Les agreed. 'Nothing a bit of home cooking won't put right.'

'Was it awful, the food out there?' Lily was keen to know, as the story back home was that they had to do without to keep the Army marching on its stomach. Though frankly Les looked as if though he hadn't eaten for weeks.

'Not bad. A bit repetitive, that's all.'

'Sounds like here,' said Gladys. She'd arrived earlier and was helping Susan, still holding the baby, settle herself in an easy chair. 'Anyway, it's lovely to see you home. And congratulations on being a dad!'

'Isn't he a little smasher?' Les beamed at his son. 'Hasn't Beryl done wonders?'

Beryl glowed as everyone showered praise on her, the baby, and the general miracle of creation.

'Don't you want to sit down, son? It's nearly wiped him out walking over here.' As she spoke, Ivy was removing her coat and lowering her own sizeable behind onto the luckless dining chair which had drawn today's short straw. Dora nodded in agreement. Physical opposites, Ivy large and expansive, Dora neat and trim, they'd become fast friends since Les and Beryl's marriage, united by their unswerving devotion to their families.

'Pull him up a chair, Jim.'

Common sense and a desire to appear manly tussled in Les's face, but he gave in to the inevitable.

'Maybe I will.' He took a chair. 'Just for a minute or two. I'm a lot better than I was!' he added bravely.

***

'I think he looks awful, don't you?' Lily asked Jim under the hiss of the kettle. They'd been sent out to the kitchen to make the tea.

'Not great.'

The worry about Les had started after the battle for Tobruk back in June. Nothing had been heard of him, or Lily's brother Reg, who was also out in North Africa, for weeks. Finally, Reg had managed to send a wire saying he was OK. From Les, though, there'd been nothing till Beryl got a letter saying he'd been in hospital – and nowhere near the fighting! He'd been taken with something called West Nile fever – from a mosquito bite.

'I don't like it,' said Lily. 'Do you think it was more serious than he let on?'

Jim shrugged.

'I can't think why else a simple fever case would mean him being shipped home and discharged for good.'

Lily sighed.

'Oh, Jim. This war! If so, where does that leave Beryl and Bobby?'

Heartache for the Shop Girls
is available to pre-order now!